Title Page

The Sicilian Defense

A Conning Couple Novel, Volume 4

Shane Reed

Published by Shane Reed, 2024.

Copyright

This is a work of fiction. Similarities to real people, places, or events are entirely coincidental.

THE SICILIAN DEFENSE

First edition. March 2, 2024.

Copyright © 2024 Shane Reed.

ISBN: 979-8224039814

Written by Shane Reed.

Chapter 1

Nate Everhart's jaw clenched as he slammed his fist down onto their sleek glass kitchen table. "It's unbelievable, Amy! How can these people just walk away with everything and nobody does a damn thing?"

Amy looked up from her MacBook, her fiery red hair framing her face like a lioness on the prowl. She shared her husband's frustration. "This city is rotting from the inside out," she spat. "And it seems like we're the only ones trying to pick up the pieces."

"Sometimes I feel like we're fighting an uphill battle," Nate sighed, running a hand through his dark hair. The weight of their missions pressed heavily on his broad shoulders, and the fatigue of countless sleepless nights had etched itself into every line on his face.

"Maybe so, but we can't give up," Amy replied fiercely. Her own eyes burned with determination, and she knew that Nate felt the same fire in his heart. They were survivors, after all – both of them had faced injustice and emerged stronger for it. And now they had dedicated their lives to ensuring others wouldn't suffer the same fate.

"Speaking of which," Nate said, his tone shifting to a more serious note, "we need to check our Proton email account. It's been a few days since we last logged in. We might have some new leads."

"Good idea." Amy nodded in agreement, her fingers flying across the keyboard as she opened the encrypted email service. As investigative journalists and ethical hackers, secure communication was essential for their work. They needed to share sensitive information without the risk of being intercepted by any prying eyes. ProtonMail offered the confidentiality they required to operate effectively, with end-to-end encryption and a Swiss-based location ensuring the highest levels of privacy.

"Let's see what we've got," Nate said, leaning over her shoulder to get a better view of the screen. The anticipation and excitement of a new case momentarily alleviated their exhaustion, replaced with a renewed sense of purpose.

"Here's hoping for something big," Amy whispered, her fingers hovering over the trackpad as they prepared to dive headfirst into another case, another fight for justice in a city desperately in need of heroes like them.

An unassuming ping cut through the air, punctuating the tense silence that had settled between Nate and Amy. Their eyes locked for a moment before darting to the screen, where a new email notification flashed like a beacon amidst the darkness.

"Looks like someone needs our help," Nate said, his voice low and measured as he reached over Amy's shoulder to click on the message. The curiosity in his eyes was unmistakable, fueled by the tantalizing prospect of a fresh case and the adrenaline rush that accompanied it.

As the email opened, they found themselves face-to-face with a plea from a woman named Caterina Bianchi, the owner of a Sicilian cafe in the city. Her words were laced with desperation and hope, each sentence painting a vivid picture of a life thrown into disarray by an unjust turn of events.

"Mi chiamo Caterina," the message began, introducing herself in her native Italian before continuing in English. "Three months ago, I've worked hard to make the Sicilian cafe I own successful. It has been and my goal is to grow the business by franchising the cafe. I had come fairly close to gaining the funds needed to start franchising. I invested my lifesavings into a project led by Edward Hewlett. He promised me that my money would be safe and that the investment would quickly grow sufficiently to provide the funds needed to take my cafe to the next level. But now, my money is gone, and Edward is nowhere to be found. Per favore, ti imploro, can you help me recover what I have lost?"

Nate felt a surge of anger rise within him as he read Caterina's story – another innocent victim preyed upon by a heartless con artist. He clenched his fists at his sides, feeling the familiar burn of injustice course through his veins. It was stories like these that drove him and Amy to fight back against the corruption plaguing their city, using their unique skills to make a difference one case at a time.

"Edward Hewlett," Amy whispered, her brow furrowing as she committed the name to memory. "He won't be getting away with this." Her determination was palpable, mirrored in the steely resolve that shone in Nate's eyes. Together, they were a force to be reckoned with, united by their unwavering quest for justice.

"Let's reply to Caterina and see if we can set up a meeting," Nate suggested, already formulating plans in his head as he turned to Amy for agreement. "We need much more information if we are to recover her investment."

"Agreed," Amy nodded, her fingers dancing across the keyboard as she composed a response to Caterina's email. "We'll get her money back, Nate. We have to."

Nate's fingers tapped a rhythm on the table as he stared at the screen, the words of Caterina's email echoing in his mind. He glanced over at Amy, who was lost in thought, her lips pursed and eyes narrowed in concentration. The air between them crackled with a shared sense of urgency.

"Damn it," Nate said, breaking the silence. "We need to help Caterina. She's one of the good ones – they're getting rarer these days."

"True," Amy replied, her voice heavy with determination. "Let's analyze what we know so far and figure out our next move."

Nate leaned back in his chair, his mind whirring through the details of Caterina's story. "So, Edward Hewlett wooed her with promises of high returns on her investment and then vanished without a trace, taking her money with him?"

"Seems that way," Amy confirmed. "And from what Caterina mentioned, it seems like she's probably not the only victim. He's likely running some sort of elaborate Ponzi scheme. We'll have to dig deeper, uncover the extent of his operations."

"Once we find him, we'll need to gather enough evidence against him to take to the authorities," Nate said, tapping his fingers on the table again.

Amy smiled, the fire of justice burning bright in her eyes. "But first, let's get in touch with Caterina again. We need to assure her that we'll do everything we can to recover her investment and bring this bastard to justice."

The clock on the wall ticked loudly, emphasizing the urgency of their newfound mission. Nate glanced at Amy, and without a word, they both knew what needed to be done.

"First things first," Nate said, his voice steady and determined. "We need to meet with Caterina in person. It's important to assess her credibility and gather as much information as possible before we dive into this."

Amy nodded in agreement, her eyes locked onto Nate's. "You're right. Let's set up a meeting with her at her cafe tomorrow. That way, we can get a feel for her environment and potentially spot any clues that could aid our investigation."

"Perfect," Nate replied, already typing out a reply to Caterina. "I'll let her know that we'd like to meet with her and discuss her case further."

***

Amy began gathering their equipment. Her movements were swift and efficient, a testament to the countless times they had prepared for similar missions. She grabbed their MacBook and her iPhone, ensuring that they would have all the necessary tools at their disposal when they met with Caterina.

While Amy packed their gadgets, Nate's thoughts raced with anticipation. He couldn't help but feel a sense of excitement mixed with trepidation. They had embarked on numerous missions before, but this one felt different - more personal. Perhaps it was the raw emotion conveyed through Caterina's words, or maybe it was the fact that they were dealing with a fellow fighter for justice who had been wronged.

"Hey," Amy called out to Nate, snapping him out of his thoughts. "We're all set. Are you ready?"

Nate took a deep breath, steeling himself for the task ahead. "Yes," he said, offering Amy a determined smile. "Let's go get us some justice for Caterina."

They strode towards the door, their resolve and commitment to justice fueling each step. As they embarked on their mission, they knew that they would stop at nothing to ensure that Caterina's stolen investment was returned and that Edward Hewlett paid for his crimes. And so, with a renewed sense of purpose and a desire to make a difference in their city, Nate and Amy stepped out into the night, ready to face whatever challenges lay ahead.

***

Nate and Amy stepped out of the car, and the scent of garlic and tomatoes hung heavy in the air. The vibrant chatter and laughter of customers spilled from the open door of Caterina's Sicilian cafe, beckoning them inside. Their mouths watered as they caught sight of a waiter carrying a steaming plate of pasta to a nearby table.

"Smells amazeballs," Amy said, her eyes widening with anticipation. "I can't wait to try the food."

"Me neither," Nate agreed, his stomach rumbling in agreement. "But let's stay focused. We're here to help Caterina first and foremost. Oh, and no-one says amazeballs any more."

As they entered the bustling cafe, Nate scanned the room, taking in the colorful wall murals, checkered tablecloths, and animated conversations of diners enjoying their meals. He felt a sense of warmth and camaraderie permeating the atmosphere, making it easy to understand why Caterina had become so successful.

"Excuse me," Nate said, flagging down a server. "We're looking for Caterina Bianchi. Is she around?"

"Si, signore," the young waiter replied with a smile. "She's in the back. You are Mr Nate and Ms Amy, no? She said you would be coming today. I'll let her know you're here."

"Thank you," Amy said, her eyes darting around the room as if trying to take in every detail at once.

As they waited for Caterina to arrive, Amy and Nate sat at a nearby table, sipping on espresso and discussing their plan of action.

"We need to make sure we have all the evidence before we confront Edward," Nate said, tapping his finger on the table. "We can't rely on just Caterina's word."

Amy nodded in agreement. "I'll do the digging into his finances, see if there are any other shady dealings going on."

"Good idea," Nate replied. "And I'll talk to some of my contacts in the legal world, see if there are any pending lawsuits against him."

Their conversation was interrupted by the arrival of Caterina. She greeted them with a warm smile and hugged them both tightly.

Caterina's dark hair fell in glossy waves down her shoulders, framing her angular face and sharp cheekbones. Her olive skin was smooth and flawless, and her dark eyes held a fierce determination.

As she spoke, her voice was clear and melodic, like a soft symphony playing in the background.

"Thank you so much for coming," she said, clasping Nate's hand with genuine appreciation before turning to Amy and offering her an affectionate hug. "I am truly grateful for your help."

"Of course," Amy reassured her, returning the embrace. "We're here to do whatever we can for you."

"Please, sit down," Caterina gestured towards a cozy corner table. "I've prepared some dishes for you to try. You must be hungry after your journey."

As they settled into their seats, Caterina served them heaping plates of pasta and fragrant garlic bread. The plates were large and filled to the brim with steaming pasta, drizzled with a rich, red sauce. The garlic bread was golden and glistening with melted butter. The aroma of fresh herbs and spices wafted from the plates, mingling with the rich scent of tomato and garlic.

The flavors exploded on Nate's tongue, a perfect combination of tangy tomato sauce, savory herbs, and the rich, nutty taste of parmesan cheese. The garlic bread provided a burst of garlic flavor, perfectly complimenting the pasta.

"Your cooking is phenomenal, Caterina," Amy praised between mouthfuls. "No wonder your cafe is so popular."

"Thank you," Caterina blushed, clearly touched by the compliment. "Now, let's discuss how we can recover my lost investment."

Nate nodded, swallowing a bite of pasta. His mind shifted gears, focusing on the task at hand. He knew that they were about to embark on a complex and dangerous mission, but seeing the gratitude in Caterina's eyes only fueled his determination.

"Alright," Nate began, his tone serious and focused as he rested his cutlery on his plate. He pulled out his iPhone and launched the recorder app. "Let's get started."

Caterina's dark eyes glistened with unshed tears as she recounted her story, her voice trembling with emotion. "Edward Hewlett approached me several months ago with a seemingly foolproof investment opportunity," she began. "He claimed that by investing in his tech startup, I could help my cafe grow and expand into an international franchise."

Nate listened intently, taking mental notes of every detail as Amy gently squeezed Caterina's hand, offering silent support.

"Everything seemed legitimate," Caterina continued, her face a mask of pain. "I trusted him because he was so convincing, and I thought this was my chance to make my dream of becoming a franchise come true. But it was all a lie. He took everything from me—my money, my trust, my hope. I can barely pay my staff at the moment." Her voice cracked, and Amy handed her a napkin to wipe away the tears that finally spilled out.

"Edward Hewlett is known for his schemes," Nate said, his voice steely with resolve. "We've been tracking some of his activities. I promise you, Caterina, we will do everything in our power to recover your lost investment and bring him to justice."

"Our expertise in cybersecurity and investigative journalism will give us an edge," added Amy, her red hair blazing like a flame against the backdrop of the cozy cafe. "We'll piece together the puzzle and find a way to get your money back."

Caterina looked at them both, her eyes red-rimmed but hopeful. "Grazie mille," she whispered, her gratitude palpable. "You have no idea what this means to me."

"Helping people like you is what we're here for," Nate replied with a reassuring smile. "We've dealt with similar cases in the past, and we won't let Hewlett slip through the cracks this time. We'll keep you updated on our progress every step of the way."

"Thank you," Caterina said again, her voice stronger now. "I knew I could trust you."

Nate and Amy exchanged a determined glance, their minds already racing with strategies and plans to bring Edward Hewlett down and recover Caterina's hard-earned money. They knew that the road ahead would be filled with danger and challenges, but they were more than ready to face them head-on in the pursuit of justice.

Caterina's eyes sparkled as she clasped her hands together, a newfound sense of hope settling in. She reached across the table, placing a piece of paper with her phone number on it. "Please," she implored, "do keep me informed and let me know if I can help in any way."

"Of course," Nate assured her, taking the paper from her grasp and carefully folding it into his wallet. "We're in this together. You'll know everything we do."

"Thank you," Caterina whispered, her voice barely audible over the hum of chatter and laughter that filled the cafe.

"Alright then," Amy said, pushing back her chair and rising to her feet. "Let's get started." The determination in her emerald eyes was unmistakable. Nate followed suit, standing up and extending a hand toward Caterina.

"Until we meet again, signora," he said, his grip firm and reassuring.

"Arrivederci," Caterina replied, her eyes glistening with unshed tears as she shook Nate's hand and then Amy's.

With a final nod, the couple turned away from the table, weaving their way through the bustling cafe. The scent of freshly baked cannoli and brewing espresso lingered in the air, mingling with the excited chatter of customers sharing stories and laughter. As they made their way to the door, Nate's mind raced at breakneck speed, sifting through the details of Caterina's story and formulating a plan of action.

Amy noticed the slight furrow in Nate's brow as he held the door open for her. "What are you thinking?" she asked, stepping out into the warm sunlight.

"Hewlett won't be easy to pin down," Nate replied, his dark eyes narrowing as they scanned the bustling street. "But I reckon we've got the skills and the motivation to see this through."

Amy sighed, her gaze lingering on the cafe's sign. "I just find it hard to believe how people would want take advantage of such a warm-hearted person. Caterina deserves better."

"Money," Nate murmured, wrapping an arm around Amy's shoulders as they walked away from the cafe.

As the couple disappeared into the crowd, their determination to bring justice to Edward Hewlett and recover Caterina's lost investment burned brighter than ever. They knew the stakes were high, the risks even higher. But for those like Caterina, who had been dealt a cruel hand in life, they were willing to face whatever challenges lay ahead.

And so, with the scent of Sicily still clinging to their clothes and the taste of sweet cannoli lingering on their lips, Nate and Amy Everhart embarked on a mission that would test their skills, their resilience, and their unwavering dedication to the pursuit of justice.

***

"Alright, let's break it down," Nate began, his voice low and steady as he leaned against the brick wall. "We've got a target: Edward Hewlett. And we've got a mission: recover Caterina's lost investment."

"An investment that could have been her ticket to a brighter future," Amy added, her eyes reflecting the fierce determination that fueled them both. "We need to gather intel on this guy, find out how he operates, and figure out how to hit him where it hurts."

"Agreed." Nate pulled out his iPhone, scrolling through the information they had already collected. "While I dive into the digital world, you focus on the human angle – talk to people who might know something about Hewlett or have crossed paths with him. Every little detail counts."

"Sounds like a plan." Amy nodded, mentally organizing her approach. "I'll start by digging into his background, maybe even get a word with some of his previous victims if I can track them down. There has to be a pattern to his schemes, something we can exploit."

"Good call. As for me, I'll search for any weak spots in his social media. his bank accounts, communication channels, anything that might give us an edge." Nate's fingers danced across the screen. "And once we've gathered enough intel, we'll formulate a strategy to take him down and get back what he stole from Caterina."

"Remember our motto, Nate: 'Justice prevails when good people refuse to stand idly by.'" Amy's voice was soft but unwavering, her gaze locked onto his. "We can't let Hewlett get away with this."

"Never," Nate whispered, sealing their pact with a firm embrace. "Now let's get to work."

Tthe streetlamp outside cast a long shadow across the pavement, a silent witness to the unfolding story of justice, revenge, and the relentless pursuit of truth that would soon consume Nate and Amy Everhart. As they delved deeper, they would no doubt find themselves entwined in a web of intrigue, deception, and danger – all against the backdrop of a vibrant Italian culture that refused to be silenced.

For Caterina Bianchi, and for countless others like her, Nate and Amy would stop at nothing to ensure that those who preyed upon the innocent would be brought to justice, no matter the cost.

Chapter 2

Nate Everhart could almost taste the tangy tomato sauce and fresh basil as he stepped through the door of Caterina's cafe, the tantalizing aroma of Sicilian cuisine enveloping him like a warm embrace. He held the door open for his red-haired wife, Amy, who took in the cozy atmosphere with a smile.

"Welcome to my humble little cafe," Caterina greeted them, her olive-skinned face lighting up with a warm smile that showcased a few laugh lines around her eyes. Her dark hair was pulled back into a neat bun, revealing gold hoop earrings that shimmered as she moved.

"Thank you for having us, Caterina," Nate replied, his voice deep and charismatic, matching the charm of the woman before them.

"Of course! Please, follow me." She waved a hand towards a table near the window, where sunlight streamed in. As they walked, Nate noticed the way Caterina carried herself – a proud, passionate woman with a dream of expanding her cafe into something greater.

"Here you are," Caterina said, pulling out chairs for them both. Nate and Amy sat down, their eyes meeting briefly in a silent exchange of understanding. They were here to help Caterina recover her lost funds and bring the man behind the investment scheme to justice.

"Thank you, Caterina," Amy said, offering a reassuring smile as she settled into her seat. "The cafe is lovely, and it smells amazing."

"Ah, grazie mille, Amelia," Caterina responded, beaming at the compliment. "I do my best to bring a little piece of Sicily to everyone who walks through that door."

As they settled into their seats, Nate began to formulate a plan in his mind. His past experiences in the military had honed his instincts, allowing him to quickly assess situations and devise strategies. But more importantly, his empathetic nature drove him to protect people like Caterina – vulnerable, trusting individuals who had been wronged.

"Shall we start with the Caponata and Arancini?" Amy suggested, her eyes scanning the menu before glancing at Nate for approval.

"Sounds delicious," he agreed, his thoughts turning to how they could use their combined skills of ethical hacking and investigative journalism to unravel the intricate web of deceit that now entrapped Caterina.

Caterina clasped her hands together with a nod. "I'll get your order started right away. And don't worry; we'll save room for the Cannoli." With that, she whisked herself away, leaving Nate and Amy to solidify their resolve and strategize on how best to bring justice to those who preyed on dreams and trust.

Nate's eyes were immediately drawn to the vibrant colors of the walls adorned with Sicilian artwork, each piece capturing scenes of daily life and the island's lush landscapes. He felt a deep appreciation for the culture Caterina had brought to life within this cozy cafe.

"Isn't it beautiful?" Amy whispered, her gaze following Nate's as they took in the intricate details of the paintings. Her keen eye for detail, honed through years of investigative journalism, allowed her to see the layers of meaning hidden within each brushstroke.

"It is," Nate agreed, his mind briefly wandering back to their mission – seeking justice for those who'd been wronged by Hewlett's investment schemes. The warmth and authenticity of Caterina's cafe only strengthened his resolve to help her.

Caterina approached them, her dark eyes gleaming with pride as she presented the menu. "Here at my cafe, I try to bring Sicily to your plate. Each dish is prepared with love and tradition," she explained, her voice filled with passion. "Our Caponata is made from fresh vegetables cooked in a sweet and sour sauce, topped with capers. And our Arancini... Ah! These are rice balls stuffed with mozzarella and peas, coated in breadcrumbs, and fried. Simply delicious."

"Everything sounds amazing, Caterina," Amy said, excitement evident in her voice. As she spoke, Nate noticed how Amy effortlessly connected with people, putting them at ease with her genuine interest and empathy.

"Thank you, Amelia," Caterina replied, her smile broadening. "I take great pride in preserving the flavors of my homeland. It's important to me that every guest leaves feeling like they've experienced a little taste of Sicily."

As Caterina described each dish, Nate could sense her vulnerability. The pain of her investment loss was palpable, and he couldn't help but feel a twinge of anger toward Hewlett for taking advantage of her trust. He looked over at Amy, reading the same determination in her eyes. They both knew they had to right this wrong, not just for Caterina, but for all those who had been deceived by Hewlett's schemes.

"Your passion truly comes through, Caterina," Nate said, his voice full of conviction. "We're looking forward to tasting these authentic Sicilian dishes."

"Thank you," Caterina replied, her eyes brimming with gratitude. "I hope you enjoy everything."

Nate exchanged a glance with Amy as Caterina retreated to the kitchen. They were ready to embark on their mission, to help Caterina recover her lost funds and bring Hewlett to account. But first, they would savor the flavors of Sicily, drawing strength from the culture that inspired Caterina's resilience and passion.

Nate's eyes scanned the menu, his anticipation building as he took in the descriptions of each dish. He glanced over at Amy, who was already nodding her agreement. They shared a mutual love for Italian cuisine and were eager to experience the true taste of Sicily.

"Let's start with the Caponata, Arancini, and Cannoli," Nate suggested, his voice filled with enthusiasm.

"Excellent choices!" Caterina beamed. "I'll have those out for you shortly."

As they waited for their food, Nate couldn't help but admire the intricate artwork on the walls, each piece telling a different story of Sicilian culture and tradition. It was evident that Caterina had poured her heart into every detail of the cafe.

When the dishes arrived, the rich aroma of spices and fresh ingredients wafted through the air, causing Nate's mouth to water. The Caponata was a symphony of flavors, with perfectly cooked eggplant, tangy olives, and a hint of sweetness from the raisins. The Arancini, crispy golden orbs filled with creamy risotto and gooey cheese, were irresistible. And the Cannoli, perfectly crisp shells encasing sweet, velvety ricotta, transported them straight to the sun-soaked streets of Palermo.

"Your food is truly remarkable, Caterina," Amy praised between bites. "It's clear how much passion and dedication you've put into your craft."

"Thank you," Caterina replied, her voice tinged with sadness. Nate could see her eyes glistening, as if she was holding back tears. "But I'm afraid my dreams of expanding my cafe have been shattered."

"Please, tell us what happened, we have the gist but need the detail" Nate urged gently, his empathy towards vulnerable individuals driving him to understand Caterina's plight.

Caterina hesitated for a moment before taking a deep breath and beginning her tale. She recounted how she had invested in Hewlett's scheme to expand her cafe, only for him to swindle her out of her hard-earned money.

As Caterina spoke, Nate and Amy listened intently, their hearts heavy with sympathy for her. She recounted how she had been approached by Hewlett, who promised to help her expand her cafe into a thriving chain across the country.

"At first, I was hesitant," Caterina explained. "I've always been cautious with my money, but Hewlett was so convincing and charming.

He showed me all these fancy charts and projections, and I could see my dream becoming a reality."

Caterina's eyes filled with tears as she continued her story. She explained how she had invested a large sum of money into Hewlett's scheme, believing that it would bring her success and security.

"But then everything started to fall apart," Caterina said, her voice trembling with emotion. "Hewlett vanished with all my money, leaving me with nothing but debt."

Nate clenched his jaw in anger at the injustice of it all. How could someone take advantage of hardworking individuals like Caterina? It was sickening.

"We're so sorry this happened to you," Amy said sincerely.

"Thank you," Caterina replied with a sad smile. "I should have known better. But I refuse to let this defeat me. I will find a way to make things right and rebuild my cafe on my own terms."

As Nate listened to Caterina's story, his anger toward Hewlett simmered beneath the surface. It was infuriating to learn that someone could take advantage of such a warm-hearted and trusting woman. He instinctively reached across the table, placing a reassuring hand on Amy's arm.

Nate admired Caterina's determination and resilience. She refused to let this setback bring her down.

"We want to help you," Nate declared firmly, exchanging a knowing look with Amy.

Caterina's eyes widened in surprise as she realized what they were suggesting.

"Absolutely," Nate said firmly. "We'll do whatever it takes to bring Hewlett to justice."

Caterina's face lit up with gratitude, and she reached out to squeeze Nate's hand.

"Your food is exceptional, Caterina. You deserve better than what's happened to you," Nate said, his voice resolute.

"Thank you, Nathaniel," Caterina whispered, her eyes welling up with gratitude. "I just want my life back."

Nate exchanged a determined glance with Amy, silently reaffirming their commitment to helping Caterina recover her lost funds and bring Hewlett to justice. They would use their unique blend of investigative journalism, ethical hacking, and military expertise to right this wrong, driven by their shared belief that no one should ever fall victim to such deception and cruelty.

But first, they took a moment to finish their meal, savoring the flavors of Sicily that had brought them all together. Every bite served as a reminder of the passion and resilience that defined both Caterina and her homeland – qualities that would undoubtedly inspire Nate and Amy in their quest for justice.

Caterina's dark eyes shimmered with unshed tears as she recounted her trust in Hewlett and his elaborate scheme. Nate and Amy focused on her every word, their expressions mirroring the pain and sense of betrayal etched onto Caterina's face.

"His charisma...it was intoxicating," Caterina confessed, twisting a napkin in her hands. "He seemed so genuine, like he truly cared about my dream of expanding the cafe. I never would have imagined that he could be capable of such deceit."

Nate clenched his jaw, the muscles in his neck tensing. As a former military man, he understood the weight of misplaced trust all too well. "Hewlett is a master manipulator, Caterina. He preys on people's vulnerabilities, exploiting them for his own gain."

"Nothing excuses what he did to you," Amy added, her voice firm yet gentle, her green eyes softening with empathy. The investigative journalist in her couldn't help but feel drawn to Caterina's story – another victim of injustice who needed their help.

Caterina looked from one to the other, her gaze pleading for reassurance. "You truly believe that you can help me?"

The couple exchanged a determined glance, silently agreeing to do everything within their power to recover Caterina's lost funds and bring Hewlett to justice. Their unwavering resolve was evident in the intensity of their locked eyes, fueled by their shared dedication to fighting for those who had been wronged.

"Absolutely," Nate replied, his voice steady and confident. "We will make sure that Hewlett pays for his crimes. You deserve justice, Caterina."

"Thank you," Caterina whispered, her voice thick with emotion. She dabbed at her eyes with the napkin, taking a deep breath to steady herself. "Grazie mille."

As the three of them sat in the cozy cafe, surrounded by the vibrant colors and comforting aromas of Sicilian cuisine, a shared sense of purpose united them. They knew that the road ahead would be challenging, but with their combined strengths and unwavering commitment to justice, they were determined to right the wrongs that had been done – not just for Caterina, but for all those who had fallen victim to Hewlett's predatory schemes.

The scent of garlic and basil hung heavy in the air as Nate and Amy considered their next move, each lost in their own thoughts about the web of deceit they were about to unravel. But for now, they were together in this warm, inviting space - a reminder that there was still goodness in the world, and a reason to fight for it.

Nate's eyes locked onto Caterina's as he leaned forward, the intensity in his gaze leaving no room for doubt. "Caterina," he said, his voice brimming with conviction, "we're going to do everything in our power to make things right." He paused, allowing the words to sink in before continuing. "Hewlett messed with the wrong people this time."

Amy reached across the table and placed a comforting hand on Caterina's, her green eyes softening with genuine concern. "We'll be there every step of the way," she promised, her grip firm but gentle.

"Thank you," Caterina whispered, her own hand trembling beneath Amy's steady touch. "I don't know what I would do without you both."

As Nate studied Caterina's face, a montage of past victims flickered through his mind – each one a testament to his determination to fight for those who had been wronged. The weight of their collective pain pressed down on him, fueling his resolve like an unquenchable fire.

"First," Amy interjected, breaking the heavy silence, "we need to gather more information about Hewlett and his operation. We'll use our combined skills to dig deep and expose the truth." Her background in investigative journalism had honed her talents for uncovering hidden secrets, while Nate's mastery of ethical hacking allowed them access to the darkest corners of the digital world.

"Agreed," Nate nodded, already mentally mapping out the steps they'd need to take. "Once we have enough evidence, we can work on dismantling his scheme and recovering your lost funds."

Caterina squeezed Amy's hand in gratitude, her eyes glistening with renewed hope. "Grazie mille. I cannot express how much this means to me."

"Think nothing of it," Amy replied, her expression warm yet determined. As she withdrew her hand, her thoughts echoed Nate's – they were in this together, ready to face whatever challenges lay ahead.

In that moment, the cozy Sicilian café seemed to radiate an almost palpable sense of camaraderie, a testament to their shared commitment to justice. The aroma of garlic and basil, mingled with the rich fragrance of espresso, enveloped them like a protective cloak – a reminder of the beauty and warmth that still existed in a world too often marred by deceit and corruption. And as the three of them sat there, united by purpose and fortified by friendship, they vowed to fight not only for Caterina but also for all those who had been ensnared in Hewlett's web of lies.

The sun cast a warm glow through the café window, bathing Caterina's face in light as she looked up at Nate and Amy, her eyes brimming with gratitude. "Thank you," she whispered, her voice full of emotion. "I never thought I would find people willing to help me like this."

Nate glanced at Amy, seeing the resolve mirrored in her green eyes. They had faced challenges before, but something about this mission resonated with them on a deeper level. He could feel it in the shared glance between them, the silent understanding that they were committed to helping Caterina regain what she had lost.

"Of course, Caterina," Amy said softly, giving the woman a reassuring smile. "You deserve justice, and we'll do whatever it takes to make sure you get it."

"Si," Caterina agreed, wiping away a stray tear with the back of her hand. "And when you succeed, I will cook for you the most magnificent feast!"

Nate chuckled, appreciating the levity amidst the seriousness of their conversation. He could envision the celebratory meal, the delicious Sicilian dishes filling the table, evidence of Caterina's immense talent and passion.

"Sounds like a plan," he replied, flashing a confident grin. "Now, let's get to work."

As one, Nate and Amy stood from their chairs, the creaking of the wooden floor beneath their feet signaling the beginning of their new journey. Their minds raced with strategy, considering angles to approach Hewlett's scheme and potential vulnerabilities to exploit.

"Remember," Nate said, his thoughts shifting to his military background and expertise in ethical hacking, "our first step is gathering intel. We need to know exactly how Hewlett operates and who else might be involved."

"Right," Amy concurred, her investigative journalism instincts kicking in. "We'll start by tracking down any leads we can find – former employees, business partners, victims. We'll build our case piece by piece."

Caterina watched them with admiration, her heart swelling with appreciation for their dedication. She could see the fire in their eyes, the determination to right the wrongs that had been done to her and countless others.

"Buona fortuna," she murmured, pressing her hands together in a silent prayer for their safety and success.

"Thank you, Caterina," Nate replied, his voice steady and strong. "We'll be in touch soon."

As they stepped out of the café, leaving behind the comforting scents of Sicilian cuisine, Nate and Amy felt a renewed sense of purpose. Together, they were a formidable team, and they knew that whatever battles lay ahead, they would face them head-on – united by their mission, their love, and their unwavering belief in justice.

Chapter 3

Nate Everhart leaned back in his chair, the dim glow of the computer monitors casting a blue hue on his chiseled features. His eyes darted between the screens as he scanned the sheets of financial data spread across their home office desk. He could feel the tension radiating from his wife, Amy, who sat beside him, her fiery red hair cascading over her shoulders like an autumn sunrise.

"Alright, babe, we're going to make this work," Nate said, his voice low and determined. "We create a fake High Yield Investment Program, one so enticing that Edward Hewlett can't resist taking the bait. If we can get him to invest, then we'll have a direct line to expose his fraudulent activities and bring justice to Caterina Bianchi."

Amy looked up from her own research, her green eyes meeting Nate's with an intensity that matched his own. "I'm with you, Nate. We just need to make sure our HYIP looks legitimate enough to hook him."

Nate nodded, running a hand through his dark hair as he considered the task ahead. "First things first, we need to research successful investment programs. We want to emulate the best to create something that Hewlett will find irresistible."

"Agreed." Amy's fingers began flying across her keyboard, pulling up browser windows and typing search queries with practiced ease. Her background in investigative journalism had honed her ability to find the information they needed quickly. "Let's start by looking at some reputable programs, see what elements we can incorporate into our own scheme."

As Amy delved deeper into her online investigation, Nate found himself reflecting on their mission. The injustice Caterina had suffered at the hands of Hewlett ignited a fire within him. He knew that he and Amy were uniquely qualified to set things right and bring retribution to those responsible. It was a personal crusade, one that they had undertaken out of love for Caterina and the memory of Amy's father, who had been wrongly convicted years before.

"Look at this, Nate," Amy said, breaking into his thoughts. "This HYIP has been successful for over five years. They have a clean, professional website and they offer a wide range of investment options. I think we can draw inspiration from this."

"Good find." Nate leaned in to examine the screen, taking note of the elements that made the site appear legitimate. He knew that creating a convincing facade would be crucial to their plan's success. "Let's start by gathering information on how these programs work, what makes them tick. We'll need to build a solid foundation for our fake program."

Nate swirled the last sip of his espresso. "Alright, let's brainstorm," he said, looking at Amy. "We need to craft an HYIP so enticing that Hewlett won't be able to resist it. What do you think are the key elements we should focus on?"

Amy tapped her pen against her chin, deep in thought. "Well, the financial projections need to be inflated enough to catch his attention. High returns and low risk – that's exactly what he'll be looking for."

"True," Nate agreed. "And we need a sleek website design that screams professionalism. Something that will make him feel secure investing his money."

"Exactly," Amy said, nodding enthusiastically. "I'll start working on the financial analysis, I know how to dig into the details and create convincing projections."

"Perfect." Nate leaned back in his chair, watching as Amy started scribbling down numbers and calculations. He knew he had married the right woman. She was brilliant, resourceful, and fiercely determined – qualities he admired and relied upon.

As Amy worked, Nate reflected on the path that had led them to this point. From his time serving in the military where he learned discipline and strategy, to his days as a carefree hacker having fun with his skills. Now, they were using their combined talents to bring down a dangerous criminal mastermind. It was an unusual love story, but one he wouldn't trade for anything.

"Hey, Nate, take a look at this," Amy said, breaking his reverie. She passed over a sheet of paper with her initial financial projections. "I've calculated the returns to be high enough to entice Hewlett, but not so absurd that they're immediately suspicious. What do you think?"

Nate studied the numbers, impressed by Amy's attention to detail. "I think this is perfect. It's exactly the kind of bait we need to hook Hewlett."

"Great," Amy said with a satisfied smile. "Now all we have to do is reel him in."

"Let's do it," Nate replied, clinking his espresso cup against her pen in a toast to their shared mission.

Nate's fingers danced over the keyboard as he quickly designed a draft of the fake website, his eyes flicking between multiple computer screens. The room was bathed in a soft glow from the monitors, casting an ethereal light on Amy as she continued analyzing investment data. Nate felt a renewed sense of purpose surging through him as he worked. This was a chance at justice, and they couldn't afford to fail.

"Alright, I've found a clean, modern template for the site," Nate announced, turning to Amy. "I'll customize it to make it look convincing. We need to seem like an established, trustworthy investment program."

"Good idea," Amy replied, glancing over at the website design. "Make sure it's user-friendly too. No one will buy into our scheme if they can't navigate the site."

Nate nodded and continued working, his fingers flying as he added compelling content and images that showcased their bogus High Yield Investment Program. He knew that first impressions were crucial, and he was determined to create a website that would hook even the most skeptical investor. As he glanced back at Amy, he could see the same determination mirrored in her eyes. They were in this together, and together, they would bring down Edward Hewlett.

"Okay, we also need some fake reviews to make this seem legit," Nate said, leaning back in his chair and stretching his arms above his head. "We should reach out to our network of friends and contacts – see if they're willing to help us out."

"Great idea," Amy agreed, pulling out her phone. "Let me send out a few messages." She began typing rapidly, outlining their plan and asking each person to write a fake testimonial for their investment scheme. In the message, she emphasized the importance of focusing on profitability and legitimacy, knowing that these factors would be crucial in convincing potential investors.

As they waited for responses, Nate continued tweaking the website design, and Amy sifted through financial data. The room hummed with quiet determination, punctuated only by the clicking of keys and the scratching of Amy's pen against paper.

"Hey, we've got our first testimonial!" Amy announced, excitement bubbling in her voice. "Listen to this: 'I was skeptical at first, but after seeing the impressive returns on my investment, I'm a true believer in their program. Highly recommended!'"

"Perfect," Nate said, grinning. "That's exactly the kind of review we need."

"Let's hope the others are just as convincing," Amy replied, her eyes glued to her phone as more messages began pouring in.

Nate felt a wave of gratitude for the incredible network of friends and contacts they had built over the years. These were the people who believed in them, who supported their quest for justice, and who would stand by them no matter what challenges lay ahead.

"Here's a good one," Nate said, his voice low and focused. "Listen – 'As a seasoned investor, I've seen my fair share of investment opportunities. This one stands out from the rest with its consistent, above-average returns. I couldn't be happier with my decision to invest.'"

Amy nodded approvingly, her emerald eyes sparkling with anticipation. "That'll catch Hewlett's attention. Keep that one."

Their conversation flowed easily between them like a well-practiced dance, each partner knowing when to lead and when to follow. As they continued sorting through the testimonials, Nate found himself in awe of how seamlessly they worked together, not only in pursuit of justice but also in their unwavering support for one another.

"Alright, let's go over everything one more time," Amy suggested, her tone shifting into a sharp, decisive rhythm. "We need this to be perfect."

Together, they scrutinized aspects of their elaborate scheme - the investment proposal, the website, and the carefully crafted fake reviews. Nate's mind raced with thoughts of Caterina Bianchi, the innocent young woman whose life had been destroyed by Edward Hewlett. He knew they had to do everything in their power to bring him to justice.

"Wait," Amy whispered, her brow furrowing as she spotted something on the screen. "This review mentions a specific percentage return. We should change that. It might seem too specific, too staged."

"Good catch," Nate agreed, quickly making the edit. "We don't want any red flags."

As they combed through details, Nate marvelled at Amy's keen eye and unwavering commitment to their cause. She was the embodiment of justice - precise, relentless, and fiercely protective. And as he looked into her determined eyes, he knew that together, they were an unstoppable force.

"Okay," Amy said, her voice resolute. "I think we've done it. Everything looks professional, convincing... perfect."

"Let's hope it's enough to reel in Hewlett," Nate replied, his heart pounding with anticipation.

With one final check for inconsistencies, they leaned back in their chairs, a rare moment of stillness settling over them. In the quiet of their home office, surrounded by the soft hum of computers and the ever-present scent of strong Italian coffee, Nate and Amy Everhart shared a look of unspoken understanding. They needed to see if their prey would take the bait.

The haze of computer screens cast a dim glow over the room as they sat shoulder to shoulder, their fingers dancing across the keys. Though they had accomplished a lot so far, they knew the devil was in the details.

"Alright," Nate said, rubbing his eyes before focusing on the task at hand. "Let's set up the email address and social media accounts for our little project."

"Perfect," Amy murmured, already scrolling through various social media platforms, setting up profiles under the same pseudonym. As she added logos, cover photos, and contact information, the digital presence of their fabricated investment program began to take shape.

"Let's post some updates on these accounts, make them look active and thriving," Nate suggested, his voice low and steady. Together, they crafted and scheduled posts about market trends, investment strategies, and shared articles from reputable financial sources, all aimed at reinforcing their credibility.

Amy paused, chewing her lower lip thoughtfully. "We need to be ready to respond to potential investors who might reach out with questions or concerns. We need to maintain a consistent narrative."

"Right," Nate agreed, opening a new document. "Let's create a list of frequently asked questions and prepare scripted responses."

They dove into the task, anticipating the inquiries that would arise from cautious investors. Nate reveled in the challenge, crafting responses that addressed doubles while subtly pushing the read toward taking the plunge.

"Here's one," Amy said, reading aloud from her screen. "'How can I trust that my investment is safe?'" She looked over at Nate, her fiery red hair spilling over her shoulder as she waited for his input.

Nate tapped his chin, considering the question. "We could mention the use of secure, encrypted transactions and emphasize the expertise of our team in managing investments." His fingers danced across the keys, translating his thoughts into a polished response.

"Good," Amy nodded, her eyes filled with determination. "And if they ask about the high returns, we should reference the aggressive investment strategies and unique market opportunities that our program offers."

"Exactly," Nate replied, adding the suggested explanation to their list. As they continued to refine their answers, Nate couldn't help but be impressed by Amy's analytical mind and unyielding pursuit of justice.

Satisfied with their prepared responses, they leaned back in their chairs, exchanging a glance of quiet confidence. They had crafted a web of deception aimed at ensnaring the one who had eluded justice for too long – Edward Hewlett. Now it was time to see if their masterful creation would hold up under scrutiny.

With a shared nod, Nate and Amy returned to their work, their keystrokes echoing through the room like a promise whispered in the night – a promise of retribution, of justice served, and of a future where even the most cunning of criminals could not escape the determined reach of those who sought to make things right.

A single bead of sweat trickled down Nate's temple as he typed the final lines onto the web page, the room illuminated only by the soft glow of multiple computer screens. The tension in the air was palpable, like a coiled spring waiting to be released. He glanced over at Amy, who had just finished reviewing their meticulously crafted investment proposal one last time, her red hair framing her face like a halo of fire.

"Alright," he said, his voice low and steady. "I think we're ready."

"Are you sure?" Amy asked, her green eyes searching his face for any hint of doubt. "Once we launch this, there's no turning back."

Nate nodded, his jaw set with determination. "I'm sure. We've covered all our bases – the inflated financial projections, the sleek website design, the fake reviews... Everything is in place to lure Hewlett into our trap."

"Let's not forget the social media presence," she added, a wry smile playing at the corners of her lips. "We have to give him the illusion of a thriving investment opportunity."

"Exactly."

"Edward Hewlett won't know what hit him," Amy mused, the satisfaction evident in her voice. Her past as an investigative journalist had honed her instincts for uncovering the truth, and now they were using those same skills to serve justice on Hewlett's silver platter.

"Justice for Caterina," Nate murmured, his thoughts drifting to the warm-hearted Italian woman who had fallen victim to Hewlett's schemes. The image of her cafe, filled with the tantalizing aroma of Sicilian dishes and the laughter of her patrons, fueled his resolve. This was about more than merely outsmarting a criminal mastermind; it was about restoring Caterina's faith in humanity and giving her the chance to pursue her dreams once more.

"Justice for Caterina," Amy echoed, her hand finding his and giving it a reassuring squeeze. "And for all those who have suffered at Hewlett's hands."

The plan was now ready to be set in motion – a high-stakes game of cat and mouse where the stakes were measured not in dollars, but in the lives and dreams of those they sought to protect.

Chapter 4

The chime of the coffee shop door announced Nate and Amy's entrance, with a whirlwind of autumn leaves chasing them inside. They spotted Tom Harding sitting in a quiet corner, his short, graying hair giving him an air of authority as he sipped his black coffee. Tom looked up from his newspaper and waved them over.

"Tom, good to see you," Nate said, shaking hands with the seasoned detective before sliding into the booth.

"Thanks for meeting with us," Amy added, her red hair gleaming under the warm lighting.

"Of course, I'm always here to help," Tom replied, folding his newspaper and setting it aside. "What do you need?"

"Let me start by introducing you to Caterina Bianchi," Nate began, pulling out his phone to show Tom a picture of the dark-haired, olive-skinned woman. "She owns a Sicilian cafe here in town, and she's recently become entangled in one of Edward Hewlett's schemes."

"Ah, Eddie Hewlett. It's been a while since I've heard that name." Tom leaned back in his seat, taking a careful sip from his coffee. "I remember when he got away with that art heist a few years back. What's he up to now?"

Amy pulled out her notebook, filled with detailed notes from her investigation. "We believe he tricked Caterina into investing in a fake expansion plan for her cafe. She lost a significant amount of money, and we're determined to bring justice to her and expose Hewlett's scheme."

"We've already started gathering intel on Hewlett's movements, but we need your expertise, Tom," Nate interjected, his eyes reflecting his determination. "We have to play this smart and stay one step ahead of him."

"Seems like you two are getting yourselves involved in something dangerous, as usual," Tom said with a sigh, rubbing the back of his neck.

"Alright, I'll help you out. But you need to be careful. You know how ruthless he can be."

"Trust me, we have no intention of underestimating him," Nate reassured Tom, his military background evident in his unyielding focus. "But it's not just about us – it's about Caterina and her dream."

"Thank you, Tom," Amy expressed, her investigative journalism instincts kicking in. "We promise to keep you updated on our progress and provide any evidence that might help your own investigation."

"Then let's get started," Tom said, leaning forward and lowering his voice. "First things first, you need to dig up as much information on Hewlett's current activities as possible. Find his weak spots, and use them against him."

As they continued discussing their plan, Nate and Amy knew they were walking a tightrope between justice and revenge, with the fate of an innocent woman hanging in the balance. But with Tom Harding's guidance and their unwavering determination, they were ready to face whatever challenges lay ahead.

A bead of sweat formed on Tom Harding's brow despite the chill of the air-conditioned coffee shop. He took a slow sip of his black coffee, his eyes never leaving Nate and Amy. "Alright," he began, wiping his damp hand on his pants leg, "we're dealing with a man who's well-versed in staying under the radar - which means we need to be extra thorough."

"Exactly," Nate agreed, his fingers tapping an impatient rhythm on the table. "That's why we need your expertise, Tom."

"Step one is gathering as much evidence as possible," Tom continued, his voice lowered to a near whisper. "You two have the skills to hack into Hewlett's systems, but you'll need to do it without leaving a trace."

Amy nodded, her red hair catching the light as she leaned in closer. "We've been working on that. We've got a few leads, but we need to know what to look for."

"Documentation is key," Tom advised, his gray eyes serious. "Bank records, emails, anything that directly links Hewlett to Caterina's situation. And maintain a clear paper trail. If it comes down to a legal battle, you'll need solid evidence to back your claims."

"Understood," Nate said, his dark eyes filled with determination. He mentally catalogued each piece of advice, his mind racing with thoughts of potential avenues to explore. His past experiences had taught him that understanding people's motivations could make or break their chances at justice, and Edward Hewlett was no exception. It was crucial to dig deep, to uncover the secrets Hewlett hid behind his charming facade.

"Remember," Tom added, "Hewlett's a cunning adversary. You'll need to think several steps ahead of him to avoid detection." He paused, watching as Nate and Amy absorbed his words like sponges, eager for any insight that would help them in their mission.

"Thanks, Tom," Amy said, her voice soft but laced with steel. "We'll do whatever it takes to bring him down and save Caterina."

"Of course," Nate chimed in, his military training evident in the resolve etched on his face. "And we won't let you down, either."

"Good," Tom replied, finishing his coffee and glancing at the door. "Now get out there and expose this bastard for what he really is. Just be careful, alright?"

Nate and Amy rose from their seats, exchanging a grateful look before turning back to Tom. "We will," they promised in unison, their shared determination fueling them as they prepared for the challenges ahead. With one final nod, they left the coffee shop, ready to put their plan into action and bring justice to both Caterina and all the others Hewlett had wronged.

The aroma of freshly brewed coffee hung in the air as Nate and Amy leaned in, their focus entirely on Tom's words. The detective's eyes darted around the coffee shop, ensuring no eavesdroppers were privy to their conversation.

"Listen closely," Tom warned, his voice low and serious. "Hewlett won't go down without a fight. He has connections, resources, and won't hesitate to use them against you if he feels threatened. Be prepared for anything."

Nate's fingers tapped rhythmically on the tabletop, betraying his eagerness to act. "We'll be careful, Tom. We won't take any unnecessary risks," he assured the detective.

"Good," Tom replied, taking a sip of his lukewarm coffee, leaving a faint mustache of foam on his upper lip. "And remember, stay within the confines of the law. It's tempting to bend the rules, but it'll only weaken your case against him."

Amy nodded, her red hair catching the sunlight streaming through the window. "Don't worry, Tom. We know the stakes are high, and we won't jeopardize our mission by straying from the legal path."

"Thanks, Tom," Nate added, sincerity in his eyes. "Your guidance means everything to us. We couldn't do this without you."

Tom smiled, the lines around his eyes softening momentarily. "I believe in what you're doing, and I know you'll succeed. Just stay vigilant and trust your instincts." Internal thoughts raced through Tom's mind, memories of past cases flooding back—those that had ended well and those that hadn't. He knew Nate and Amy were capable, but the weight of responsibility still weighed heavy on his shoulders.

"Alright, then," Nate said, clapping his hands together. "Let's get to work. We'll keep you updated with our progress, Tom."

"Please do," Tom replied, his no-nonsense attitude returning. "And remember, I'm here to help in any way I can."

As Nate and Amy stood up to leave, the detective couldn't help but feel a sense of pride watching them. They were the embodiment of justice, and though their methods at times unconventional, they fought with honor and dedication. In a world of corruption and deceit, they were a beacon of hope.

"Good luck," Tom called out as they exited the coffee shop, his eyes following them until they disappeared into the bustling street. He knew they would face challenges ahead, but also understood that their pursuit for justice was unwavering. And as the sun set on another day, the wheels of their plan began to turn, driven by determination, passion, and an unquenchable thirst for justice.

Rain pattered against the coffee shop's window, a rhythmic, steady beat that seemed to underscore the gravity of their conversation. Tom Harding leaned forward in his seat, his short, graying hair catching the dim light as he fixed Nate and Amy with a serious gaze.

"Look," he said, his voice low and no-nonsense. "I understand that in situations like this, sometimes you have to bend the rules a little. I'm willing to turn a blind eye to any...creative methods you might need to employ in your pursuit of justice."

Nate and Amy exchanged a glance, relief flickering across their faces. They knew that having Tom on their side meant they could take actions they otherwise wouldn't dare.

"But," Tom continued, holding up a finger to emphasize his point, "you need to be cautious and discreet. Remember, you're taking on a potentially dangerous adversary who will stop at nothing to protect his scheme. Hewlett won't hesitate to eliminate anyone who threatens him."

Nate's fingers drummed on the table, his mind racing with thoughts of Caterina and the countless victims of Hewlett's nefarious investments. "We'll be careful, Tom. We know what's at stake here."

Amy nodded, her eyes narrowing in determination. "We've faced dangerous situations before, but we always manage to come out on top. This time won't be any different."

Tom studied them for a moment, his expression softening as he recognized the fire burning within them, fueled by their unyielding commitment to justice. He knew he had placed his trust in the right people.

"Alright," he agreed, his tone still firm. "Just remember: patience and discretion are your allies. Don't let anger or impulsiveness cloud your judgment."

"Understood," Nate replied, his hand instinctively reaching for Amy's, their fingers intertwining in a silent vow to stand together against the darkness that threatened to engulf them.

As they stood up to leave, Tom's gaze lingered on their retreating forms. He knew the risks they were taking, and he couldn't help but feel a pang of worry for their safety. But in his heart, he believed in their ability to bring Hewlett to justice and protect those who had fallen prey to his treacherous schemes.

"Stay safe," he whispered into the rain-soaked air, hoping that somehow, his words would find their way to Nate and Amy, guiding them through the treacherous path they now walked.

Nate and Amy exchanged a glance as they pulled out their notebooks, their pens at the ready. The rain continued to tap against the coffee shop windows, creating a rhythmic background for Tom's words of wisdom.

"Tom," Nate began, his voice steady and resolute, "you've seen it all in your years as a detective. What other insights can you share with us that might help our case?"

Tom leaned back in his chair, his eyes narrowing thoughtfully as he recalled past cases. He took a sip of his black coffee before responding. "Remember that every investigation is a chess game. You need patience, persistence, and the ability to think several steps ahead of your opponent."

Amy's pen danced across the pages of her notebook, capturing the essence of Tom's advice. Nate nodded, an intense look in his eyes as he considered the implications of the detective's words.

"Let me tell you about a case I worked on a few years back," Tom continued, his gravelly voice captivating the couple. "There was this crime boss – real nasty piece of work – who had half the city wrapped around his finger. Everyone feared him, but nobody could pin anything on him. It took months of careful observation, gathering evidence, and anticipating his moves before we finally managed to bring him down."

"Sounds like a dangerous game," Amy commented, her gaze never leaving Tom's face.

"Very much so," Tom agreed. "But sometimes, that's what it takes to expose the truth and bring justice to those who have been wronged. You two have the skills and determination to make it happen, but you'll need to play it smart."

Nate tapped his pen against his notebook, deep in thought. "We're not unfamiliar with playing the long game, but we must be cautious not to lose sight of our ultimate goal: helping Caterina and exposing Hewlett's scheme."

"Exactly," Tom said, his expression serious. "Never lose sight of why you're doing this. That's what will keep you going when things get tough – and believe me, they will."

"Thank you, Tom," Amy murmured, her voice filled with genuine gratitude. "Your insight is invaluable."

As the rain continued to pour outside, Nate and Amy absorbed every word Tom shared, taking comfort in the knowledge that they were not alone in their fight for justice. Each story, each piece of advice, served as a reminder that patience, persistence, and strategic thinking would ultimately guide them to victory over Edward Hewlett and the darkness he represented.

And with that determination burning within them, they prepared to face whatever challenges lay ahead.

The worn leather of the booth creaked as Tom Harding leaned back, his fingers drumming rhythmically on the table. The steam from their now lukewarm coffees mingled with the afternoon sun filtering through the blinds, casting a warm glow over the three of them.

"Listen," Tom began, his voice firm but reassuring. "I've seen my fair share of criminals, and Hewlett is no different. Cunning, ruthless, and always hiding behind a veneer of charm – but he's not invincible. I believe in you two, Nate and Amy. If anyone can bring him down, it's you."

Nate looked into Tom's eyes, searching for any sign of doubt, but found only steadfast conviction. He nodded slowly, allowing himself to feel a spark of hope. "We'll do whatever it takes, Tom. Hewlett's caused enough pain. It's time to stop him."

"Exactly," Tom said, leaning forward again. "And I want you to know that I'll be here every step of the way. You update me on your progress, and if there's anything I can do to help, just let me know."

"Thank you, Tom," Amy chimed in, her green eyes shimmering with determination. "Your expertise and advice have been invaluable to us. We promise to keep you informed and share any evidence we find that could assist in your investigation."

"Good," Tom replied, giving them both a small, tight-lipped smile. "Just remember what I told you: patience, persistence, and staying ahead of your opponent. Those are the keys to success in this game."

Nate absently traced the rim of his coffee cup, mulling over Tom's words. He knew that their mission was complex and dangerous, but Tom's faith in them bolstered his own confidence. They had faced challenges before, and they would face them again – together.

"Alright," Nate said, closing his notebook and tucking it under his arm. "We'll be in touch, Tom. And trust me: we won't rest until justice is served."

"Neither will I," Tom replied, a steely glint in his eyes. "Take care of yourselves, and don't hesitate to call if you need anything. We're all in this together."

With that, the trio exchanged nods of understanding and mutual respect, their bond strengthened by their shared pursuit of justice. As they prepared to part ways, Nate and Amy couldn't help but feel a renewed sense of determination, ready to face whatever obstacles lay ahead in their mission to bring Edward Hewlett to justice and protect Caterina from his nefarious schemes.

The Sicilian sun cast golden beams of light through the coffee shop window, illuminating the swirling steam from Nate's half-empty cup. He glanced at Amy, her red hair glowing like a phoenix in the warm sunlight. Their eyes met, and she gave him a subtle nod, signaling that it was time to go.

"Tom," Nate said, extending his hand. "Thank you for everything."

"Stay safe, both of you," Tom replied, clasping Nate's hand firmly.

"Always," Amy chimed in with a warm smile.

With a final exchange of knowing glances, Nate and Amy turned towards the door, their footsteps echoing on the polished tile floor as they left the comforting aroma of espresso behind them. The bustling street outside seemed almost surreal after the intensity of their meeting. Nate tightened his grip on his notebook, feeling the weight of Tom's advice settle into his bones.

"Are you ready for this?" Amy asked, her green eyes searching Nate's face for any sign of hesitation.

"Absolutely," he responded without a moment's delay, his voice steady and resolute. "Hewlett won't know what hit him."

"Good," she replied, linking her arm through his. "We've got Caterina counting on us, and I'm not about to let her down."

Nate's thoughts drifted back to their first encounter with Caterina, her dark eyes filled with equal parts fear and determination. The memory only served to strengthen his resolve. He had seen firsthand the devastation wrought by Hewlett's schemes, and he wouldn't rest until justice was served.

"Neither am I," he murmured, more to himself than to Amy. "We'll find the evidence we need, expose Hewlett's operation, and put an end to his reign of terror."

"Speaking of which," Amy said, pulling out her phone and opening a secure messaging app. "I think it's time to get back in touch with our favorite hacker friend. We're going to need all the help we can get."

"Agreed," Nate replied, his mind already racing ahead to their next move. "Let's not waste any more time. There's work to be done."

"Right," Amy said, a fierce determination lighting up her eyes. "Let's get to it."

As they walked arm in arm through the crowded streets, Nate couldn't help but feel that they were on the cusp of something momentous. This was bigger than just Caterina's case – it was about exposing a dangerous criminal and protecting countless other victims from falling prey to Hewlett's web of deceit.

With Tom Harding's advice still ringing in their ears and their unwavering conviction fueling them onward, Nate and Amy strode into the Sicilian sunlight, ready to take on whatever challenges lay ahead in their relentless pursuit of justice.

Chapter 5

Nate leaned back in his swivel chair, the dim glow of the computer screen casting eerie shadows across his face. "This is going to be a tightrope walk, Amy," he said, rubbing his temples. "But I know we can pull it off. We just need the right people with the right skills to make our fake High Yield Investment Program look legitimate."

"Right," Amy agreed, her red hair shimmering in the screen's light as she tapped away at her keyboard. "And we have such a diverse group of friends who would be perfect for this job." Her focus shifted from the screen to Nate, eyes narrowing ever so slightly. "You remember Sarah, don't you? Our tech-savvy entrepreneur friend?"

"Of course," Nate replied, the corners of his mouth twitching into a smile. "She's got the skills and connections we need to make the website appear professional and convincing."

"Then there's Mark, the venture capitalist," Amy continued, ticking off names on her fingers. "His financial expertise and network will help us create the illusion of a successful investment program."

"Lisa, the social media influencer, is a natural choice for spreading the word about our 'amazing opportunity.'" Nate mimed air quotes before continuing. "Her reach and ability to generate buzz will lend credibility to the scheme."

"Tony, the stockbroker, and Maria, the business owner, will round out our team nicely," Amy concluded. "Their respective knowledge of the market and business operations will give our fake program the appearance of stability and sustainability."

"Perfect," Nate said, nodding in agreement. "These friends are the key to luring Eddie Hewlett into our trap and recovering Caterina's stolen investment. If we can convince them to join us, we'll be one step closer to justice."

"Let's just hope their sense of loyalty outweighs any potential doubts," Amy mused, biting her lower lip.

"Trust me, babe," Nate reassured her, his voice brimming with confidence. "By the time we're done explaining our plan and appealing to their individual motivations, they'll be on board. We've got this."

With a determined nod, Amy turned back to her computer screen. The room fell silent, save for the rhythmic tapping of keys and the hum of the computer's cooling fan – each keystroke bringing them closer to retribution against one Eddie Hewlett.

In the shadows of their makeshift command center, Nate and Amy plotted the downfall of a swindler, armed with only their wits, their talents, and the steadfast support of their friends. They knew that together, they would weave a web of deception so intricate, even the most discerning eye would be fooled.

For in the high-stakes game of justice and revenge, sometimes the best way to fight fire is with an equally blazing inferno.

Nate's eyes narrowed as he stared intently at the computer screen, his fingers tapping a staccato rhythm on the desk. "Okay," he said, turning to face Amy, who was perched on the edge of her chair, her fiery red hair pulled back into a loose ponytail. "We need to tailor our approach for each friend. Let's start with Sarah."

"Right," Amy agreed, nodding thoughtfully. "She's all about innovation and cutting-edge technology. We'll need to show her how our fake High Yield Investment Program incorporates the latest advancements in cybersecurity and investment strategies."

"Exactly," Nate responded, his voice exuding confidence. "We can also emphasize that once we've taken down Eddie Hewlett, she can use this experience to bolster her own tech reputation."

Amy grinned, knowing full well that Sarah would be unable to resist such an opportunity. "Now, what about Mark?"

"Ah, Mark," Nate mused, rubbing his chin. "He's all about the bottom line – the potential return on investment. We'll need to demonstrate that our fake program has a proven track record of success, even if it's entirely fabricated. He won't be able to resist the allure of high returns."

"Perfect. And Lisa?" Amy asked, her eyes sparkling with anticipation.

"Lisa's a social media influencer, so she's always looking for new, exciting content to share with her followers," Nate explained. "We can offer her exclusive access to our operation, allowing her to document and share the process with her audience. She'll love the idea of being part of something so thrilling and unique."

"Alright, let's go meet Sarah first," Amy said, grabbing her purse. "The sooner we get this ball rolling, the better."

***

As Nate and Amy entered Sarah's sleek, minimalist office, the scent of freshly brewed coffee wafted through the air. Sarah, a woman in her late 20s with short, jet-black hair and an ever-present smirk, greeted them with raised eyebrows.

"Alright, you two," she said, leaning back in her ergonomic chair. "What brings you here? I assume it's something more interesting than your usual small talk."

"Sarah, we've got a proposition for you," Nate began, his voice smooth and persuasive. "We've created a fake High Yield Investment Program designed to entice Eddie Hewlett into investing – allowing us to regain the funds he's stolen from Caterina, our dear friend and owner of that Sicilian cafe we all love."

"Interesting," Sarah replied, her skepticism evident as she adjusted her glasses. "But why involve me?"

"Because we need your expertise in technology to help sell the legitimacy of this program," Amy chimed in. "Your reputation in the tech world is invaluable, and your involvement will make the whole scheme more convincing."

"Plus," Nate added, "once we've brought Hewlett down, think of how this experience could strengthen your own standing in the industry. You'll be the entrepreneur who helped take down a notorious scammer – that kind of publicity is priceless."

For a moment, Sarah seemed to mull over the proposal, her eyes darting back and forth between Nate and Amy. Then, she leaned forward, the spark of determination igniting within her.

"Alright," she said, her voice laced with intrigue. "Tell me everything I need to know about this fake High Yield Investment Program."

Sarah's eyes narrowed as she scrutinized the High Yield Investment Program website displayed on her laptop. Nate and Amy held their breath, waiting for her verdict.

"Your design is clean," Sarah admitted, tapping a well-manicured finger on the screen. "The encryption seems secure, and I can't find any glaring loopholes that would give us away." She glanced up at them with a sly grin. "Alright, I'm in. Let's catch this scammer."

Nate gave Sarah a grateful nod; he could feel the gears shifting into place. One down, several more friends to go. As they left Sarah's office, his mind raced with thoughts of how to approach Mark, their next target.

"Mark's a tough cookie," Amy murmured, reading Nate's thoughts as they walked side by side. "He'll need concrete proof of success before he even entertains the idea."

"Agreed," Nate replied, the corners of his mouth lifting into a half-smile. "But we both know our venture capitalist friend loves a good challenge. And what's more challenging than getting back Caterina's stolen funds?"

Amy chuckled, her green eyes dancing with excitement. "I like your style, Everhart."

They arrived at a posh downtown lounge, where Mark was already waiting in a secluded booth. His immaculate suit and confident posture screamed power, but Nate knew better than anyone that Mark possessed an innate sense of justice. He just needed some convincing.

"Ah, the dynamic duo!" Mark greeted them, a wide grin stretching across his face. "What brings you to my humble abode?"

"Mark, we have a proposition for you," Nate began, leaning forward and lowering his voice. "We're creating a fake High Yield Investment Program to recover the funds stolen by an online scam from Caterina, our favorite Sicilian cafe owner."

"Interesting," Mark mused, his brow furrowing. "But why should I get involved? I have a reputation to maintain, after all."

"Your reputation is exactly why we need you," Nate responded, his voice calm but persuasive. "Your connections and influence are essential to our plan's success. And besides, think of the satisfaction you'll feel when we right this wrong and help Caterina rebuild her dream."

Mark considered their words, his eyes searching Nate and Amy's faces for any sign of doubt. After a moment, he let out a slow breath and nodded.

"Alright," he said, determination flickering in his gaze. "I'm in. But I'll need to see some solid evidence of how this scheme will work before I put my full weight behind it."

"Of course," Amy assured him, a victorious smile lighting up her face. "We wouldn't have it any other way."

As they shook hands with Mark, Nate could feel the pieces of their intricate plan falling into place. One by one, they were building an unstoppable team – fueled by justice, revenge, and just a touch of that irresistible Italian charm.

The conference room was a sea of crisp white paper and numbers, some typed up in neat rows, others scrawled hastily by hand. Nate watched as Amy expertly spread out the fabricated financial reports and testimonials, her fingers dancing like a conductor orchestrating a symphony of deception. Mark's eyes narrowed as he scrutinized each document, searching for any trace of doubt.

"Look," Nate began, maintaining eye contact with Mark and gesturing to the documents. "These are just a few examples of our success stories. We've made sure that all the i's are dotted and the t's crossed. Our investors –" he added a knowing wink, "– have given rave reviews."

Amy chimed in, her voice steady and assertive. "We've gone to great lengths to make this look as legitimate as possible. Rest assured, your reputation will remain intact."

Mark leaned back in his chair, his gaze unwavering. Finally, he let out a long exhale and nodded. "Alright, you've convinced me. I'm in."

"Great," Nate smiled, shaking Mark's hand before turning to Amy. "Now we just need a little help from our friend, Lisa."

***

Nate and Amy found themselves at an upscale coffee shop, the kind of place where the WiFi was free-flowing and the lattes were served with a side of Instagram-worthy latte art. They spotted Lisa in the corner, tapping away on her phone, her fingers flying across the screen with the precision of a pianist.

"Lisa!" Amy called out, pulling her into an enthusiastic hug. "Thanks for meeting us. We have a proposition for you."

"Spill it," Lisa said, setting her phone down and giving them her full attention.

"Remember Caterina?" Nate asked, watching as Lisa's face lit up with recognition. "Her cafe was robbed by Eddie Hewlett through an online scam. We've created a fake High Yield Investment Program to get him to invest and return Caterina's funds."

"Sounds risky," Lisa replied, her eyes flickering with excitement.

"Here's where you come in," Amy continued. "We need you to use your social media prowess to promote our fake program. Make it the next big thing everyone's talking about."

"Are you sure?" Lisa asked, hesitating for a moment. "If this goes south, it could ruin me."

"Trust us," Nate reassured her, placing a hand on her shoulder. "We've carefully crafted every detail of this plan, and we'll make sure nothing traces back to you. This is for Caterina – and justice."

"Alright, I'm in," Lisa agreed, a fire igniting in her eyes as she shook hands with Nate and Amy. "Let's take down Eddie Hewlett and bring Caterina's dream back to life."

The sun dipped below the horizon, painting the sky in shades of pink and orange as Lisa finally agreed to help Nate and Amy. "Okay, but remember, if it starts looking too dangerous, I'm out."

"Understood," Nate replied with a nod. "We'll be careful."

"Good," Lisa said, shaking hands with them before she disappeared into the growing shadows of the city.

As Nate and Amy walked away from their meeting with Lisa, they felt the weight of their mission settling on their shoulders. They had one more friend to recruit – Tony, a seasoned stockbroker whose knowledge and connections could make or break their plan. The scent of freshly baked bread wafted through the air as they approached the upscale Italian restaurant where they'd arranged to meet him.

"Tony!" Nate called out, spotting his old friend at the bar nursing a glass of red wine. "Fancy seeing you here."

"Ah, Nate, Amy," Tony greeted, his deep voice filling the room as he stood up to hug them both. "What brings you two to my favorite spot?"

"Let's grab a table and we'll tell you all about it," Amy suggested, her green eyes sparkling with determination.

Seated in a cozy corner booth, the trio exchanged pleasantries before Nate got down to business. "Tony, we need your expertise for something. It's a bit... unconventional."

"Go on," Tony urged, swirling his wine thoughtfully.

"We're trying to recover stolen funds from a man named Eddie Hewlett. He scammed Caterina, a Sicilian café owner who makes the most incredible cannoli you'll ever taste. We've created a fake High Yield Investment Program to bait him into investing, and then we'll return the money to Caterina."

"Sounds like quite the operation," Tony remarked, eyebrows raised. "But what do you need from me?"

"Your connections and advice, mainly," Nate explained. "We want this to look as legit as possible."

"Also," Amy chimed in, "we need you to help us navigate the financial side of things. We're confident in our plan, but your expertise would be invaluable."

Tony took a slow sip of his wine, considering their proposal. "It's risky, but I like that you're doing it for the right reasons. Besides, I owe Caterina for the countless espresso shots she's given me over the years. Count me in."

"Thank you, Tony," Nate said, relief washing over him. With their team assembled, they were one step closer to outsmarting Eddie Hewlett and reclaiming Caterina's stolen funds.

"Let's enjoy some good food and wine tonight," Tony suggested. "Tomorrow, we can discuss the details and plot our course of action."

As they clinked glasses, Nate couldn't help but feel a sense of camaraderie and purpose. Their eclectic group was united by a common goal – to bring justice to those who had been wronged. And with their combined skills and unwavering determination, there was no doubt in his mind that they would succeed.

The sun dipped below the horizon, casting an orange glow over the city's skyline. From the rooftop terrace of his luxury apartment, Tony surveyed the view, a glass of Chianti in hand. Nate and Amy stood beside him, their expressions a blend of determination and anticipation.

"Before we move forward with this plan," Tony began, swirling the wine in his glass, "I need to know how you plan on making this

High Yield Investment Program appear sustainable. Market volatility is always a concern, especially for high net worth investors like Hewlett."

Nate nodded, understanding Tony's concerns. He withdrew a sleek tablet from his briefcase, tapping the screen to display a detailed analysis of the program's investment strategy. "We've meticulously researched and created a diverse portfolio designed to weather market fluctuations," he explained. "Our investments will be spread across multiple sectors, reducing the risk associated with relying too heavily on any one industry."

"Additionally," Amy chimed in, "we've employed a series of algorithms to monitor market trends and adjust our strategy accordingly. This will allow us to stay ahead of the curve and maintain the illusion of consistent returns."

Tony studied the information presented to him, nodding in approval. "Impressive work. I can see that you've put a lot of thought into this. I'll do my best to add any further refinements."

"Thank you, Tony," Nate said, shaking his friend's hand. "Now, there's just one more person we need to bring on board."

***

Nate and Amy entered Maria's restaurant, the scent of garlic and basil wafting through the air as they made their way to her office at the back. A successful business owner, Maria had turned her small family-run trattoria into a thriving chain of Italian eateries across the city.

"Maria, thank you for meeting with us on such short notice," Amy greeted her warmly, placing a gentle hand on her shoulder.

"Of course," Maria replied, her eyes filled with curiosity. "You said it was important, and I trust you both. What's going on?"

Nate wasted no time in outlining their mission, describing how they planned to deceive Eddie Hewlett with a fake High Yield Investment Program to recover the funds he had stolen from Caterina.

"Interesting," Maria mused, stroking her chin thoughtfully. "But what do you need from me?"

"Your business savvy and connections," Amy explained. "We want to ensure that our program not only looks legitimate but also garners respect within the investment community. Your endorsement would go a long way."

Maria considered their request, her eyebrows furrowing as she weighed the risks against the potential rewards. Finally, she nodded, an air of determination settling over her. "I'm in," she declared, extending her hand to Nate and Amy. "Let's take this crook down and make things right for Caterina."

Maria's office was a testament to her tenacity and drive, adorned with framed newspaper clippings featuring her success story and sleek mahogany furniture that exuded authority. As Nate and Amy settled into the plush armchairs before her desk, they could sense Maria's steely determination – a trait that had undoubtedly played a pivotal role in her rise to prominence.

"Alright," Maria began, her fingers drumming rhythmically on the desktop. "I'm intrigued by your plan, but I have to ask – what if someone has reservations about investing in a scheme they might not fully understand?"

Nate nodded thoughtfully, his eyes glinting with anticipation. "It's a valid concern, Maria. But our objective is to make this High Yield Investment Program as convincing as possible. To do that, we need to ensure potential investors have access to all the information they need to feel confident in their decision."

Amy chimed in, her red hair catching the light as she leaned forward, her enthusiasm palpable. "We've already created a comprehensive and detailed website for the program, complete with graphs, charts, and projections. However, you're right – we should also provide an explanation of how it all works for those who might be less familiar with these types of investments."

"Exactly," Maria agreed, her eyes narrowing as she regarded them both. "Transparency is crucial in gaining trust and maintaining credibility."

"Maria, we hear you," Nate reassured her, his voice steady and resolute. "We'll create a dedicated page on our website outlining the intricacies of the program, so that anyone visiting the site can easily understand what we're offering and how it works."

Amy nodded in agreement, adding, "And we'll ensure that the language used is clear and accessible, without unnecessary jargon that might confuse people."

"Good," Maria said, a satisfied smile playing at the corners of her lips. "I'm glad we're on the same page."

"Thank you, Maria," Amy beamed. "We truly appreciate your support."

As they exited Maria's office and stepped into the bustling streets outside, Nate couldn't help but feel a surge of adrenaline coursing through his veins. They had done it – they had secured the support of their friends, each with unique skills and connections that would contribute to the success of their plan.

"Can you believe it?" Amy exclaimed, her eyes shining with excitement. "We've actually managed to pull this off!"

Nate grinned, the thrill of their accomplishment igniting a fire within him. "We're one step closer to taking down Hewlett and recovering Caterina's lost investment." His thoughts turned to Caterina, her warm-hearted generosity and love for her cafe, and how she deserved justice after being so cruelly duped by Hewlett.

"Here's to us," Amy said, raising an imaginary toast as they walked arm-in-arm down the crowded sidewalk. "And to making things right for Caterina."

"Cheers to that," Nate agreed, his mind already racing ahead to the next phase of their plan.

Nate and Amy stood on the rooftop terrace of their apartment, watching the sun dip below the horizon, casting an orange glow across the city skyline. The warmth of the day still lingered in the air, and with it, the exhilaration of having secured the support of their friends for their daring plan.

"Alright," Nate said, his voice low but firm, "we've got everyone on board. Now comes the tough part – making sure our High Yield Investment Program appears legitimate."

Amy nodded, her fiery hair catching the last rays of sunlight. "We've got the website up, and our friends will bring credibility to the program, but we need to make certain that no one suspects anything."

"Absolutely," Nate agreed, his military background kicking into gear as he focused on the logistics. "We need to ensure our digital tracks are covered. We can't take any chances with Hewlett finding out what we're up to."

"Right." Amy's investigative journalism instincts sharpened her gaze. "I'll follow up with Sarah tomorrow. She'll know the best ways to maintain our online presence while keeping our identities secure."

"Good idea," Nate replied, rubbing his chin thoughtfully. "And I'll touch base with Tony about the financial side of things. We have to keep our investment strategy solid and believable."

"Meanwhile," Amy said, tapping a slender finger against her lips, "I think we should also prepare a contingency plan, just in case things don't go as smoothly as we hope."

"Always one step ahead," Nate remarked, admiration shining in his eyes. "What do you have in mind?"

"Maria mentioned a concern that some investors might not fully understand the intricacies of the program. I think we should create a FAQ section on our website, addressing potential questions and concerns."

"Smart thinking," Nate agreed. "That'll add another layer of authenticity to our scheme."

As the last sliver of sun disappeared beneath the horizon, Nate and Amy stood side by side, their thoughts swirling with the intricate details of their plan. The weight of what they were about to do pressed down on them, but it was tempered by the knowledge that they were seeking justice for Caterina.

"Are you ready for this?" Amy asked, her voice barely audible over the hum of the city below.

"More than ever," Nate replied, his eyes reflecting the determination that coursed through his veins. "We've come too far to turn back now."

"Then let's do it," Amy said, a fierce resolve settling upon her features. "Let's take down Eddie Hewlett and make things right for Caterina."

"Agreed," Nate said, clasping Amy's hand in his own. Together, they turned away from the darkening skyline and walked back into their apartment, ready to face whatever challenges lay ahead in their quest for justice.

Chapter 6

The steam from the espresso machine hissed and sputtered, competing with the low hum of conversation in the small coffee shop. Nate leaned over a table strewn with papers, his eyes narrowed as he dissected the details of their latest plan. Amy sat opposite him, her red hair catching the sunlight streaming through the window as she tapped a pen against her lips, deep in thought.

"Okay," Nate said, his voice steady and decisive. "We need to build our team. The more diverse the skillsets, the better we can pull this off."

"Agreed," Amy replied, her fingers drumming on the table. "We have connections, people who owe us favors. We just need to find the right approach to convince them to join our cause."

Nate grinned, his eyes lighting up with mischief. "We've done it before, haven't we? They won't be able to resist the allure of bringing down those HYIP scammers."

"True," she conceded. "But let's start with someone we know we can trust implicitly and has the skills we need." She paused, considering their options. "What about Mark?"

"Mark?" Nate raised an eyebrow, mulling over the suggestion. "He does have experience in web development. That could be valuable for building the fake HYIP website."

"Exactly," Amy said, nodding with determination. "And he's always been a loyal friend. If we explain the endgame, I'm sure he'll want to be a part of this."

"Alright." Nate pulled out his phone and began scrolling through his contacts. "Let's set up a meeting with Mark at his office. We can show him what we've got so far and see if he's interested."

Amy watched Nate, her mind already racing ahead to the next steps. *We'll need someone in marketing, maybe Sarah... And Lisa would be perfect for the graphics...* She took a deep breath, reining in her thoughts. *One step at a time, Amelia.*

"Done," Nate announced, slipping his phone back into his pocket. "Meeting with Mark is set for tomorrow afternoon."

"Great." Amy smiled, feeling the gears beginning to turn. "Now we just need to perfect our pitch."

Nate reached across the table and squeezed her hand, his dark eyes meeting hers. "We've got this," he said softly. "Our cause is just, and we have the skills and connections to make it happen. One scammer at a time, we'll get justice for those who have been hurt."

Amy squeezed back, her resolve solidifying. Together, they would expose the HYIP scammers and protect unsuspecting victims from falling prey to their schemes. And with each ally they recruited, their mission would grow stronger – until justice was served.

The midday sun bathed the busy streets in golden light, sending shadows dancing across the faces of the bustling lunchtime crowd. Amy leaned against a wrought iron railing outside a charming Italian bistro, her fingers tapping out an impatient rhythm on her phone. She was about to meet Sarah, her former colleague from their days in investigative journalism. A few years back, they had been a formidable duo, chasing down leads and exposing corruption in high places. Now, she needed Sarah's expertise in marketing to spread the word about the fake HYIP.

"Amelia!" a voice called out, accompanied by the click-clack of heels on cobblestones. Amy looked up to see Sarah striding towards her, blonde hair pulled back into a neat ponytail that swayed with each step. "It's been too long!"

"Sarah!" Amy grinned, hugging her friend tightly. "You're looking fabulous as always."

"Thank you," Sarah replied, cheeks flushed with pleasure. "Shall we go inside? I'm starving."

"Of course." Amy held the door open, allowing Sarah to sweep past her into the cozy bistro.

They settled at a corner table near a window, the scent of garlic and tomato sauce heavy in the air. As they perused the menu, Amy steeled herself for the conversation ahead. *Remember, Amelia, you need Sarah on your side. Convince her it's worth her while.*

"Alright, Amelia, spill it," Sarah said, setting down her menu with a smirk. "I know that look. You have a story for me."

"Actually," Amy began, her heart pounding in her chest, "it's not a story. It's... a project Nate and I are working on. We need someone with your marketing expertise to help us get the word out."

"Interesting." Sarah raised an eyebrow, her curiosity piqued. "What's the project?"

"Have you heard of High Yield Investment Programs, or HYIPs?" Amy asked, watching her friend's reaction closely.

"Of course. They're all over the internet – most of them are scams."

"Exactly," Amy nodded. "Nate and I have been investigating these scams, and we've hatched a plan to expose the fraudsters and help their victims. But we need your help."

"Go on," Sarah urged, her eyes narrowing in anticipation.

Amy pulled out a sleek black folder from her bag and slid it across the table. "This is what we've got so far: marketing materials for a fake HYIP. We need to make it look as professional as possible to draw the scammers in."

Sarah opened the folder, her eyes scanning the pages with practiced speed. As she read, her lips curled into a smile. "This is... brilliant," she breathed, looking up at Amy. "You want me to help promote this HYIP, but it's actually a trap for the scammers?"

"Exactly," Amy confirmed, relief flooding through her. "We'll use their greed against them and bring them down. Will you help us?"

"Absolutely." Sarah's eyes sparkled with excitement. "I'm in."

"Thank you," Amy said sincerely, warmth spreading through her chest. "Now, let's order some food and celebrate our new partnership."

Later that evening, Nate found himself nursing a cold beer at a dimly lit bar, the clink of pool balls echoing through the smoky haze. He scanned the room and spotted Jake, his old military buddy, leaning against the bar with a half-empty glass in hand.

"Jake!" Nate clapped him on the back, grinning widely. "How's life treating you?"

"Can't complain," Jake replied, returning the grin. "What brings you here, Nate?"

"Got a proposition for you, my friend." Nate leaned in conspiratorially. "You still working as a financial analyst?"

"Sure am," Jake confirmed, eyeing him curiously. "Why do you ask?"

"Because I need your expertise in that field," Nate explained, pulling out his phone and showing Jake a series of financial projections. "Amy and I are setting up a fake HYIP to catch scammers. We've got the website and marketing covered, but we could use your help making these numbers look realistic."

"Sounds like fun," Jake mused, studying the projections closely. "I haven't done anything this exciting since our days in uniform."

"Perfect." Nate clapped him on the shoulder. "Let's grab a booth and dive into the details."

As Nate and Jake huddled together, deep in discussion over profit margins and investment strategies, they were united by a common desire for justice – a desire that drove them to use their skills to protect the innocent and bring down the unscrupulous.

The sun dipped low in the sky, casting a warm golden glow on the cityscape as Nate and Amy sat huddled together at their favorite coffee shop. They were deep in conversation, mapping out the next steps of their plan.

"Lisa's got an amazing eye for design," Amy said, sipping her cappuccino thoughtfully. "She could really make our website pop."

"Your cousin, right?" Nate asked, nodding in agreement. "Let's set up a video call with her."

"Great idea." Amy pulled out her phone and quickly texted Lisa, arranging a time for the call.

Later that evening, Nate and Amy settled into their home office, the room illuminated by the flickering glow of their computer screens. As Lisa's face appeared on the screen, Amy greeted her warmly. "Hey, Lisa! Thanks for making time for us."

"Of course!" Lisa smiled. "What's this project you're working on?"

Amy shared the screen, revealing the basic layout they had in mind for the fake HYIP website. "We're creating a sting operation to catch scammers preying on vulnerable investors. We need your help to design visuals that'll make it look legit."

"Wow, that sounds intense," Lisa replied, examining the layout closely. "I love the concept. I'm thinking we could use some bold colors and sleek lines to convey professionalism and trustworthiness. What do you think?"

"Spot on," Nate chimed in. "We want people to feel confident when they see the site."

"Leave it to me," Lisa assured them, her enthusiasm contagious. "I'll have some designs ready for you soon."

"Thanks, Lisa," Amy said gratefully. "We couldn't do this without you."

With Lisa on board, Nate and Amy turned their attention to finding seed investors. They knew their friend Alex had connections in the investment world, so they arranged a meeting at a trendy Italian wine bar.

"Buonasera!" Alex greeted them, his eyes twinkling with curiosity. "I've been dying to hear about this project of yours."

"Alex, we need your help," Nate began, taking a sip of his Montepulciano. "We're setting up a fake HYIP to catch scammers, but for it to be believable, we need seed investors who can play the part convincingly."

"Ah, I see," Alex said, swirling his wine thoughtfully. "You want people who know how to talk the talk and walk the walk."

"Exactly," Amy confirmed. "Do you think you can find us some trustworthy allies for this mission?"

"Leave it to me," Alex grinned, his excitement palpable. "I know just the right people who'd love to stick it to those scammers."

"Perfect," Nate replied, clinking glasses with Alex. "Grazie, amico mio."

As they toasted to their growing team, Nate's thoughts raced with anticipation. Each new ally brought them one step closer to justice, one step closer to righting the wrongs inflicted by the very criminals they sought to bring down. And in this high-stakes game of deception, every move counted.

The aroma of freshly brewed coffee wafted through the air as Nate and Amy sat hunched over a laptop at their favorite local coffee shop, Café Italia. Mark, their tech-savvy friend, had joined them in their mission to create the perfect facade for their fake HYIP website.

"Alright," Nate began, his fingers tapping rhythmically on the table, "we've got Lisa's brilliant visuals, but we'll need your expertise, Mark, to bring this site to life."

"Consider it done," Mark replied, adjusting his glasses with a smirk.

Amy chimed in, her emerald eyes gleaming with determination. "We also have the financial projections from Jake and some testimonials ready for you. Just make sure everything looks professional and legitimate."

"Piece of cake," Mark assured them, fingers already flying across the keyboard.

Over the next few days, Nate, Amy, and Mark worked tirelessly, bouncing ideas off one another, refining the layout, and adding content that would entice potential scammers while keeping unsuspecting victims at bay. With each passing hour, the website transformed into a convincing masterpiece.

"Great work, team," Nate praised, sipping his cappuccino as he surveyed the screen. "Now, we just need a final touch to seal the deal – authentic-sounding reviews."

"Leave that to me," Amy responded, reaching for her phone. "I'll get Sarah on board for that."

"Sounds like a plan," Nate agreed, leaning back in his chair and allowing himself a moment to savor the progress they'd made.

"Hey, Sarah," Amy greeted her former colleague warmly when she picked up the call. "I need your marketing expertise. Can you help us create some convincing testimonials for our fake HYIP? We want to ensure the reviews sound authentic and varied."

"Absolutely, Amy," Sarah replied, her enthusiasm palpable even through the phone. "I'll get started on them right away."

"Thanks, Sarah. You're a lifesaver," Amy said, her voice filled with gratitude.

With Sarah on board, the group dove into crafting compelling testimonials that showcased the supposed success and profitability of their scheme. They spent hours perfecting each review, ensuring they sounded genuine and diverse enough to avoid suspicion.

"Alright, everyone," Nate announced after days of intense collaboration, "I think we've got ourselves a solid product." His eyes scanned the room, appreciation evident in his gaze. "You've all done an incredible job, and I can't thank you enough."

"Here's to sticking it to those scammers!" Mark cheered, raising an imaginary glass.

"Indeed," Amy agreed, her eyes meeting Nate's. "It's time for justice to be served."

As they packed up their laptops and drained the last drops of their coffee, Nate couldn't help but feel a renewed sense of purpose. With each step they took toward dismantling this criminal world, they were proving that even in the darkest shadows, light could still prevail.

The sun cast a golden hue on the cobblestone streets of Rome as Nate and Amy walked purposefully toward their meeting with Jake. They could feel a palpable energy in the air, as if the ancient city was urging them forward, like gladiators entering the Colosseum to fight for justice.

"Ready to crunch some numbers?" Nate asked, his voice steady and confident.

"Always," Amy replied with a smirk, her red hair catching the sunlight as they entered the charming Italian café where they had arranged to meet their friend.

"Ah, there he is!" Nate spotted Jake sitting at a corner table, his laptop open, and a steaming espresso at his side. The aroma of freshly-baked pastries filled the room, but the trio's focus was solely on the task at hand.

"Jake, good to see you again," said Nate, extending a firm handshake.

"Likewise, Nate," Jake responded, standing up to greet him. As a financial analyst and former military buddy of Nate's, Jake had seen his fair share of high-stakes situations. He eyed Amy appreciatively. "And you must be Amelia. I've heard great things."

"Thanks, just call me Amy," she replied with a warm smile. "Now, let's get down to business." The three settled into their seats, laptops open, ready to finalize the financial projections for their fake HYIP.

"Alright," Jake said, rubbing his hands together. "I've been analyzing market trends and potential investor expectations. We need to make sure these projections appear realistic and enticing."

"Absolutely," Nate agreed, his fingers already flying across the keyboard, adjusting figures based on Jake's expertise. "We can't afford any slip-ups."

As they worked, Amy observed the two men, her mind racing with thoughts of their mission. She knew that justice wasn't always served through conventional means and that sometimes, the best way to fight fire was with fire. Her father's wrongful conviction had taught her that.

"Okay," Jake announced after an hour of intense number-crunching. "These projections should do the trick. They're solid, believable, and most importantly, tempting."

"Great work, Jake," Amy said, relieved. "Now we just need to make sure the website visuals are on point."

"Speak of the devil," Nate said as he received a notification on his phone. "Lisa just sent over her designs." He opened the email and glanced at the attached files. "Wow, these look incredible."

Amy leaned in closer, examining Lisa's designs for the website visuals. The sleek, professional layout perfectly matched their overall theme and message, making their fake HYIP scheme appear legitimate and trustworthy.

"Lisa has outdone herself," she murmured, impressed by her cousin's creativity and attention to detail. "Let's give her some feedback so we can refine the visuals even further."

Nate and Amy spent the next half hour providing constructive criticism to Lisa over a video call, ensuring that every element of the design aligned seamlessly with their plan. As they wrapped up the conversation, Nate couldn't help but feel a sense of pride in their progress.

"Alright," he said, closing his laptop with a satisfying click. "We've got the numbers, the testimonials, and the visuals. We're one step closer to making those scammers pay."

"Here's to justice," Amy whispered, raising her espresso cup in a toast.

"Justice," Nate echoed, clinking his cup against hers. And as they sipped their coffee, they knew that their mission was more than just personal revenge. It was about restoring balance in a world where too often, the scales were tipped in favor of the corrupt.

Nate glanced at the array of documents, printed emails, and laptop screens scattered across their kitchen table, each one a crucial piece of their meticulously crafted plan. The smell of freshly brewed coffee filled the air, mixing with Amy's subtle perfume that always reminded him of sunlit afternoons in Venice.

"Alright, let's do this," he said, rubbing his hands together and casting a determined look at his wife. "Time to make sure all our ducks are in a row."

Amy nodded, her fiery red hair catching the light as she leaned in to examine the materials. "We need to ensure everything is consistent, from the website design to the fake reviews."

"Speaking of which," Nate interjected, "did Sarah send you those revised testimonials?"

"Yep," Amy replied, scrolling through her email on her phone. "She really captured the essence of satisfied investors. It's almost scary how convincing they are."

"Perfect. We'll go over those together," Nate suggested, opening a shared document where they could review and edit each testimonial.

As they worked, their conversation was punctuated by the occasional burst of laughter, the absurdity of creating such a detailed web of deception not lost on them.

"Imagine if we used our powers for evil," Amy joked, sipping her coffee. "We'd be unstoppable."

"True, but where's the fun in that?" Nate smirked, a glint of mischief in his eyes. "Besides, I like to think we're evening out the playing field for those who've been wronged."

"Agreed. Now let's finish this up so we can present our masterpiece to the team and get their input," she said, refocusing on the task at hand.

Once they had reviewed every element of their scheme – from the website Mark had built to the marketing materials Sarah contributed

– they were confident they had a convincing package to present to potential investors.

"Alright, team meeting time," Nate announced, shooting off a group text to Mark, Sarah, Jake, and Lisa. "Let's gather at our place in an hour."

As their friends arrived, the atmosphere was a mix of excitement and apprehension. They all knew the stakes were high, but they also believed in Nate and Amy's mission.

"Thank you all for being here," Nate began, as they settled around the table. "Amy and I couldn't do this without your expertise and support. We've come a long way, and now it's time to finalize our strategy and assign roles."

"Mark, obviously you'll continue managing the website, ensuring it stays functional and secure," Amy added. "Sarah, your role will be crucial in spreading the word and creating buzz about our fake HYIP through social media and targeted campaigns."

"Jake, as our financial analyst, you'll make sure the numbers stay plausible and enticing, while also monitoring any trends or changes we need to adapt to," Nate continued. "And Lisa, your graphics are the icing on the cake – keeping those visuals polished and engaging is key."

"Lastly, we'll need to reach out to our seed investors," Amy concluded. "Having their support will lend credibility to our scheme, and that's where you come in, Alex. We're counting on your connections to help us find those who can convincingly play the part."

As they discussed the details of their plan, the room buzzed with energy and determination. They were a team forged by friendship and a shared sense of justice, ready to take on an unjust world.

"Remember," Nate said, looking around at his allies, "we're doing this to protect the vulnerable and level the playing field. It might be risky, but we're doing it for the right reasons."

With a shared nod of agreement, they clinked their coffee mugs together, knowing that they were prepared and ready to move forward – not just as partners in crime, but as champions of justice.

The sun dipped below the horizon, casting long shadows across the room as the meeting came to an end. Nate and Amy exchanged a knowing glance, their expressions a mixture of gratitude and determination. They stood up from the table that was littered with diagrams, financial projections, and design mock-ups.

"Guys," Nate began, his voice steady and strong, "I just want to say thank you. This wouldn't be possible without your help, and we really appreciate your dedication to this cause."

"Absolutely," Amy chimed in, her eyes sparkling with sincerity. "We know it's not going to be easy, but together, we can make a difference."

Mark leaned back in his chair, crossing his arms confidently. "Hey, I'm always down for sticking it to the bad guys." A grin spread across his face, highlighting the mischievous glint in his eyes.

"Same here," Sarah agreed, her fingers tapping rhythmically on the table. "It's not every day you get to use your marketing skills for something so... exhilarating."

"Count me in," Jake said, his military background evident in the determined set of his jaw. "I've got your six, Nate."

"Thanks, Jake," Nate replied, clapping him on the shoulder. "I know we can count on you."

Lisa looked up from her sketchpad, her fingers smeared with charcoal. "I'm glad I can contribute my talents to such a worthy cause. It's about time my art made an impact on more than just gallery walls."

As the team members expressed their enthusiasm, Nate felt a surge of pride and gratitude. These were more than just friends or colleagues – they were allies in a mission to restore balance and justice, using their unique skills to bring down the corrupt and powerful who preyed on the innocent.

"Alright, then," Amy said, gathering up her notes. "Let's get to work. We have a lot to accomplish, and time is of the essence."

"Remember," Nate added, looking each of them in the eye, "we're doing this for the people who don't have anyone else on their side. For those who've been taken advantage of by predators hiding behind computer screens and fancy titles."

As they filed out of the room, Nate couldn't help but feel a renewed sense of purpose coursing through him. They had come together as a team, united by their desire to make a difference, and he knew that nothing could stand in their way.

"Here's to taking down the bad guys one fake HYIP at a time," Amy said, linking her arm through Nate's as they stepped into the fading light.

"Cheers to that," Nate replied with a determined grin, knowing that their mission – and their dedication to it – was only just beginning.

Chapter 7

Nate's eyes sparkled with excitement as he leaned closer to Amy, their faces lit by the soft glow of the computer screen. "I've got him, babe," he whispered. "Eddie Hewlett is attending a high-end event at that fancy new hotel downtown."

Amy's heart raced as she took in the news. She had been waiting for this moment since they began their mission to bring Eddie to justice, and now it was finally within reach. "What kind of event?" she asked, trying to keep her voice steady.

"An exclusive investment gathering," Nate replied, his fingers dancing across the keyboard as he pulled up more information. "The guest list is small but filled with influential individuals. It's the perfect opportunity for us to get close to Eddie."

"Let's see what else we can find out about this event," Amy suggested, her investigative instincts kicking in. Nate nodded, and together they dove into the digital realm, their hacking skills working in tandem to uncover every detail they could.

As Nate infiltrated the hotel's security system and examined the floor plans, Amy focused on the event's attendees. Their combined efforts painted a vivid picture of the opulent surroundings and the high-stakes conversations that would unfold within them. The stakes were high, but so was their determination.

"Looks like there are multiple entry points," Nate muttered, pointing out the various doors and windows on the screen. "We'll need to bypass the biometric scanners, though. That'll be tricky."

"Leave that to me," Amy said confidently, her red hair blazing like a fiery halo around her head. "I've dealt with tougher security systems before."

Nate smiled at his wife's unwavering confidence. He knew he could always count on her to rise to the challenge, no matter how difficult.

"Alright, let's make a plan," he said, turning his attention back to the screen. "We'll need to blend in with the crowd, look the part."

"Plus, we should have a good cover story," Amy added, her mind already racing with ideas. "Something that'll draw Eddie's interest and get him talking to us."

"Exactly," Nate agreed. As they brainstormed together, their shared passion for justice and their unbreakable bond fueled their creativity. They knew they had to be careful – one misstep could ruin everything – but they were more than ready for the challenge.

"Once we're there, it's just a matter of waiting for the perfect opportunity to approach him," Nate said, his eyes narrowing with determination. "And when we do, we'll make sure he never forgets us."

"Justice is coming for you, Eddie Hewlett," Amy whispered, her voice fierce and filled with resolve. "And we won't stop until we see you behind bars."

As they continued to gather information and refine their plan, Nate and Amy knew they were closer than ever to achieving their goal. With every click of the keyboard, they were one step closer to outsmarting the cunning criminal mastermind, and ensuring that he faced the consequences of his actions.

Nate's fingers danced across the keyboard, his eyes locked on the screen as he delved deeper into the event's security system. Beside him, Amy was busy browsing through images of high-end fashion, selecting outfits that would help them blend in with the wealthy crowd.

"Got it," Nate announced triumphantly, bypassing the last firewall. "We're in."

"Nice work," Amy praised, her gaze shifting from the designer dresses to their newly-acquired guest list. "I think we can pull this off."

"Of course we can," Nate replied confidently, a mischievous glint in his eye. "Now, let's focus on our cover story. We need something that'll draw Eddie's attention and make him believe we're the real deal."

Amy thought for a moment, her journalistic instincts kicking in. "How about a High Yield Investment Program?" she suggested. "It's risky and lucrative – right up his alley."

"Perfect," Nate agreed, nodding. "We'll pose as successful investors who've made a fortune from it. He won't be able to resist."

With their plan in motion, they set about creating an elaborate façade for their HYIP. Nate focused on crafting a convincing website, complete with testimonials, charts, and graphs showcasing impressive returns. His hacking skills were put to good use as he manipulated search engine results to lend credibility to their scheme.

Meanwhile, Amy worked on designing brochures and financial projections that could rival any legitimate investment firm's. Her keen eye for detail ensured everything appeared professional and enticing, tempting even the most discerning investor.

"Check this out," Nate said, pulling up the completed website on his monitor. Amy studied it, impressed by its sleek design and persuasive content. Their fake HYIP looked like a surefire winner.

"Excellent job," she complimented, handing him a stack of freshly printed brochures. "These should do the trick."

"Couldn't have done it without you," he replied, grinning. Together, they packed their materials into a leather briefcase, ready to be unveiled at the event.

As Nate and Amy prepared for their infiltration, their shared desire for justice fueled their determination. The stakes were high, but they were confident in their abilities and unwavering in their pursuit of revenge. They would bring Eddie Hewlett to his knees – whatever it took.

"How do I look?" Amy asked, adjusting her elegant gown as she stepped out of their makeshift dressing room.

"Like a million bucks," Nate replied, adjusting his cufflinks with a smirk. "Ready to take down a criminal empire?"

"Always," she answered, her eyes blazing with resolve. Arm in arm, they strode towards the door, their hearts pounding with anticipation. This was it – their chance to make Eddie pay for his crimes.

"Let's get this show on the road," Nate declared, his voice steady and determined. "Justice awaits."

The chandeliers cast a warm glow across the opulent ballroom, illuminating the polished marble floors and intricate gold-leafed moldings. Nate and Amy entered the high-end event, their tailored attire and confident demeanor drawing admiring glances from the powerful elite gathered there.

"Feels like we're walking into a lion's den," Amy murmured under her breath as she surveyed the crowd. Her eyes flicked from one influential individual to another, taking in the designer gowns and expensive watches that adorned them.

"Relax, we've got this," Nate reassured her quietly, his grip tightening around the leather briefcase containing their meticulously crafted HYIP materials.

As they sipped champagne and exchanged pleasantries with fellow guests, an undeniable tension simmered beneath the surface. They were outsiders in this world of wealth and corruption, driven by a thirst for justice that set them apart from those around them.

"Look over there," Amy whispered, nodding discreetly toward a man with slicked-back dark hair and an impeccably tailored suit. "That's Eddie Hewlett."

"Got it," Nate replied, his pulse quickening at the sight of their target. His military instincts kicked in, assessing Eddie's position in the room and calculating the most efficient approach.

"Let's work our way over," he suggested, leading Amy through the throng of attendees. Their plan hinged on timing, on seizing the perfect opportunity to introduce their HYIP and ensnare Eddie in their web.

They strategically positioned themselves near Eddie, pretending to engage in lighthearted conversation as they carefully observed him. He was laughing animatedly with a group of people, a glass of whiskey in hand.

"His guard is down," Amy thought, her keen journalistic intuition sensing an opening. "We need to act now."

"Agreed," Nate concurred, reading her thoughts in the subtle shift of her expression. Despite the air of joviality that surrounded them, he knew that their mission was anything but a game. They had come here to avenge the wrongs Eddie had committed, and they would not leave until justice had been served.

"Ready?" Nate asked quietly, his dark eyes meeting Amy's fierce gaze.

"Always," she replied, steeling herself for the task at hand. The time had come to put their plan into motion, to bring Eddie Hewlett one step closer to his downfall.

Taking a deep breath, they moved in tandem, the moment of truth suddenly upon them.

Nate locked eyes with Eddie across the crowded ballroom, the clink of crystal glasses echoing like a symphony around them. With a reassuring squeeze of Amy's hand, they moved toward their target, their steps as fluid and synchronized as dancers in a grand waltz.

"Edward Hewlett, is it?" Nate asked, his voice smooth as he extended his hand for a firm shake. "I'm Nathaniel Everhart, but please call me Nate. And this is my lovely wife, Amelia."

"Charmed," Eddie replied, clearly captivated by Amy's radiant smile and warm demeanor. "What brings you to this event?"

"Business, mostly," Nate answered casually, feigning nonchalance. "We've been fortunate enough to find success in a variety of ventures. Some might even call us serial entrepreneurs."

"Indeed," Amy chimed in, her laughter lilting like a melody. "Our latest project has been quite rewarding, wouldn't you say, darling?"

"Absolutely," Nate agreed, his eyes never leaving Eddie's. He could see the spark of interest igniting behind those calculating eyes. It was time to reel him in. "We have been involved in a high-yield investment program that's been generating significant returns."

"Really?" Eddie inquired, sipping his whiskey with renewed curiosity. "I must admit, I've always had a penchant for lucrative opportunities."

"Ah, well then," Amy said, her tone playful yet conspiratorial. "You're certainly in good company. We've been able to help a select few individuals grow their wealth exponentially."

"Exponential growth, you say?" Eddie's gaze flickered between Nate and Amy, the allure of untapped riches tugging at his greed. "I'd love to hear more about this venture of yours."

Nate could sense the momentum shifting in their favor, the weight of their carefully crafted lies settling comfortably on their shoulders. They had Eddie's attention, and more importantly, his trust.

"Of course," he replied, a sly grin spreading across his face. "But perhaps we should discuss it in a more private setting. After all, opportunities like this don't come around every day."

"Agreed," Eddie said, his eagerness barely concealed. "Lead the way."

Seated in a dimly lit corner of the exclusive event hall, Nate and Amy laid out their elaborately designed materials for Eddie. The way the candlelight danced across the gold-embossed brochures only added to the allure of the HYIP they were about to unveil.

"Here we are," Amy said smoothly, handing Eddie a sleek black folder containing all the necessary information. "Our high-yield investment program."

Eddie opened the folder with a mixture of curiosity and skepticism, scrutinizing the contents as Nate and Amy watched him closely. His eyes widened at the sight of the financial projections, showcasing the impressive returns their fake venture promised.

"Twenty-five percent return on investment within just three months?" Eddie asked, his voice a mix of disbelief and interest. "That's extraordinary."

"Indeed," Nate chimed in, leaning back confidently in his chair. "And that's just the beginning. As our program grows, so do the returns."

Eddie flipped through the pages, finding himself increasingly drawn into their web of deception. He paused at the testimonials of their bogus investors, each one singing praises of the HYIP and its life-changing potential.

"Are these your seed investors? Their stories are quite... compelling," Eddie remarked, unable to hide his intrigue.

"Only the best for our inner circle," Amy replied with a coy smile. "We've handpicked each individual, ensuring that they possess the right qualities to help our venture thrive."

"Which brings us to the exclusivity of this opportunity," Nate interjected, his gaze steady and unwavering as he locked eyes with Eddie. "We don't let just anyone join our ranks. In fact, only a select few have been invited to participate."

"Really?" Eddie asked, clearly flattered by the idea of being considered for such a restricted group.

"Absolutely," Amy confirmed. "We believe that true success lies in working with those who share our vision and values."

"Understandably so," Eddie said, his expression shifting from surprise to determination. "But your program... it's unlike anything I've ever seen before."

"Good," Nate thought to himself, sensing the hook sinking deeper. "You're falling for it."

"Sometimes, the best opportunities are the ones that defy expectation," Amy added, her eyes never leaving Eddie's face.

"Indeed," Eddie agreed, closing the folder and placing it on the table. "I must say, this has been quite enlightening."

"Enlightening" was an understatement. Eddie had fallen for their ruse, just as they'd hoped. But there was still much work to be done, as Nate and Amy knew all too well. For now, however, they were one step closer to bringing Eddie Hewlett to justice. And that was a victory worth savoring.

Eddie leaned back in his chair, the flickering candlelight casting a sinister glow on his face as he studied the documents Nate and Amy had presented. He twirled an expensive fountain pen between his fingers, lost in thought. The air was thick with anticipation, like a summer night before a thunderstorm.

"Your projections are... impressive," Eddie admitted, his eyes narrowing as he considered the potential for financial gain. "I must say, I can see the appeal of this program."

Nate exchanged a subtle glance with Amy, their silent communication honed after years of working side by side. They knew they had him, but now it was time to reel him in.

"Thank you, Mr. Hewlett," Nate replied, his voice dripping with false humility. "We've worked hard to create something that offers real value to our investors."

"And we're confident that someone with your experience would appreciate the opportunity this HYIP presents," Amy added, her green eyes sparkling with mischief. She watched as Eddie absorbed her words, gauging the impact they were having on his ego.

"Ah, yes," Eddie said with a thin smile, tapping the folder on the table. "A chance to be part of something truly innovative - that's always been my aim, you know."

"Of course," Nate agreed, sensing the opening they needed. "And it's precisely why we believe you'd be a perfect fit for our exclusive circle of investors. Someone with your background and reputation... well, let's just say it would only enhance the prestige of our enterprise."

"Really?" Eddie asked, raising an eyebrow. His interest now fully piqued, he leaned forward, resting his chin on his hand. "Tell me more about this circle of yours."

"Let's just say it's a group of visionaries who recognize the potential in our HYIP," Amy explained. "They understand that being part of something this groundbreaking will only serve to solidify their status as successful investors. Like you, they're always looking for the next big thing."

"Exactly," Nate chimed in. "And by joining us, you'd be making a statement that Eddie Hewlett is not only a force to be reckoned with but also a leader in the world of investments."

Eddie's eyes gleamed in the candlelight as he considered their words. It was clear that his ego had been stroked just the right amount, and he couldn't help but imagine himself at the helm of an empire built on the foundation of this seemingly lucrative HYIP.

"Alright, you've got my attention," he said finally, a wicked grin spreading across his face. "Let's talk specifics."

Nate and Amy exchanged another knowing look, their hearts pounding with adrenaline as they prepared to take the next step in their intricate plan. The game was on, and they were ready to play.

The sound of clinking glasses and murmured conversations filled the opulent event hall, as Nate leaned in closer to Eddie. "We're only offering this opportunity to a select few," he said, his voice barely audible above the hum of the crowd. "And I must emphasize that spots are filling up quickly."

Amy chimed in, her eyes locked onto Eddie's calculating gaze. "Time is of the essence, Eddie. If you want to be part of this exclusive group, we need your commitment soon."

Eddie leaned back in his chair, drumming his fingers on the table as he considered their words. The urgency in their tone was palpable, and he could feel the weight of the decision pressing down on him. He glanced around the room, taking in the gilded chandeliers and marble pillars, as if trying to find an answer hidden among the extravagance.

"Alright," he finally conceded, his voice laced with both excitement and apprehension. "I'll give it some thought tonight. Can we meet tomorrow to discuss the details?"

"Of course," Nate replied, extending his hand for a firm shake. "We'll be in touch."

With their mission accomplished, Nate and Amy subtly excused themselves from the table, weaving through the crowd of elegantly dressed attendees. As they walked away, they couldn't help but glance back at Eddie, who was now deep in conversation with one of his associates, no doubt discussing the merits of their HYIP.

As they neared the exit, Amy felt a sudden wave of anxiety wash over her. "Do you think he bought it?" She asked Nate in a hushed tone, her heart pounding in her chest.

"Keep your cool," Nate murmured, his eyes scanning the room for any signs of suspicion. "We've played our cards right so far. Now, we just wait and see how he reacts."

With one final look back at Eddie, Nate and Amy slipped out of the event, leaving behind a world of wealth and influence that seemed almost surreal in its opulence. They knew that Eddie would be eager to explore the potential of their HYIP and, most importantly, how it could elevate his own standing within the world of high-stakes investments.

As the cool night air enveloped them, they couldn't help but feel a sense of satisfaction knowing that their carefully crafted plan was moving along smoothly. The game continued, with each move bringing them closer to achieving the justice they so desperately sought. The weight of their purpose kept them grounded as they disappeared into the shadows, ready to face whatever challenges lay ahead.

Nate and Amy stood outside the lavish venue, the faint sound of laughter and clinking glasses still audible from within. The night was ripe with possibilities, and the adrenaline in their veins made the stars above seem to shimmer with an electric intensity. A sleek black car pulled up to the curb, the engine purring like a predator stalking its prey. Nate held open the door for Amy, who slid into the leather seat with grace.

"Home, James," Amy quipped, a playful smirk on her lips as Nate took his place behind the wheel.

"Very funny," Nate responded, his voice laced with good-natured sarcasm. He expertly navigated the car through the narrow streets, the ancient cobblestones a stark contrast to the cutting-edge technology that hummed beneath the hood.

As they drove, Amy couldn't help but replay the evening's events in her mind. "Do you think Eddie will take the bait?" she asked, her voice a mix of hope and concern.

"Hard to say," Nate admitted, his knuckles tightening around the steering wheel. "He's a smart man, but I think we've given him enough incentive to at least consider our offer."

Amy stared out the window, watching as the opulent villas gave way to more modest homes. She thought about the countless victims Eddie had swindled and manipulated, their lives forever altered by his greed. She couldn't shake the feeling that the stakes were higher than ever before.

"Remember what we're fighting for," she murmured, almost as if speaking to herself.

Nate glanced over at her, his eyes filled with understanding. "Justice," he said simply, knowing that it was the one thing that drove them both forward. They were two sides of the same coin, each with their own reasons for wanting to see Eddie brought to his knees.

"Justice," Amy echoed, the word tasting like a promise on her tongue. She turned to Nate, her green eyes fierce and determined. "We'll bring him down, no matter what it takes."

"Agreed," Nate replied, his voice steady and unwavering. They shared a look that spoke volumes, their bond stronger than any force that might try to tear them apart.

As they sped through the darkened streets, anticipation crackling in the air like electricity, Nate and Amy knew that they were one step closer to achieving their goal. The game was far from over, but with each calculated move, they were inching closer to victory – and to the justice they both so desperately sought.

Chapter 8

Nate's phone buzzed against the cool marble countertop, shattering the silence that had enveloped their temporary hideout. With a furrowed brow, he reached for the device, his fingers tapping rapidly as he unlocked it and read the terse message. The tension in his jaw was palpable, and Amy couldn't help but notice the way his knuckles turned white as he gripped the phone.

"Something wrong?" she asked cautiously, her green eyes narrowing with concern.

"Maybe," Nate replied tersely. "We just got a message from one of our fake investor friends. They want to meet in person, urgently."

"Which one?"

"Doesn't say," he murmured, his dark eyes scanning the message again. "Whoever it is, they're clearly spooked."

"Let's not waste any time, then," Amy suggested, already on her feet and grabbing her coat. "The sooner we find out what's going on, the better."

***

The abandoned warehouse loomed like a giant specter above Nate and Amy as they approached its rusted metal doors. A chill wind whipped through the empty streets, sending shivers down their spines, and the distant howl of a siren only added to the unease that hung heavy in the air.

"Are you sure this is the right place?" Amy whispered, her breath fogging up in the cold air. She scanned the area warily, her instincts honed from years of investigative journalism screaming that something was off.

"It's the location they sent," Nate confirmed, his voice low and tense. He rapped sharply on the door, and after an agonizing few seconds, it creaked open to reveal their fake investor friend, Marco.

"Thank God you came," Marco breathed, his face pale and drawn. He ushered them inside quickly, casting nervous glances around the dimly lit warehouse as he did so.

"Marco, what's going on?" Nate demanded, studying their friend closely. "You sounded desperate in your message."

"Things are moving faster than we expected," Marco replied evasively, his eyes darting around the room as if searching for an escape. "We need to adjust our plan, take some new steps."

"Slow down," Amy interjected, her voice firm but gentle. "What exactly happened?"

Marco hesitated, wringing his hands together anxiously. "I can't tell you here. It's not safe."

Nate's eyes narrowed, and he exchanged a worried glance with Amy. Whatever was causing Marco's distress, it was serious enough to have him spooked - and that meant trouble for their entire operation.

"Look, I don't have much time," Marco stammered, beads of sweat dotting his forehead despite the chill in the warehouse. "Hewlett's been pushing me for results, and my family...we're in a tight spot financially."

Nate crossed his arms, his jaw clenched as he studied Marco intently. "So what? You've been playing both sides?"

"Please understand," Marco pleaded, desperation etched into every line on his face. "I didn't want to betray you. But Hewlett is ruthless, and I needed to protect my family. I thought if I could give him something, anything, it would buy us some time."

Amy looked at Nate, her eyes filled with hurt. The unspoken question hung in the air between them: how could someone they trusted do this to them?

"Marco," Nate said slowly, keeping his voice even. "Tell us exactly what information you gave to Hewlett."

"I-I told him about the fake HYIP," Marco admitted, swallowing hard. "I didn't give him your names, but I mentioned that there were two masterminds behind it all. He's smart, Nate. He'll figure it out soon enough."

"Damn it, Marco!" Amy erupted, her fists clenched at her sides. "You've put us all in danger!"

"Please, let me make it right," Marco begged, his voice cracking under the weight of his guilt. "Let me help you come up with a plan to throw Hewlett off your trail."

Nate stared down at Marco, his eyes cold and calculating. Inside, a storm of emotions raged – betrayal, anger, disappointment – but he couldn't afford to let those feelings cloud his judgment now. They had to act fast to mitigate the damage Marco had caused.

"Alright," he finally said, his voice low and steady. "We'll give you a chance to fix this. But if you cross us again, we won't hesitate to cut you loose."

"Thank you," Marco whispered, relief flooding his face. But as the gravity of his actions weighed on him, he couldn't help but feel a pang of fear. He had betrayed two people who were like family to him, and there was no going back.

Marco's fingers hovered over the keyboard, hesitating. His heart pounded in his chest, each beat echoing louder in his ears as he stared at the anonymous email addressed to Hewlett. The words on the screen seemed to blur together, yet every detail about the fake HYIP and Nate and Amy's involvement screamed out at him. With a deep breath, he tried to steady his shaking hands.

"Damn it," Marco muttered under his breath, his voice barely audible. Why was this so hard? He'd already betrayed them once; what difference did it make if he did it again?

As his mind raced, memories of late-night dinners in Nate and Amy's cozy kitchen filled with laughter and camaraderie flashed before him. They had taken him in when he needed it most, when he was drowning in debt and struggling to keep his head above water. Was he really about to throw away their friendship – their trust – for a chance at Hewlett's protection?

"Get a grip, Marco," he scolded himself, clenching his jaw. "This is your only shot."

With trembling fingers, he typed out the last few details about the plan, his stomach churning with guilt. As he hesitated, his cursor hovering over the 'send' button, the pressure from Hewlett's threats loomed over him like storm clouds. He knew there was no turning back now.

"Forgive me," Marco whispered, his voice laden with remorse, and hit send.

***

Hewlett leaned back in his plush leather chair, his eyes narrowing as he read the anonymous email that had just arrived in his inbox. His lips curled into a sly smile as he took in the information, his interest piqued.

"Interesting," he murmured, his fingers drumming against the polished mahogany desk. It seemed someone had decided to gift him valuable intel on this mysterious HYIP, and he couldn't help but feel a sense of intrigue.

"Who would betray their friends like this?" Hewlett wondered aloud. He had always admired loyalty, even in those who opposed him. But as much as it disappointed him to see such betrayal, it also presented an opportunity.

"Let's see what you're hiding," he said to himself, his determination growing by the minute. With each keystroke, he delved deeper into the world of the fake HYIP, his mind racing as he pieced together the puzzle before him.

As the information unraveled, so did his suspicions. There was no doubt in his mind that someone was pulling strings behind the scenes, and he was hell-bent on discovering their identities. Whoever they were, they had made a grave mistake by crossing paths with Edward Hewlett.

"Game on," he whispered, his eyes glinting with excitement. And as he prepared to dive further into the depths of the conspiracy, he knew one thing for certain: he wouldn't stop until he'd uncovered every last secret.

The room was dimly lit, the flickering glow of a single candle casting eerie shadows on the walls. The seed investor friend, his face pale and sweaty, paced nervously as he awaited Hewlett's arrival.

"Pull yourself together," he muttered under his breath, his hands trembling. The weight of betrayal weighed heavily on him, and he knew there would be consequences if Nate and Amy discovered his actions. But what choice did he have? His financial troubles had only grown worse, and Hewlett promised protection in exchange for his loyalty.

The door creaked open, and Hewlett stepped into the room, a predatory smile on his face. "I must say, I didn't expect to find an ally amongst Nate and Amy's friends," he said, closing the door behind him.

"Desperate times call for desperate measures," the investor replied, voice wavering. "I need your help, Mr. Hewlett. And I'm willing to do whatever it takes to save myself."

"Let's not get ahead of ourselves," Hewlett warned, leaning against the wall. "Tell me more about Nate and Amy's plan."

Back at their safe house, Nate's phone beeped with an urgent notification. He glanced at the screen and felt his blood turn cold. He locked eyes with Amy, who immediately sensed something was wrong.

"What is it?" she asked, her heart racing.

"Someone leaked information about the HYIP," Nate said, anger seeping into his voice. "We've been betrayed."

"Who would do this?" Amy demanded, her hands clenching into fists. Their trust in their friends had been shattered, and they couldn't afford any more setbacks.

"Doesn't matter right now," Nate replied, his mind working furiously. "We need to assess the damage and ensure our team's safety."

As the two strategized, the seed investor recounted the intricate details of Nate and Amy's plan to Hewlett. His voice shook with fear, as he realized there was no going back.

"Very interesting," Hewlett mused, his eyes glinting with anticipation. "I'll admit, I'm impressed by their audacity. But they won't get away with it. Not now."

"Please, Mr. Hewlett," the friend stammered. "You promised me protection if I cooperated. You have to keep your word."

"Of course," Hewlett replied smoothly. "But remember, you're in my debt now. And I expect loyalty."

The seed investor nodded, swallowing hard. He had made a deal with the devil, and only time would tell if he'd live to regret it. Meanwhile, Nate and Amy continued to scramble, their minds racing as they tried to salvage their plan and protect their friends.

Alliances had been broken, and trust shattered. The stakes were higher than ever, and there was no turning back now.

Nate's eyes darted across the dimly lit room, his fingers tapping a rapid rhythm on the wooden table. He could almost feel the tension hanging in the air like a heavy cloud, casting a shadow over their once unbreakable team. Amy paced back and forth, her red hair a fiery blur as she clenched and unclenched her fists.

"Alright," Nate said finally, breaking the silence. "We need to minimize the damage and protect ourselves and our friends. We'll intensify our efforts with the HYIP to keep Hewlett invested."

Amy nodded, pausing her pacing. "Okay, but how do we ensure everyone's safety?"

"First things first, we need to reach out to our seed investor friends. Warn them about the leak, advise them to be cautious," Nate replied, his mind racing with possibilities.

"Right." Amy picked up her phone and sent a group message to their trusted allies. The response was almost immediate, a flurry of questions and concerns pouring in.

"Guys, listen," Nate began, adopting a tone of leadership that he had honed during his military days. "We've been betrayed. Hewlett knows about the HYIP. It's crucial that we all stay vigilant and protect ourselves."

"Can we trust each other, though?" came a hesitant question from one of their friends, echoing the doubt that had begun to creep into each of their minds.

"Whoever did this will be dealt with accordingly," Amy said, her voice laced with anger. "But for now, let's focus on keeping the rest of us safe."

As the conversations continued, Nate couldn't help but feel a pang of sadness at the disintegration of their once tight-knit group. They had been through so much together, but now suspicion hung between them like an invisible barrier.

"Nobody makes any moves without checking in," Nate instructed. "If you suspect anything, let us know immediately. We need to be more careful than ever."

The group murmured their agreement, but Nate could sense the unease simmering beneath the surface. Trust had been a cornerstone of their operation, and now it was crumbling.

"Stay strong, everyone," Amy added with determination. "We've faced worse before. We'll handle this together."

As the virtual meeting came to an end, Nate and Amy exchanged worried glances. They knew that they were navigating uncharted waters, and the path ahead was uncertain at best.

"Whatever happens," Nate said quietly, his hand finding Amy's in a silent pledge of solidarity, "we won't let Hewlett win."

Nate's fingers danced across the keyboard, his eyes flicking between the multiple screens as he and Amy worked feverishly to create a smokescreen of false evidence. Their small home office had been transformed into a command center, with every available surface covered in hastily scribbled notes and half-empty coffee cups.

"Got another fake testimonial ready," Amy announced, her voice tinged with exhaustion but still determined. She emailed it to Nate, who added it to their rapidly growing collection.

"Good work," he praised her briefly, before returning to his own task of fabricating financial documents that would lend credibility to the HYIP scheme.

"Hey, Nate?" Amy said hesitantly, pausing for a moment. "Do you think we can really pull this off? I mean, Hewlett's no fool, and now he's on our trail."

Nate glanced at her, his eyes filled with a mixture of concern and conviction. "We have to try, Amy," he responded, his tone firm. "We've come too far to give up now, and there are too many people counting on us. Besides," he added with a wry smile, "we've outwitted him before, haven't we?"

Amy returned his smile, reassured by his confidence. "You're right," she agreed, taking a deep breath and diving back into her work.

As they continued their frantic efforts, Nate couldn't help but replay the events of the past few days in his mind. The betrayal by their supposed friend had shaken them both, and the knowledge that someone they had trusted was now working with Hewlett gnawed at him.

"Enough is enough," he muttered under his breath, pausing in his typing. "It's time we confronted our traitor."

Amy looked up from her screen, her green eyes narrowing in agreement. "Let's do it."

***

The door to the small, dimly-lit café swung open, admitting Nate and Amy. Their eyes scanned the room, finally coming to rest on the figure hunched over a table in the corner. The fake investor friend – who they once believed to be an ally – tried to make themselves invisible, but there was no hiding from the cold fury that emanated from Nate and Amy.

"Mind if we join you?" Nate asked icily, his voice barely above a whisper as he pulled out a chair and sat down. Amy followed suit, her gaze never leaving the face of their betrayer.

"Look, I-I can explain," stammered the friend, their eyes darting around the room as if searching for an escape. "I didn't want to do it, I swear. But Hewlett...he's dangerous, and he had me backed into a corner."

"Save it," Amy snapped, her patience wearing thin. "You knew what you were getting into when you joined us. We all took risks to bring about justice, and you turned your back on us."

"Please," the friend begged, tears welling up in their eyes. "I know I messed up, but I'll do anything to make it right. Just give me a chance."

Nate leaned in closer, his expression hardening. "You crossed a line that can't be uncrossed," he said, his voice low and menacing. "But if you truly want to make amends, you'll help us mislead Hewlett and put this right."

The friend nodded vigorously, clearly desperate for any chance at redemption. "I'll do it," they agreed, wiping away their tears. "Whatever it takes to fix things."

"See that you do," Nate warned, holding their gaze for a moment longer before standing up. "We'll be in touch."

As Nate and Amy left the café, the weight of their situation pressed heavily on them. But despite the challenges they faced, they remained steadfast in their commitment to righting wrongs and protecting those who couldn't protect themselves – even if it meant navigating treacherous waters and facing down their own demons.

The sun dipped below the horizon as Nate and Amy sat on a park bench, their breath visible in the chilling air. The once bustling area was now desolate and quiet, allowing them to finally process the weight of their situation. Nate stared at the ground, clenching his fists, while Amy gazed at the darkening sky, her eyes searching for answers.

"Can you believe it?" Nate asked, breaking the silence. "After all we've been through, one of our own betrays us."

Amy sighed, her heart aching for the friend they'd just confronted. "I understand why they did it," she said softly. "Desperation can drive people to do things they never thought possible."

"Doesn't make it right, though," Nate muttered, anger simmering beneath his calm exterior. "We trusted them. We let them into our lives, and they threw it all away for what? A chance at protection from Hewlett?"

"Sometimes fear gets the better of us," Amy replied, her voice tinged with sadness. "But we can't let this setback deter us. We have a mission to complete, Nate. We need to stay focused."

"Focus..." Nate repeated, rubbing his temples as he tried to clear his mind. "It's getting harder and harder to maintain that when everything seems to be crumbling around us."

"Then let's regroup," Amy suggested, determination shining in her eyes. "We'll strengthen our defenses, protect our allies, and mislead Hewlett at every turn. We're still a strong team, Nate. Betrayal or not, we'll see this through."

"Right," Nate agreed, taking a deep breath. "Let's get back to work."

As they stood up, ready to leave the park, Amy's phone buzzed with an incoming message. She glanced at the screen, her face paling as she read the contents aloud.

"Anonymous tip," she said, her voice trembling. "Hewlett's hired a private investigator. They're digging into our pasts."

Nate's eyes widened as he felt his pulse quicken. The stakes had just been raised, and time was running out. He clenched his jaw, fury igniting in his chest.

"Looks like we don't have a choice," Nate gritted out. "We need to act now. We'll have to play our hand sooner than expected."

Amy nodded, her resolve hardening. "Let's do this," she whispered, gripping Nate's hand as they made their way back to their safe house, ready to face whatever challenges lay ahead.

As they walked away, unseen by either of them, a figure lurked in the shadows, watching intently.

Chapter 9

Nate's fingers danced across the keyboard, his eyes locked on the screen before him. The dim light from the monitor cast eerie shadows across his face, reflecting off the determination in his eyes. Amy sat beside him, her red hair a fiery contrast to the gloom of their home office. She studied their progress carefully, her brow furrowed as she considered the next steps.

"Things are moving along," she said, "but we need to create a sense of urgency around this HYIP. If Eddie doesn't feel the pressure to act soon, we could lose our window."

"Agreed," Nate replied, pausing his work to consider their options. "We've got all the pieces in place – the seed investors, the fake testimonials. Now, we just need to push him over the edge."

"Exactly." Amy tapped her pen against her lips, deep in thought. "What if we make it seem like there are limited-time offers and exclusive benefits for early investors? That way, Eddie will feel like he can't afford to miss out on this opportunity."

Nate's lips curled into a smile as he processed Amy's suggestion. "I like that. It plays on his greed and his desire to be part of something elite. And it also adds another layer of credibility to our scheme."

"Right," Amy agreed, already scribbling down notes on her legal pad. "We can present it as a once-in-a-lifetime chance to get in on the ground floor of something big."

Nate nodded, turning back to his computer. "Okay, I'll draft up an email emphasizing the limited availability of these special offers. We'll make it clear that time is running out, and Eddie needs to make a decision quickly if he wants in."

As he typed, Nate couldn't help but feel a surge of adrenaline coursing through his veins. For years, he had used his hacking skills for fun and amusement. But now, as he and Amy worked together to bring justice to those who had wronged Caterina, he found a new sense of purpose.

"Let's make sure we really sell it," Amy said, her voice low and intense. "We need Eddie to feel like he's got the world at his fingertips if he takes this opportunity."

Nate felt the weight of their mission settle on his shoulders. Their time in the military and Amy's background in investigative journalism had prepared them for this moment. They were ready to see this through, to ensure that Caterina's memory was honored and that Eddie paid for his crimes.

"Absolutely," Nate replied, his fingers flying across the keys once more. "We'll give him an offer he can't refuse."

"High returns, Nate," Amy said, a gleam in her eyes. "That's what'll really reel him in. We have to make Eddie believe he's going to make a fortune if he doesn't hesitate."

Nate looked up from his computer screen, his fingers hovering above the keyboard. He considered her words, thoughts racing through his mind. It made sense. They needed to appeal to Eddie's greed if they wanted him to take the bait.

"Alright, we'll emphasize that," Nate agreed, his voice firm. "But how do we present all of this information in a way that'll truly capture his attention? How do we tap into his desires and motivations?"

Amy chewed on her lip for a moment, thinking. "Eddie's always been drawn to power and wealth. What if we create a presentation that speaks directly to those desires? Something visually impactful – charts, graphs, maybe even a few staged photos of our fake investors living the high life."

"Good idea," Nate said, nodding. "We can also include some testimonials from these so-called investors, raving about their success thanks to the HYIP."

"Perfect," Amy replied, her lips curving into a sly smile. "We'll make it impossible for him to resist the allure of such an incredible opportunity."

As Nate continued typing, he could feel the gears turning in his head. Their plan was starting to come together, each piece of the puzzle falling into place. Caterina's memory fueled their determination, pushing them forward in their quest for justice.

"Let's not forget to stress the urgency," Nate reminded Amy. "We need Eddie to feel like he has to act now, or he'll miss out."

"Of course," she agreed, running her fingers through her fiery red hair. "The fear of missing out is a powerful motivator. We'll make sure to hammer that point home."

"Then we're set," Nate said, his voice steady and filled with resolve. "We'll craft a presentation that's impossible to resist – one that appeals directly to Eddie's desires and fears. And once he's hooked, we'll reel him in and finally achieve justice for Caterina."

The room seemed to hum with anticipation as Nate and Amy got to work, their shared passion for their mission driving them forward. Together, they would bring down the man responsible for so much pain and suffering, and in doing so, honor the memory of a woman who deserved nothing less than justice.

"Justice for Caterina," Amy whispered, her voice filled with determination and a hint of sadness. "And for all the others who've been hurt by people like Eddie."

"Justice," Nate echoed, his eyes meeting hers in a moment of quiet understanding. And with that, they continued their careful preparation, each keystroke bringing them one step closer to their goal.

A thin, pale hand closed around the silver pen, its weight both a comfort and a reminder of the task ahead. Nate stared out the window at the bustling city streets, his dark eyes narrowing in determination. "We need to make this meeting feel like a once-in-a-lifetime opportunity," he mused aloud. "Somewhere upscale, exclusive... a place that will appeal to Eddie's sense of luxury."

"Agreed," Amy replied, her green eyes scanning their carefully crafted list of potential venues. "How about La Dolce Vita? It's one of the top Italian restaurants in the city, and their private dining room is perfect for our needs."

"Perfect," Nate said with a nod. "Book it."

As Amy picked up her phone to make the reservation, Nate turned back to his computer, pulling up several financial charts and graphs. He knew they needed hard data to support their claims, but more importantly, they needed to weave a story – a story that would resonate with Eddie on a deeply personal level.

"Look at this," Amy said, drawing Nate's attention to an article she had found during her research. "It's about a group of investors who got in early on a similar HYIP, and now they're all multi-millionaires. We could use this as a case study, show Eddie what he stands to gain if he acts quickly."

"Good find," Nate praised, already imagining how he would incorporate the information into their presentation. "I'll get started on the visuals while you work on the testimonials from our fake investors."

As they worked, Nate couldn't help but marvel at the way their skills complemented each other. Amy's background in investigative journalism had taught her how to dig deep, uncovering the hidden truths that others might miss. Meanwhile, Nate's time in the military and experience as an ethical hacker had honed his instincts and ability to think strategically.

"Okay," Amy announced a short while later, her voice tinged with satisfaction. "I've got three glowing testimonials from our seed investors, each one emphasizing the incredible returns they've seen and the need to act fast before it's too late."

"Excellent," Nate replied, adding the finishing touches to a visually striking bar graph that illustrated the HYIP's projected growth. "I think we're about ready. Let's go over our talking points one more time, make sure we're on the same page when it comes to emphasizing urgency and exclusivity."

As they reviewed their plan, Nate could feel the familiar thrill of anticipation coursing through his veins. They were so close now, just one carefully orchestrated meeting away from achieving justice for Caterina – and all the others who had suffered at Eddie's hands.

"Remember," he said quietly, his voice firm and resolute, "we can't afford any mistakes. Not when we've come this far."

Amy met his gaze, her eyes shining with a fierce determination that mirrored his own. "We won't fail, Nate," she promised. "Not this time."

And with that, they turned back to their work, each keystroke and carefully chosen word bringing them one step closer to the endgame they had been working towards for so long.

The sun dipped below the horizon, casting an orange and pink glow over the sleek glass-and-steel building that housed Le Ciel Étoilé, one of the city's most exclusive restaurants. Nate's pulse quickened as he watched the valets park luxury cars in front of the entrance, their crisp uniforms adding to the air of sophistication that permeated the place.

"Remember, Amy," Nate murmured, his gaze locked on their target, "act like we belong here, like we're part of this world."

Amy flashed him a reassuring smile, her red hair cascading down her back like a fiery waterfall. "When have I ever let you down?"

With that, they stepped out of their car and strode confidently into the restaurant. They had arrived early to ensure everything was in place for their pitch, from the private table tucked away in a secluded corner to the carefully arranged props that would lend credibility to their presentation.

"Mr. Everhart!" the maître d' greeted them with a wide smile, expertly masking any surprise he may have felt at seeing a couple like Nate and Amy in his establishment. "Your table is ready. Please, follow me."

As they walked through the dimly lit dining room, Nate couldn't help but marvel at the elegant surroundings – from the crystal chandeliers that sparkled overhead to the impeccably dressed patrons who murmured quietly over plates of exquisite cuisine.

This is Eddie's world, he thought grimly. A world built on the suffering of others.

They reached their private table, and Nate nodded his approval at the discreet screen they had requested to shield them from curious eyes. He quickly set up their laptop, Amy double-checking the charts and graphs that illustrated the HYIP's potential success. Everything had to be perfect if they were to hook Eddie and achieve justice for Caterina.

"Showtime," Nate whispered, just as the maître d' announced Eddie's arrival.

Eddie sauntered into the restaurant, his expensive suit impeccably tailored to accentuate his broad shoulders and lean frame. His slicked-back hair gleamed under the soft lighting, and an air of confidence and curiosity radiated off him as he scanned the room.

"Edward!" Nate called out with a warm smile, rising from his seat to greet the criminal mastermind. "So glad you could make it."

"Wouldn't miss it for the world," Eddie replied smoothly, his eyes darting between Nate and Amy, clearly appraising their every move.

"Please, have a seat," Amy offered, gesturing to the empty chair at their table.

Eddie sat down, his gaze never leaving Nate's face. The tension in the air was palpable, but beneath it all, Nate could sense Eddie's curiosity – his desire to learn more about this too-good-to-be-true investment opportunity that had been dangled before him like bait on a hook.

"Shall we get started?" Nate asked, opening the laptop and turning the screen to face Eddie.

"By all means," Eddie replied, leaning back in his chair and steepling his fingers. "I'm eager to see what you have to offer."

As Nate began his pitch, he couldn't help but feel a thrill of anticipation. With each passing moment, they were drawing Eddie further into their web, one carefully crafted lie at a time. And soon, justice would finally be served.

The first slide of the presentation illuminated Eddie's face, casting an almost sinister glow. Nate watched Eddie's eyes narrow as he took in the impressive numbers and charts on display.

"Edward, let me start by saying that this High-Yield Investment Program is unlike any other you've seen," Nate began, his voice smooth and captivating. He kept his military posture, exuding authority. "The returns are truly exceptional, and I'm sure you'll agree."

Eddie leaned forward, intrigued. "I'm listening."

Amy observed the exchange from the corner of her eye, her investigative journalist instincts kicking in as she analyzed Eddie's reactions.

"Take a look at these graphs," Nate continued, gesturing to the screen. "Our HYIP has generated consistent profits for our early investors, far surpassing any traditional investment vehicle."

"Interesting," Eddie mused, rubbing his chin. "And how do you achieve such high returns?"

"Ah, that's where our expertise comes in," Amy interjected, her confident demeanor matching Nate's. "We have a unique combination of cutting-edge algorithms and carefully selected investments that ensures maximum profitability."

"Can you give me some examples of these investments?" Eddie asked, his curiosity growing.

"Of course," Amy replied, pulling up a new slide filled with detailed information. "We invest in a diversified portfolio of cryptocurrencies, commodities, and even some highly profitable start-ups. Our algorithms monitor the markets 24/7, allowing us to capitalize on any sudden changes."

Nate couldn't help but notice Eddie's slight shift in body language, indicating his increasing interest. He knew they had him hooked, but they needed to reel him in further.

"Edward, I understand you're a man who appreciates exclusivity and opportunity," Nate said, leaning in closer. "That's why we've reserved a limited number of spots for investors like yourself – those who recognize the potential of this HYIP and are ready to seize it."

"Is that so?" Eddie asked, raising an eyebrow.

"Yes," Amy chimed in. "And we've already received interest from several high-profile investors, so I'd advise you not to wait too long if you're considering joining us."

Eddie's eyes flickered back and forth between Nate and Amy, no doubt weighing his options. He took a deep breath, then leaned back in his chair, the gears turning in his cunning mind.

"Alright," he said finally. "You've got my attention. Let's discuss the specifics."

Nate and Amy exchanged a subtle, satisfied glance. They knew their plan was working – and they were one step closer to achieving justice for Caterina.

Eddie's fingers drummed rhythmically on the polished wooden tabletop, his eyes narrowing as he scrutinized the data-laden presentation slides. The dim glow of candlelight flickered across his face, casting shadows that accentuated his calculating expression.

"Edward," Nate began, the urgency in his voice unmistakable. "We cannot stress enough the time-sensitive nature of this opportunity. As Amy mentioned earlier, we've already received interest from several influential investors. If you want to secure your spot and reap the maximum rewards, you must act immediately."

Amy nodded in agreement, adding, "The early investors will have access to exclusive benefits, such as priority access to new investment channels and higher potential returns. These incentives won't last long, so it's crucial to seize this chance while it's still available."

Eddie's gaze shifted from the presentation back to Nate and Amy, his hands steepled beneath his chin. The wheels in his mind were turning rapidly, fueled by a mixture of curiosity and ambition. Nate could sense Eddie's growing desire for power and wealth, and he knew exactly how to exploit it.

"Think about it, Edward," Nate urged, leaning forward with intensity in his eyes. "With our HYIP, you'd be at the forefront of cutting-edge investments – far ahead of your competitors. The potential for financial success is immense... but only if you act now."

Amy chimed in, her voice soft yet determined. "Imagine the prestige and influence you'd gain from being an early investor in such a lucrative venture. We're talking about life-changing returns here, Edward. But they'll only be within your grasp if you make your move quickly."

For a moment, silence enveloped the private dining room, broken only by the distant clinking of glassware and murmured conversations from the restaurant beyond. Eddie appeared deep in thought, weighing the tantalizing prospect of untold riches against the inherent risks of any investment scheme.

"Alright," Eddie said finally, a predatory gleam in his eye. "I'm in. I'll invest – but only if you can guarantee my spot among the exclusive early investors."

Nate and Amy exchanged a knowing glance, their plan working like clockwork. All that remained was to secure Eddie's commitment and set their trap in motion.

"Consider it done, Edward," Nate replied with a smile. "Welcome aboard."

The room was awash in the golden glow of candlelight, casting flickering shadows on Eddie's expectant face. Nate leaned back in his chair, a picture of calculated confidence as he assessed their quarry. Amy mirrored his posture, her gaze steady and unwavering.

"Edward," Nate began, his voice laced with just the right amount of urgency, "we need to emphasize that time is of the essence here. We've already had several high-profile investors express interest in this opportunity – but we're holding a spot for you. However, it won't be open indefinitely."

Amy glanced at her watch, feigning a momentary sense of urgency. "We can only guarantee your spot for the next 48 hours. After that, I'm afraid we'll have no choice but to offer it to someone else."

Eddie's eyes narrowed, his mind racing with thoughts of missed opportunities and potential rivals snapping up the lucrative deal before he could stake his claim. He drummed his fingers on the table, each tap echoing his mounting anxiety.

"Alright, alright," he conceded, unable to contain his eagerness any longer. "You've made your point. I don't want to miss out on this opportunity. Consider my investment secured."

Nate allowed himself a small, satisfied smile as he watched the flames of urgency dance in Eddie's eyes. Their plan was proceeding flawlessly, each step bringing them closer to justice. But there was still work to be done, and Nate knew better than to let his guard down now.

"Excellent decision, Edward," he praised, extending a hand to seal the deal. "You won't regret it."

As Eddie clasped Nate's hand firmly, Amy made a mental note of every subtle nuance in Eddie's expression – the glint of greed, the flicker of uncertainty, the palpable hunger for success. All would serve as crucial ammunition when the time came to bring their plan to fruition.

"Welcome to the future, Edward," she murmured, offering her own hand in a gesture of partnership. "Together, we'll make history."

Eddie's departure left a lingering scent of expensive cologne in the air, his confident stride carrying him towards the restaurant exit. Nate and Amy remained seated, their eyes meeting in the dimly lit private dining area. The tension between them evaporated with a shared glance, replaced by satisfaction and relief. They had done it – convinced Eddie to invest, and placed him right where they wanted him.

"Buon lavoro," whispered Nate, offering a nod of approval to his wife. Their time spent with Caterina had taught them more than just the art of Sicilian cooking; Italian phrases now punctuated their conversations, adding a touch of spice to their partnership.

"Gracias, mi amor" replied Amy, her smile as warm as the Sicilian sun. She felt the weight of responsibility on her shoulders lighten ever so slightly. Caterina's dream of expanding her café could become a reality if they continued down this path.

Nate leaned back in his chair, eyes scanning the room for any potential threats or unwelcome eavesdroppers. His military background never allowed him to fully relax, even when things appeared to be going well. Amy admired his vigilance, knowing that it was part of what made them such an effective team.

"Next step," said Nate, his voice low and cautious, "is to make sure our fake investors stay convincing enough for Eddie. He'll probably do some digging."

"Leave that to me," Amy assured, her journalistic instincts kicking in. "I have everything covered."

"Good," Nate nodded, his fingers tapping a rhythmic pattern on the tablecloth. "We have to stay ahead of him at all times."

Amy could sense the wheels turning in Nate's mind, his thoughts undoubtedly focused on Caterina and the countless others who had fallen victim to Eddie's schemes over the years. Their pursuit of justice was personal, fueled by empathy for those who had suffered at the hands of ruthless predators.

"Justice will be served," Amy vowed, her voice firm with conviction. "For Caterina and all the others."

Nate looked into her eyes, his gaze steady and resolute. "I have no doubt," he said quietly. "Together, we'll make sure of it."

As they rose from the table, Nate's hand found Amy's, their fingers intertwining in a silent promise of solidarity. With unwavering determination, they strode out of the restaurant, the click of Amy's heels echoing through the empty space like the ticking of a clock – a reminder that time was on their side, and justice would not be denied.

Chapter 10

The sun dipped below the horizon, casting the city in a warm amber glow as Nate and Amy walked into the high-end restaurant, their steps confident and purposeful. The sharp clink of glasses and the hum of conversation filled the air. Eddie sat at a corner table, his eyes scanning the room like a hawk, his fingers drumming impatiently on the linen tablecloth.

"Edward Hewlett," Nate greeted him with an easy smile, sliding into the cushioned booth across from him. "You're looking well."

"Cut the small talk, Everhart," Eddie replied, his lips curling into a smirk. "I know you didn't invite me here for a friendly chat. What have you got?"

"Right to business, then." Amy pulled out a sleek black binder and slid it across the table towards Eddie, her eyes never leaving his face. "Take a look at these financial reports. You'll find that your initial investment has grown quite significantly."

Eddie raised an eyebrow as he flipped through the pages, his skepticism visible in the furrow of his brow. But as he absorbed the numbers, something shifted in his expression - a glimmer of intrigue sparked in his eyes.

"Interesting," he murmured, pausing on a particularly impressive chart. "How did you manage this?"

"Trade secret," Nate replied, leaning back in his seat. He could see the wheels turning in Eddie's mind, the hunger for wealth beginning to gnaw at his composure. "But I can tell you that our methods are innovative and effective."

"Clearly," Eddie said, his voice dripping with sarcasm. He glanced up at them, considering their confident expressions, the way they held themselves. They had his attention now. "So, what's in it for you two? Why share this with me?"

"Because, Eddie," Amy began, her voice soft but steady, "we believe in partnerships. We've always admired your... resourcefulness. And we think that working together could be mutually beneficial."

"Besides," Nate chimed in, a hint of a smile tugging at the corner of his mouth, "it's not every day you come across an opportunity like this. Just think of what you could achieve with the returns on your investment."

Eddie's jaw clenched as he mulled over their words. He knew they were playing him, appealing to his pride and ambition – but the allure of potential wealth was difficult to resist.

"Alright," Eddie said slowly, closing the binder and pushing it back towards Amy. "I'm intrigued. But I'll need more than just these numbers to convince me. Tell me more about how you pulled this off."

As Nate and Amy began to weave their tale of cunning schemes and cyber security mastery, they exchanged a subtle glance - one that spoke volumes about their true intent. They had Eddie right where they wanted him, and they knew it was only a matter of time before their plan came to fruition.

The glow of the candlelight flickered across Eddie's face, casting a sinister shadow that danced in tandem with his thoughts. He swirled the wine in his glass, letting the deep red liquid catch the light before bringing it to his lips. Nate watched him closely, gauging his reaction as he prepared to reel him further into their web.

"Timing is crucial," Nate began, his voice steady and confident. "The market conditions that have allowed us to achieve such incredible growth won't last forever. In fact, our analysis suggests that this window of opportunity may close within the next few weeks."

"Which means," Amy interjected, leaning forward to emphasize her point, "that now is the best time to invest more funds if you want to maximize your profits. Waiting too long could mean missing out on a once-in-a-lifetime chance."

Eddie's brow furrowed, and Nate could see the wheels turning in his mind. Greed and caution wrestled for supremacy as he weighed the risks against the rewards. But Nate and Amy had come prepared, armed with psychological tactics designed to tip the scales in their favor.

"Of course, we understand that this is a big decision for you, Eddie," said Nate. "But I think it's important to consider the other investors who have already seen substantial gains from this scheme."

"Like our friend Marco," Amy added, a casual smile playing across her lips. "He invested just a few months ago and doubled his money in no time. Now, he's using the profits to fund a lavish trip around Italy – something he'd always dreamed of doing."

Nate saw the flicker of envy in Eddie's eyes, and he knew they were making progress. The fear of missing out – FOMO, as it was often called – was a powerful motivator, and one that they intended to exploit to its fullest potential.

"Then there's Lucia," Nate continued, his voice taking on a conspiratorial tone. "She was initially hesitant to invest, but after seeing the returns that others were enjoying, she decided to take the plunge. I heard she's planning to open her own cybersecurity firm with the profits she's made."

"Imagine what you could do with that kind of money, Eddie," Amy chimed in, her voice laced with both encouragement and challenge. "The expansion of your criminal empire, the freedom to pursue even more ambitious schemes – all within reach if you're willing to seize the opportunity."

Eddie's fingers tapped rhythmically on the table, betraying his growing impatience and agitation. The pressure was mounting, and Nate and Amy knew they had him on the edge. All it would take was one final push to send him tumbling into their carefully laid trap.

"Of course, we don't want to pressure you into making a decision," Amy said sweetly, her eyes locked onto Eddie's. "But the clock is ticking, and we'd hate for you to miss out on something so extraordinary."

As the words hung in the air, Nate and Amy exchanged a knowing glance. They were getting closer to their goal, and as the candlelight flickered across Eddie's face once more, they could see the first cracks beginning to form in his resolve.

The clinking of glasses echoed in the dimly lit restaurant as Eddie glanced at the three strangers approaching his table. Nate grinned, gesturing for them to join.

"Ah, right on time," he said smoothly. "Eddie, allow me to introduce you to our esteemed colleagues: Olivia, Darren, and Marco. All successful investors, thanks to our little venture."

"Nice to meet you," Eddie murmured, watching as they settled into their seats. The anticipation was palpable, hanging thick in the air like the scent of the rich Italian dishes being served.

"Olivia here made a modest investment six months ago," Amy began, her voice low and conspiratorial. "Now she's set to retire early, living off the profits."

"Better than I could've ever imagined," Olivia chimed in, her smile genuine and infectious. "I was able to pay off my mortgage and even take my entire family on an all-expense paid vacation to the Amalfi Coast."

"Darren's story is equally impressive," Nate continued, nodding towards a middle-aged man with salt-and-pepper hair. "He invested just before the market took off and doubled his initial input in just two months."

"Best decision I've ever made," Darren agreed, raising his glass in a toast. "This opportunity has changed my life."

Eddie's gaze shifted to Marco, whose calm demeanor and piercing eyes seemed to hide a deeper history. Seeing the curiosity in Eddie's expression, Amy filled the silence.

"Marco had a rough year. Lost almost everything in a business venture gone wrong," she explained, her tone empathetic. "But after investing with us, he's not only recovered his losses but found a newfound sense of purpose."

"Indeed," Marco confirmed, a hint of gratitude in his voice. "I have been given a second chance, and I plan to make the most of it."

The success stories washed over Eddie, each word chipping away at his resolve. His mind raced, calculating the potential returns and weighing them against the risks. Could it be possible that he was missing out on something truly life-changing?

"Of course, not everyone sees such astronomical results," Nate interjected, breaking through Eddie's thoughts. "But I think you'll agree, the potential for growth is undeniable."

Eddie's fingers drummed against his wine glass, a bead of sweat forming on his brow. The pressure was mounting, and the fear of missing out began gnawing at the edges of his consciousness. He glanced around the table, meeting the eyes of these seemingly satisfied investors, and felt the seed of doubt begin to grow.

"Fine," he said finally, his voice strained with the effort of maintaining his composure. "I'm in. I'll invest more."

Nate and Amy exchanged a discreet glance, their plan coming together seamlessly. The next move was theirs, and they knew exactly how to play it.

The dimly lit ambiance of the high-end restaurant cast an air of mystery over their secluded table. Glasses clinked, and muted conversations filled the room as Nate leaned forward, his eyes locking onto Eddie's with a steely determination. "Now, Eddie," he began, his voice low and steady, "I need you to understand something. This isn't just about the returns you've seen so far. You have the opportunity to make even more."

Eddie's eyes flickered between Nate and Amy, his interest piqued. He fidgeted in his seat, trying to maintain an air of indifference, but his desire for wealth betrayed him.

"Show him the projections," Amy suggested, her voice calm yet assertive. She handed a sleek tablet to Eddie, a smug smile playing on her lips.

As Eddie swiped through the data before him, his eyes widened with each slide. The figures danced across the screen, painting a picture of astronomical profits that would have been impossible to ignore. It was as if the very air around them hummed with anticipation, the promise of riches too tantalizing to resist.

"Look at this, Eddie," Nate said, pointing to a graph that depicted a steep upward trajectory. "These are the returns we've seen from our most successful investors – those who went all in. As you can see, the potential for growth is exponential."

Eddie's heart pounded in his chest, his pulse quickening as greed took hold. He could almost feel the weight of the gold bars and stacks of cash that seemed within reach, beckoning him with their seductive allure.

"Of course, there are no guarantees," Amy added, her words carefully chosen to heighten the sense of urgency. "But time and time again, we've seen investors like yourself reap incredible rewards."

Eddie's mind raced, the cogs turning furiously as he weighed the potential benefits against the risks. His fingers twitched, itching to reach for his phone and wire the funds that would secure his place among the financial elite.

"Remember, Eddie," Nate said, his voice taking on a conspiratorial tone, "fortune favors the bold."

Eddie stared at the screen, images of yachts, luxury cars, and lavish vacations playing in his mind like a movie reel. He took a deep breath, steeling himself for the decision that could change his life forever.

"Alright," he conceded, his voice barely audible above the din of the restaurant. "I'll do it. I'll increase my investment."

Nate and Amy exchanged a knowing glance, their plan unfolding exactly as they had anticipated. They could feel the gears of justice turning, inching them ever closer to avenging Caterina's losses – and securing their own future in the process.

As the clink of silverware against fine china and the murmurs of conversation filled the upscale restaurant, Nate leaned in towards Eddie, his eyes alight with purpose. "You know, Eddie," he began, his voice just loud enough to be heard over the din, "I've been thinking about your future, about what comes next for you."

Amy, sipping her wine, nodded in agreement. "It's true. With this High-Yield Investment Program as a stepping stone, there's no telling what heights you could reach."

Eddie paused, fork hovering above his plate, as he considered their words. The idea of greater success, of building his own empire, held undeniable appeal. He glanced between Nate and Amy, searching for any hint of deception, but found only sincere encouragement.

"Go on," he said cautiously, intrigue coloring his tone.

"Picture it," Nate continued, his words painting a vivid image in Eddie's mind. "A lucrative business venture backed by your newfound wealth – one that allows you to call the shots, to shape your own destiny."

"Imagine the power," Amy chimed in, her eyes sparkling with excitement, "the influence you could wield. You'd be unstoppable."

Eddie allowed himself a small smile, the thought of such prospects igniting a fire within him. But doubts still nagged at the edges of his consciousness, threatening to extinguish the flames of ambition.

"Sounds great," he admitted, "but how do I make sure I don't miss out? I mean, what if the opportunity slips through my fingers?"

"Ah," Nate said, seizing upon Eddie's uncertainty with the precision of a seasoned marksman. "That's where we come in." He leaned back in his chair, his expression a mix of confidence and camaraderie. "You see, Eddie, we have connections – other investors who have already reaped the rewards of this HYIP. They're living proof of what's possible."

"Time is of the essence, though," Amy added softly, her words laced with urgency. "The window to maximize your profits won't stay open forever."

Eddie's pulse quickened at the mention of scarcity, his instincts screaming at him not to let this chance slip away. He took a slow, steadying breath, trying to regain his composure.

"Alright," he said, determination settling in his voice. "I'll do it. I'll increase my investment."

Nate and Amy shared a fleeting, triumphant glance, their plan progressing as smoothly as they had hoped. With each carefully chosen word, each subtle manipulation, they guided Eddie further down the path they had laid out – one that would lead not only to justice for Caterina but also to the downfall of a man who had built his fortune on the suffering of others.

The clink of champagne glasses punctuated the low hum of conversation in the high-end restaurant. Nate and Amy exchanged a knowing smile as they laid out fabricated reports on the table before Eddie. The glossy pages were adorned with impressive figures and charts that teased at a world of wealth just within reach.

"Take a look, Eddie," Nate said, tapping the report with an air of nonchalance. "These numbers aren't just smoke and mirrors – we have testimonials from actual investors who have made substantial profits."

Eddie's eyes darted across the documents, greed flickering like candlelight behind his gaze. He couldn't help but imagine what he could do with those returns – a new car, a bigger house, perhaps even expanding his business empire.

"Listen to this," Amy chimed in, her finger tracing a line of text on one of the pages. "'I was initially hesitant to invest, but the Everhart team quickly put my fears to rest. In just a few months, my investment has more than tripled.'"

As the words left her lips, Eddie felt a knot tighten in the pit of his stomach. What if he missed out on such incredible returns? He couldn't bear the thought of being left behind, watching others reap the benefits while his own fortune stagnated.

Nate leaned in, his face a picture of sincerity. "Eddie, we understand your concerns, but these aren't empty promises. This HYIP is a once-in-a-lifetime opportunity – one that could change your life for the better. But you have to be willing to take the leap."

Eddie hesitated, his fingers drumming against the report. He knew that investing more was a risk, but the potential rewards were tempting him like a siren's song. He glanced up at Nate and Amy, their faces the embodiment of success and confidence. If they could achieve such prosperity, why couldn't he?

"Think of all the things you could do with even greater returns, Eddie," Amy whispered, her voice as smooth as velvet. "The freedom it would give you to pursue your dreams and ambitions."

Eddie's mind raced with visions of wealth and power, each one more enticing than the last. He knew the risks, but the alluring prospect of unimaginable success was too powerful to resist.

"Alright," he said, his voice barely above a whisper. "I'll increase my investment."

"Excellent choice, Eddie," Nate replied, clasping his hands together. "We're confident that you won't regret it."

As they watched Eddie depart the restaurant, Nate and Amy shared a victorious grin. Their carefully constructed web of deception had ensnared its prey, bringing them one step closer to achieving their ultimate goal – justice for Caterina and the downfall of a man who profited from the suffering of others.

Eddie's gaze lingered on the financial reports spread across the crisp white linen. The numbers seemed to dance before his eyes, seducing him with their promise of wealth and power. He could almost taste the fine Italian wines he'd be able to afford if he took the plunge.

"Of course," Nate said, leaning back in his chair with a casual air, "we can't force you to invest more. That decision is entirely up to you, Eddie."

"However," Amy chimed in, her red hair glowing like embers beneath the soft restaurant lighting, "you should consider what might happen if you don't take advantage of this opportunity." She traced a perfectly manicured finger along the edge of the reports as she spoke. "You wouldn't want to look back and regret not seizing the chance when it was right in front of you."

Eddie's fingers tightened around the stem of his wine glass, his knuckles turning white. The truth in Amy's words stung like a slap to the face. He had always prided himself on being a risk-taker, a man who knew how to spot a golden opportunity when it presented itself. Was he really willing to let this one slip through his fingers?

"Besides," Nate added, his tone light but laced with a subtle hint of warning, "think about all those other investors who have already made substantial gains. They knew when to act, when to trust their instincts. Do you really want to be the only one left behind?"

Eddie's heart hammered in his chest, a mixture of fear and adrenaline coursing through his veins. He'd never been one to shy away from a challenge, and now he was poised on the edge of a precipice, ready to dive headfirst into uncharted territory. It was a feeling he both craved and dreaded in equal measure.

"Alright," he finally conceded, his voice barely audible over the hum of conversation that filled the restaurant. "I'll increase my investment."

"Excellent decision, Eddie," Amy said, her face lighting up with a genuine smile. "You won't regret it."

"Indeed," Nate agreed, raising his wine glass in a silent toast. "To your future success and the prosperity that awaits you."

As the clink of their glasses echoed through the elegant dining room, Eddie felt a surge of excitement and anticipation coursing through him. He had taken the plunge, embraced the risk, and now there was no turning back.

"Thank you, Nate and Amy," he murmured, his eyes shining with newfound determination. "With your guidance, I'm confident that this investment will be the key to unlocking my dreams."

"Of course, Eddie," they replied in unison, their voices a harmonious blend of confidence and reassurance.

And as they shared a toast, deep within, Eddie couldn't shake off the feeling that he had just made a life-altering decision – one that would either catapult him to heights he'd never imagined or send him spiraling into the abyss. But for now, all he could do was savor the taste of the fine Italian wine and hope that fortune favored the bold.

The restaurant's doors swung open, and a cool evening breeze swept through the opulent dining room. Eddie rose from the table, buttoning his suit jacket as he prepared to leave. As he turned to face Nate and Amy, their faces were the picture of reassurance.

"Goodnight, Eddie," Nate said, offering a firm handshake. "We'll be in touch soon with more details."

"Looking forward to it," Eddie replied, his voice steady yet tinged with anticipation. He turned to Amy, who extended her hand with a warm smile. "It was lovely to see you again, Amy."

"Likewise, Eddie. Take care." She held his gaze for a moment before releasing her grip, and Eddie knew there was no turning back now.

As the doors closed behind him, sealing out the cacophony of clinking glassware and murmured conversations, Eddie couldn't help but feel an odd mixture of excitement, apprehension, and even pride. He had taken a calculated risk, one that promised to pay off handsomely if all went according to plan.

Back at the table, Nate and Amy exchanged a knowing glance, acutely aware of the weight of the decision they had just helped orchestrate. The fine wine that lingered on their palates served as a reminder of the stakes at play – not just for Eddie, but for Caterina, the woman whose losses they were determined to recover.

"Phase one complete," Nate whispered, his gaze never leaving Amy's. "Now we just need to keep him on the hook long enough to get what we need."

Amy's eyes flashed with determination, her mind racing through the intricate web of deceit they had so carefully spun around Eddie. "We've got this, Nate," she replied softly, her hand finding his beneath the table. "For Caterina."

"Agreed," he nodded, his fingers tightening around hers. "For Caterina."

As they silently toasted their progress, Nate's thoughts turned to the countless hours spent poring over code and schematics in pursuit of this ever-elusive justice. The stakes were higher than ever, but so too was his resolve. There would be no room for error – not when the lives and dreams of so many hung in the balance.

"Avanti," he murmured under his breath, invoking the Italian word for forward. It was a fitting mantra for their mission, and one that would carry them through the challenges that lay ahead. As they finished their wine and paid the bill, Nate and Amy shared one final, lingering look – a silent acknowledgment of the battle they had won, and the war that still raged on.

Chapter 11

Nate Everhart sat in his home office, the room bathed in the glow of multiple computer screens. The hum of machines mingled with the faint scent of espresso, a reminder of their recent trip to Italy where they had first crossed paths with Eddie Hewlett. He leaned back in his chair and rubbed his eyes, weariness creeping in as he mentally reviewed the evidence they had gathered thus far.

"Any luck?" Amelia asked as she entered the room, her striking red hair framing her face like an untamed halo.

"Nothing decisive yet," Nate replied, scratching at the stubble on his chin. "We've got plenty of circumstantial evidence, but nothing that would convince Eddie to invest more in our fake HYIP."

Amy sighed and dropped into the seat next to him, her eyes scanning the documents scattered across the desk. Her keen attention to detail had saved them countless times before, and Nate could see the gears turning in her head. "So what's our next move?"

"Maybe we need to dig deeper," Nate suggested, fingers tapping rhythmically on the armrests. "Learn more about Eddie's current schemes. If we can find something he's desperate to keep hidden, we'll have leverage."

"Sounds risky," Amy said with a slight smirk, leaning closer to Nate. "But it does have a certain appeal."

"Exactly," Nate grinned, feeling a renewed sense of determination. "And I think I know just how to do it. We infiltrate his office, gather evidence of his newest scheme, and use it against him."

"Right under his nose, huh? I like it." Amy nodded, her expression serious but her green eyes sparkling with excitement. "So when do we make our move?"

"Let's find a time when he won't be there." Nate pulled up Eddie's schedule on one of the computer screens, his fingers flying over the keyboard as he searched for an opportunity.

"Perfect," Amy said, pointing to a gap in Eddie's calendar. "His weekly golf game. That gives us a two-hour window."

"Two hours should be enough," Nate agreed, his mind already racing ahead to plan their infiltration. He knew the risks they were taking, but the thought of outsmarting Eddie filled him with a sense of satisfaction and purpose. This was about more than just revenge; it was about justice for all the people Eddie had wronged.

"Alright then," Amy said, standing up and stretching her lithe frame. "Let's get to work."

As they delved deeper into their plans, Nate couldn't help but feel a sense of pride for what they had accomplished together. They were a formidable team, united by their shared experiences and mutual desire for justice. And as they prepared to face Eddie Hewlett once again, Nate knew that there was no one else he would rather have by his side.

Nate's fingers danced across the keyboard, his eyes narrowed in concentration as lines of code scrolled across the screen. He knew he had to work quickly - Eddie's weekly golf game wouldn't last forever. A bead of sweat trickled down his temple, but he ignored it, focusing instead on the complex security system that stood between them and the truth.

"Cameras disabled," Nate announced, his voice a low murmur. "You're good to go."

"Thanks, love." Amy's voice was soft in his earpiece, her tone playful despite the tension of the moment. Dressed in an impeccable disguise - a janitor's uniform complete with cap and glasses - she blended seamlessly into the background as she slipped into Eddie's office. "Let's hope Eddie isn't too attached to this mop."

Nate allowed himself a small chuckle before returning his focus to the task at hand. With each keystroke, he dismantled another layer of the digital fortress protecting Eddie's secrets.

"Alarms are down," he reported, feeling a rush of satisfaction as he bypassed the final roadblock. "You've got twenty minutes until the system resets."

"Got it," Amy replied, her voice all business now as she began rifling through Eddie's desk. Nate could hear the rustle of paper, the click of a drawer opening and closing, as she searched for any evidence that could help them expose Eddie's latest scheme.

"Nothing here," she muttered, frustration creeping into her voice. "Come on, Eddie, where are you hiding your dirty little secrets?"

"Try looking for hidden compartments," Nate suggested, recalling one of their earlier encounters with Eddie. "He likes to keep things close at hand."

"Good thinking," Amy said, and Nate could almost see the determined glint in her eyes as she redoubled her efforts. A moment later, she let out a triumphant gasp. "Found it."

"Nice work," Nate said, his heartbeat picking up in anticipation. "What have you got?"

"Project Phoenix." The words were barely more than a whisper, but they carried the weight of discovery. "This is it, Nate. This is what we've been looking for."

"Get photos of everything and get out of there," Nate urged, glancing at the countdown clock on his computer screen. Time was running out.

"Already on it," Amy replied, her voice steady as she snapped pictures of the documents with her phone. As she worked, Nate couldn't help but admire her calm under pressure - a trait that had saved them both more times than he could count.

"Ten minutes left," he warned, keeping one eye on the security feed to make sure Eddie hadn't returned early. He knew they were playing a dangerous game, but the thought of bringing Eddie down and protecting countless innocent people from his schemes made it all worth it.

"Got everything I need," Amy confirmed, her breath quickening as she prepared to make her exit. "Heading out now."

"Stay sharp," Nate cautioned, feeling the adrenaline coursing through his veins as he helped guide her safely out of the building. They had done it - they had finally found the key to unraveling Eddie's plans. And now, it was time to bring their nemesis to justice.

Nate's fingers flew across the keyboard, his eyes darting between multiple monitors that displayed live feeds from Eddie's security system. The soft glow of the screens illuminated his face, casting eerie shadows across the room.

"Alright, Amy," Nate said into the microphone attached to his headset. "I've got your back. You're clear to continue."

"Copy that," came Amy's hushed reply through the hidden earpiece. He could sense her determination, even through the static of their connection. The woman he had loved and fought alongside for years was as focused and relentless as ever.

He watched intently as Amy's disguised figure moved gracefully through the office on one of the screens, her red hair tucked neatly under a black wig. Nate couldn't help but smile at the sight – she always managed to look stunning, even in such dire circumstances.

"Computer at nine o'clock," Nate informed her, nodding towards the sleek desktop on the corner of Eddie's desk. "Might be something useful."

"Got it," Amy murmured, approaching the computer with a practiced ease. Her slender fingers hovered over the keyboard for a moment before she began typing rapidly, her mind racing as she worked to bypass the password protection.

"Come on, come on..." Amy muttered under her breath, her frustration mounting with each failed attempt. Nate knew she was running out of time – they both were. He clenched his fists, willing her to succeed.

Suddenly, the screen flickered to life, revealing a treasure trove of information. "I'm in," she whispered triumphantly, snapping pictures of the files related to Project Phoenix with her phone as quickly as possible.

"Good job, love," Nate praised, his heart swelling with pride. "Now get out of there."

"Almost done," Amy replied, her voice steady despite the pressure. She continued photographing the incriminating evidence, her fingers flying across the screen as she captured every last detail.

"Wait," Nate's voice tightened as he noticed a shadow moving in the hallway on one of his monitors. "We've got company."

"Who is it?" Amy asked, her voice suddenly tense.

"Can't tell yet," Nate admitted, squinting at the screen. "But they're heading your way. Fast."

"Alright," Amy said with forced calmness. "I'll be ready."

As the seconds ticked by, Nate found himself holding his breath, praying that whoever was approaching wouldn't discover Amy. He knew that if they were caught, everything they had worked so hard to build would come crashing down around them.

"Time to go, Amy," Nate urged, his voice barely more than a whisper. "Now."

"Understood," she replied, quickly pocketing her phone and slipping silently towards the exit. The figure was growing closer, their footsteps echoing ominously through the empty office space.

"Keep me updated, Nate," Amy whispered, her voice strained with urgency.

"Will do," he promised, his gaze never leaving the monitors as he continued to track the unknown visitor. They were playing a dangerous game – one that could cost them everything if they weren't careful.

And as Nate watched Amy disappear from view, he couldn't help but hope that luck was on their side.

Amy's heart pounded in her chest as she crouched behind the heavy oak desk, her fingers gripping the edge for support. The footsteps grew louder, echoing through the dimly lit room like a harbinger of doom.

"Get out of there now, Amy," Nate's voice buzzed in her ear, sharp and urgent. "I think it's Eddie."

"Copy that," she whispered, adrenaline surging through her veins as she darted towards a nearby closet. She slipped inside just as the office door swung open with a creak, revealing the imposing figure of Eddie Hewlett.

"Stay quiet and keep me informed," Nate instructed, his tone barely audible as he continued to monitor the situation from their makeshift control center.

"Got it," Amy mouthed silently, holding her breath as she watched Eddie through a thin crack in the closet door. He seemed agitated, pacing back and forth across the plush carpet, his expensive Italian shoes leaving faint imprints in the fibers.

Eddie pulled out his phone, dialed a number, and began speaking in hushed tones. "We need to move faster on Project Phoenix," he said, anxiety lacing his words. "There's been too much chatter. I can't risk exposure."

Project Phoenix – the very name sent shivers down Amy's spine. Whatever it was, it had the power to make a man like Eddie nervous. And that made it all the more dangerous.

"Understood, boss," a gravelly voice replied over the line, one of Eddie's associates no doubt. "We'll double our efforts."

"Good," Eddie snapped, cutting off the call. "No more delays."

As Amy listened to the conversation, the gravity of the situation weighed heavily on her. She knew they were onto something big, something that could bring Eddie and his entire operation crashing down. But they needed to act fast.

"Did you get all that, Nate?" she asked silently, her voice barely a whisper as she relayed the information to her husband.

"Every word," he confirmed, his voice grim. "This is exactly what we needed. We can nail him now."

"Let's just focus on getting out of here first," Amy reminded him, her heart still racing from the close encounter. "We're not safe yet."

"Agreed," Nate said, his voice taking on a protective edge. "Stay put for now. I'll let you know when it's clear."

As Eddie continued to pace and mutter to himself, Amy couldn't help but think of all the lives that had been destroyed by his schemes – including her own father. It fueled her determination to see him brought to justice, no matter the cost.

"Justice will be served, Eddie," she thought, a steely resolve settling over her. "One way or another."

The door clicked shut, and the echo of Eddie's footsteps faded down the hallway. Amy, still hidden in the closet, waited for Nate's signal.

"Alright, coast is clear," he whispered through the earpiece. She exhaled a breath she hadn't realized she'd been holding and quietly emerged, scanning the room one last time before making her exit. As she moved to leave, she noticed a pen on the floor beside the desk – a potential clue that someone had been there. Amy picked it up and slid it into her pocket, leaving the office as though she had never been there.

***

Back at their home office, Nate and Amy eagerly began reviewing the evidence they had gathered from Eddie's lair. The photos from the Project Phoenix folder laid out on their workstation, and the recorded conversation played back from a small speaker. They exchanged glances, both knowing the gravity of what they had discovered.

"Can you believe this?" Amy asked, her eyes wide with disbelief. "He's planning on defrauding even more people with this new scheme."

Nate shook his head, his jaw clenched in anger. "It's monstrous. But now we have everything we need to confront him. We can use this information to convince him to invest more money in our fake HYIP, and then we'll bring him down for good."

"Right," Amy agreed, her fingers brushing over the photographs. "But we have to be cautious. We don't want to tip him off that we know about Project Phoenix."

"Of course," Nate replied, his eyes narrowing as he contemplated their next move. "We'll have to play this just right. We'll present our HYIP as if it's the perfect solution to his problems, without revealing how much we know."

"Exactly," Amy said, nodding. She paused for a moment, lost in thought. "You know, this has been a long time coming. I can't help but think about my father and what he went through because of Eddie."

Nate reached across the table, his hand covering hers. "We're doing this for him, and for everyone else Eddie's hurt. We're going to make sure he never hurts anyone again."

A fire burned in Amy's eyes as she met her husband's gaze. "Let's bring him down."

"Agreed," Nate said, determination etched on his face. "We'll play this game better than he ever could. And then we'll make him pay for everything he's done."

With that, the couple dove into their preparation, fine-tuning their plan to ensnare Eddie once and for all. They knew they had one shot at bringing him to justice – and they were determined to make it count.

Nate and Amy stood in their dimly lit home office, the glow of multiple computer screens casting eerie shadows on their faces. Nate paced back and forth, his fingers tapping rhythmically against his thigh.

"Alright," he began, "we need to set up a meeting with Eddie. We'll tell him we want to discuss the progress of the HYIP and iron out some details."

"Sounds good," Amy agreed, her voice steady and focused. "But how do we bring up Project Phoenix without tipping him off?"

"Simple," Nate said with a sly grin. "We weave it into the conversation, making it seem like we've only just discovered it. Then, we use that knowledge as leverage to convince him that our HYIP is the real deal."

"Perfect," Amy replied, her eyes narrowing in determination. "He won't know what hit him."

The couple spent the next several hours preparing for their meeting with Eddie. They pored over documents and fabricated spreadsheets, crafting a narrative that would appeal to Eddie's greed and ambition. As they worked, Nate couldn't help but think about the countless victims who had been swindled by Eddie's schemes. This was their chance to make things right.

"Think about it," Amy mused aloud, her fingers flying across the keyboard as she put the finishing touches on a fake financial report. "If we can get Eddie to invest more money in our HYIP, we can take him down from the inside."

"Exactly," Nate murmured, his eyes scanning the screen as he cross-checked the information they'd gathered. "But we have to be careful not to push too hard. If he gets suspicious, we could lose everything."

Amy nodded, pausing to take a deep breath. "It all comes down to this one meeting. Let's make sure we're ready for anything."

As they continued their preparations, an unspoken understanding settled between them. They were a formidable team, and justice would be served – one way or another.

"Okay," Nate finally said, standing up and stretching his muscles as they finished their work. "We've got everything we need. Now, let's get some rest. Tomorrow is going to be a big day."

Together, they turned off the computers, plunging the room into darkness. The weight of their mission hung heavy in the air, but they knew they had each other's backs.

"Sleep well, partner," Amy whispered, pressing a soft kiss to Nate's cheek.

"Sweet dreams, my love," he replied, pulling her into a tight embrace. And with that, they headed to bed, their hearts filled with hope and determination.

For tomorrow, they would bring Eddie to his knees – and justice would finally prevail.

The weak sun cast a sickly glow across the gray concrete of the abandoned warehouse, its beams filtering through dusty windows and casting eerie shadows on the floor. Nate stood at the entrance, his tall, imposing figure backlit by the fading light, his dark eyes scanning the interior for any signs of danger.

"Remember," he whispered into the tiny microphone concealed in his collar. "Stay focused and keep your wits about you."

"I know the drill, Nate," Amy replied, her voice distorted by the earpiece hidden beneath her fiery hair. She adjusted her crisp suit jacket, her fingers trembling with anticipation.

Eddie entered the warehouse, flanked by two solemn bodyguards. Their tailored suits and polished shoes seemed out of place in the dingy surroundings. He approached Nate and Amy, eyeing them with equal parts curiosity and suspicion.

"Good to see you again, Mr. and Mrs. Everhart," Eddie said smoothly, extending a hand to Nate. "I trust you've been busy since our last encounter?"

"Indeed we have, Eddie," Nate replied, shaking Eddie's hand firmly. "We believe we've found a way to ensure the success of the HYIP and protect your interests at the same time." He glanced at Amy, who produced a sleek leather binder from her bag.

"Allow us to present our findings," she said, opening the binder and revealing an array of neatly organized documents. "As you can see, we've been monitoring the progress of several investment schemes – including one that caught our attention... Project Phoenix."

Eddie's eyes widened momentarily before narrowing once more. "And how exactly did you come across this information?" he asked, trying to maintain his composure.

"Let's just say we have our ways," Nate interjected, smirking. "But that's not what's important here. What matters is that we've discovered some vulnerabilities in Project Phoenix that could jeopardize your reputation and financial security."

"Go on," Eddie said, his voice strained.

"By investing more capital into our HYIP, you can not only avoid those risks but also significantly increase your profits," Amy explained. "The returns we're projecting far exceed those of Project Phoenix or any of your other ventures."

Nate leaned in closer, his eyes locked onto Eddie's. "We know what you're after, Eddie – power, wealth, control. Our proposal offers you all of that, without the risk of exposure or failure. But if you want to reap the rewards, you'll need to commit fully."

Eddie hesitated, clearly weighing his options. "And if I don't invest more money?"

"Then you risk losing everything when Project Phoenix inevitably goes up in flames," Amy replied coolly. "But I think you're smarter than that, Eddie. You know a good opportunity when you see one."

"Very well," Eddie conceded, his fingers tapping nervously on the surface of the binder. "You've got my attention. Show me what you've got."

As Nate and Amy presented their carefully crafted narrative, they could see the intrigue growing in Eddie's eyes. With each passing moment, he seemed to become more and more invested in the potential of their fake HYIP, captivated by the promise of untold riches.

"Alright," Eddie finally said, straightening his tie. "I'm in. But remember – if this doesn't pan out as you've promised, there will be consequences."

"Of course," Nate replied, nodding solemnly. "But we have every confidence in our plan. You won't be disappointed."

"See that I'm not," Eddie warned before turning on his heel and leaving the warehouse, his bodyguards in tow.

As the sound of footsteps faded, Amy exhaled sharply. "We did it," she whispered, her eyes wide with disbelief.

"Justice will prevail," Nate murmured, his voice filled with quiet confidence. And as they walked away from the warehouse, hand in hand, they knew that they had taken a crucial step toward righting the wrongs of the past and ensuring a brighter future for those who had suffered at Eddie's hands.

With the warehouse bathed in a chiaroscuro of light and shadow, Nate leaned forward, his eyes fixed on Eddie as he spoke with conviction about the fake HYIP. Amy, sitting next to him, shifted her gaze between Eddie's reactions and the paperwork that backed up their grand scheme.

"Imagine this, Eddie," Nate said, the rhythm of his words hypnotic. "A cutting-edge algorithm that predicts market trends before they even happen. The profits would be astronomical."

"Too good to be true?" Amy chimed in, her red hair catching a stray beam of sunlight. "It may seem like it, but we have the data to back it up." She tapped the stack of documents in front of her, a knowing smile playing on her lips.

Eddie's eyes flickered with excitement, his calculating mind already assessing the potential windfall. He drummed his fingers on the table, attempting to maintain an air of skepticism, but Nate could see through it.

"Of course, for maximum returns, we'll need to expand our current investments," Amy continued, her tone casual yet insistent. "We thought you might be interested in increasing your stake, given the potential rewards."

As Eddie pondered the proposal, Nate studied him closely, noting the minute changes in his expression and posture. It was working – Eddie's greed was getting the better of him, and it wouldn't be long before he took the bait.

"Tell me more about this algorithm," Eddie demanded, his voice betraying a hint of eagerness. "How does it work? What makes it different from everything else out there?"

"Ah, well, that's our little secret," Nate replied, a sly grin spreading across his face. "But I can assure you, it's revolutionary." He knew giving away too much information would risk exposing the ruse, but just enough mystery would keep Eddie hooked.

Amy interjected with a well-timed laugh. "We wouldn't be here if it was just another run-of-the-mill investment, now would we? You don't make it to the top by playing it safe, Eddie."

Eddie's eyes narrowed as he considered their words, his body tense with anticipation. Nate could almost hear the gears turning in his head, weighing the risks and rewards of their proposition.

"Alright," Eddie finally agreed, his fingers drumming excitedly on the stack of documents. "I'll up my investment – but this better live up to your promises. If not, you know what happens."

"Of course," Nate reassured him, his voice steady but his heart racing. "You won't be disappointed."

As Eddie nodded and signaled for his bodyguards to follow him out, Nate and Amy exchanged a glance filled with triumph and relief. They had done it – they had convinced Eddie to invest more in their scheme while remaining oblivious to their true intentions.

'Justice is in motion,' Nate thought, satisfaction swelling within him. And as they left the warehouse, hand in hand, the ghosts of those wronged by Eddie's schemes seemed to whisper their gratitude in the wind.

Chapter 12

Nate's fingers flew over the keyboard, his dark eyes locked on the screen as he sifted through the digital trail of Edward Hewlett. The room was dimly lit, casting an eerie glow over the couple as they conducted their research. Amy leaned closer to Nate, her red hair spilling over her shoulder like a fiery waterfall.

"Look at this," Nate said, pointing at a news article from years ago. "Edward Hewlett, age 12, arrested for theft."

"Wow," Amy replied, scanning the text. "He started young, didn't he?"

"Seems that way," Nate murmured, continuing his search.

As they delved deeper into Hewlett's past, an image began to form in their minds – a picture of a child brought up in a rough neighborhood, where survival often meant breaking the rules.

"Hey, Nate?" Amy asked, her voice tinged with concern. "Do you ever wonder if we're just perpetuating a cycle here? I mean, what if Hewlett had no choice but to turn to crime because of his upbringing?"

"Everyone has choices, Amy," Nate replied, his voice firm. "And while it's true that our circumstances can influence those choices, ultimately, we're responsible for our own actions."

Amy sighed and nodded, knowing deep down that Nate was right. Still, she couldn't help but feel a pang of sympathy for the young Hewlett who had grown up in such a harsh environment.

A sudden flashback pulled her thoughts back in time, presenting a vivid scene from Hewlett's childhood.

"Get outta here, ya little punk!" a gruff voice shouted. Young Eddie Hewlett ducked behind a dumpster, clutching a stolen loaf of bread to his chest. His heart pounded in his ears as he listened to the angry store owner's footsteps fade away.

"Close one," he whispered to himself, wiping the sweat from his brow. He knew that stealing was wrong, but the gnawing hunger in his stomach had driven him to desperation. In his neighborhood, it was every man for himself, and at twelve years old, Eddie was quickly learning that he'd have to rely on his wits if he wanted to survive.

"Whatcha got there, Eddie?" a voice called out from the shadows. Eddie's eyes widened as Tommy, the older boy who lived down the street, stepped into view. Tommy was known as a troublemaker – someone who always seemed to be involved in petty crimes and scuffles with other kids.

"None of your business," Eddie snapped, clutching the bread tighter.

"Aw, come on," Tommy said, grinning. "I just wanna help. You know, show you the ropes. We could be a real team, you and me."

Eddie hesitated, torn between his desire to stay out of trouble and the need to survive. As he looked into Tommy's eyes, he saw a reflection of his own desperation – a shared understanding of the struggles they faced in their rough neighborhood. And in that moment, the seeds of a criminal partnership were sown.

Nate's voice pulled Amy back to the present. "I found something interesting," he said, excitement in his tone. "Apparently Hewlett was involved in a gang as a teenager – that's where he learned most of his criminal skills. It's all starting to make sense now. The more we learn about his past, the better we can predict his next move."

"Agreed," Amy replied, her resolve strengthened. While she understood that Hewlett's upbringing had played a role in shaping him into the criminal mastermind he'd become, she also knew that Nate was right – everyone had choices. And now it was up to them to stop Hewlett from making any more victims.

The sun dipped below the horizon, casting an eerie glow over the decrepit playground where young Eddie Hewlett and his friends spent their evenings. The rusty swings creaked ominously as they swayed back and forth in the chilly breeze – a perfect backdrop for the life-changing decision that lay before him.

"Hey, Eddie, you gonna join us or what?" called out Danny, one of the older boys who had taken a liking to Eddie. His gang loitered nearby, faces obscured by shadows as they shared cigarettes and whispered conspiratorially.

Eddie hesitated, glancing over at his mother's apartment window, which flickered with the soft light of the television. If she caught him sneaking out again, he'd be grounded for weeks. But somehow, the potential consequences paled in comparison to the offer being made to him tonight.

"Come on, man," Danny urged, his voice low but insistent. "You're smart. You've got the brains to help us score big, and we can teach you everything you need to know."

Eddie weighed his options, his mind racing with thoughts of what could happen if things went south. Still, the allure of the gang's camaraderie and the promise of financial gain held undeniable appeal.

"Alright," he said finally, taking a deep breath. "I'm in."

From that moment on, Eddie's life took a sharp turn towards crime. As he entered his teenage years, the friends he once played with on the playground were replaced by a motley crew of criminals-in-training. Under the tutelage of Danny and his cohorts, Eddie learned the art of pickpocketing, lock-picking, and how to talk his way out of any situation.

"Remember, kid," Danny would often remind him, "it's not about how strong you are, it's about how smart you are. Always stay one step ahead of the game."

Eddie took these lessons to heart, his natural aptitude for deception and manipulation only growing stronger with each passing day. He reveled in the thrill of outwitting both his marks and any law enforcement officers who crossed his path.

"Maybe I was meant for this," Eddie mused one night, lying awake on his lumpy mattress, staring at the ceiling. "Maybe all those years of struggle were just preparing me for this life – a life where I can take what I want and answer to no one."

Though he knew deep down that his criminal lifestyle would eventually catch up with him, Eddie couldn't help but feel a sense of pride in his newfound skills. It was as if he had finally found a place where he belonged – a world where his intellect and cunning could be put to good use.

And as Eddie's reputation within the underworld grew, so too did his ambition. No longer content with petty theft and small-time scams, he began envisioning himself as the mastermind behind an empire of crime – an empire that would make even the most hardened criminals tremble in fear.

But first, he needed to learn from the best. And that meant finding a mentor who could show him how to transform his grandiose dreams into a reality. Little did he know that his search would lead him down a path darker and more treacherous than anything he'd ever faced before.

Eddie Hewlett leaned back in his plush leather chair, a self-satisfied grin spreading across his face as he surveyed the room of eager underlings. They were all here to learn from him – to become part of his criminal empire. For Eddie, it was more than just money and power – it was validation. Validation that he had made the right choice all those years ago when he turned his back on society's expectations in favor of a life of crime.

"Remember, gentlemen," he said smoothly, tapping his perfectly manicured fingers on the polished oak table. "The key to any successful scheme is preparation and precision. You need to know your mark inside and out, anticipate their every move, and strike when they least expect it."

As he spoke, images from his own rise to power flashed through his mind – from his humble beginnings running small-time scams to the elaborate, high-stakes cons that had earned him the nickname 'The Puppet Master.'

"Take the Bianchi job, for example," Eddie continued, gesturing animatedly as he recounted one of his most audacious heists. "We knew Caterina came from old money, but we also knew she had a weakness for gambling. So we set up a fake underground casino, lured her in, and relieved her of a few million euros without her even realizing it."

Eddie reveled in the admiring glances directed at him by his proteges. But his thoughts couldn't help but drift back to the motivations that had driven him to this point. It wasn't just about the wealth or the power – though he certainly had no complaints about either. No, what truly fueled Eddie's passion for crime was a deep-seated desire to prove himself.

"Boss?" One of the younger recruits piped up, interrupting Eddie's reverie. "How did you know you wanted to do this?"

"Good question," Eddie replied, leaning forward and steepling his fingers. "For me, it was about defying expectations. I grew up in a rough neighborhood, with everyone telling me I'd never amount to anything. And for a while, I believed them. But then I realized – why should I play by their rules? Why not make my own?"

"Exactly!" chimed in another recruit, an ambitious young woman with fiery red hair. "It's about showing the world that we're smarter than they think. That we can outwit them at every turn."

"Indeed," Eddie said, his voice gaining intensity as he recalled the thrill of each new challenge he had faced over the years. "As my schemes grew more elaborate, so did my hunger for success. It became a game – a test of wits between me and my marks. And I always made sure I came out on top."

"Which brings us back to the importance of preparation," he added, his eyes narrowing as he directed their attention back to the task at hand. "It's all about anticipating your target's next move and staying one step ahead. That's how you win this game. That's how you build an empire."

His words hung in the air like a promise – a promise of wealth, power, and unbridled freedom. And as Eddie watched the fire of ambition ignite in the eyes of his proteges, he couldn't help but feel a surge of pride.

"Welcome to the world of crime," he whispered, as if sharing a secret with himself. "Now go out there and show me what you've got."

A haze of smoke filled the dimly lit room, casting shadows that seemed to dance on the walls as Eddie Hewlett leaned back in his leather chair. A small smile played on his lips, betraying the excitement brewing within him. Across from him sat a powerful businessman, Carlo Montenegro, who was nervously shifting in his seat.

"Mr. Montenegro," Eddie began, a suave confidence lacing his words, "I believe you have a problem. And I think I can help."

Carlo glanced around the room, hesitating at first. Finally, he leaned in, lowering his voice. "The authorities are looking into my business operations," he disclosed. "I need someone to make their suspicions go away."

Eddie's smile widened. "You've come to the right place." As they discussed the details of the plan, Eddie could feel his heart pounding with anticipation – this was no ordinary scam. This was an opportunity to solidify his name among the criminal elite.

"Alright, Mr. Hewlett," Carlo said, extending his hand. "You pull this off, and you'll have the respect of the underworld."

"Consider it done," Eddie replied smoothly, sealing the deal with a firm handshake.

As Eddie set about orchestrating the elaborate scheme to throw the authorities off Carlo's trail, he couldn't shake the nagging feeling that he was crossing a line. He had always justified his actions by telling himself that he only targeted those who deserved it, the greedy and corrupt. But now, as he worked to protect a man who was undoubtedly guilty, the lines between right and wrong began to blur.

He paused, staring at his reflection in the tinted glass window. Was he becoming one of them? The very people he had sought to outwit and bring down?

For a moment, doubt flickered in Eddie's eyes. Then, just as quickly, it vanished. He had a job to do, and he was determined to see it through. Any moral qualms would have to wait.

"Focus, Eddie," he whispered to himself. "You're in this for the long game."

With renewed determination, Eddie dove back into his work, employing every trick he had learned over the years to manipulate the situation to his advantage. He hacked into databases, planted false evidence, and orchestrated a series of distractions to keep the authorities from discovering the truth.

Finally, as the last piece of the puzzle fell into place, Eddie couldn't help but marvel at his own handiwork. It was a masterpiece – the perfect blend of cunning, audacity, and sheer technical prowess.

"Mr. Montenegro," Eddie said with a satisfied grin as they met once again in the smoke-filled room, "your troubles are over."

"Amazing," Carlo replied, shaking Eddie's hand with genuine admiration. "You've more than earned your place among us, Hewlett."

As Eddie left the meeting, a sense of pride washed over him. He had done it. He had pulled off the ultimate con, solidifying his reputation as a criminal mastermind. But as the excitement faded, the weight of his actions began to settle in.

"Is this who I am now?" he wondered, silently wrestling with the moral implications of his choices. And as he stepped out into the night, the shadows seemed to swallow him whole, leaving only the echo of his footsteps behind.

A glass of whiskey, amber and half-empty, sat on the mahogany desk as Eddie reviewed his growing empire. The faint sound of opera music wafted through the air, a relic of his Italian heritage that he still held close to his heart. He leaned back in his leather chair, the gears in his mind whirring with excitement and anticipation.

"Ricardo," he called out to his right-hand man, who stood near the door. "Bring me the latest reports on our operations."

"Of course, boss," Ricardo replied, handing over a sleek black tablet. Eddie swiped through the various graphs and charts, reflecting on the progress of his criminal ventures: money laundering, fraud, forgery, and even a few instances of extortion – all executed with precision and finesse.

As his empire grew, so too did the betrayals. The most significant loss came when his closest friend and confidante, Marco, turned against him, feeding information to their enemies. The sting of betrayal burned like acid, and Eddie swore never to let anyone get that close to him again. His trust was reserved only for himself, and his thirst for revenge intensified.

"Boss, we've had a bit of a hiccup in our latest venture," Ricardo said hesitantly, breaking Eddie's reverie.

"Explain," Eddie demanded, his voice cold and unforgiving.

"Marco's intel led to the arrest of one of our men. They're trying to trace it back to us." Ricardo's voice trembled ever so slightly – he knew the magnitude of this news.

Eddie clenched his fist, feeling the rage surge within him. "This ends now," he declared. "I will not allow Marco's treachery to bring down everything I built."

"Understood, boss," Ricardo said, relief washing over his face. "What are your orders?"

"Find him. I want to look him in the eye before we make him pay for his disloyalty."

"Consider it done," Ricardo affirmed, slipping out of the room.

As Eddie sat in the dim light, surrounded by the fruits of his criminal labor, he couldn't help but ponder the consequences of his actions. The thrill of outsmarting his adversaries and the satisfaction of exacting revenge were intoxicating, but he knew that every scheme he orchestrated only served to pull him deeper into the shadows.

"Is it worth it?" he asked himself, swirling the whiskey in his glass. "What price must I pay for this empire?"

But deep down, he already knew the answer. It was a deal he had made long ago – power, wealth, and control, all at the expense of his own humanity. And as the last notes of the opera faded away, Eddie raised his glass, silently toasting to the life he had chosen, and the dark path that lay ahead.

The faint aroma of espresso wafted through the air as Nate and Amy sat hunched over their laptops in a dimly lit corner of Caterina's cafe. Their fingers danced across the keyboards, sifting through digital records and news articles that detailed Edward Hewlett's criminal escapades, piecing together the puzzle of his past.

"Check this out," Amy whispered, her eyes widening as she stumbled upon an intriguing article. "Eddie was already dabbling in money laundering and fraud, but it looks like he made a major breakthrough when he discovered the potential of investment schemes."

"Really?" Nate asked, intrigued. "What happened?"

"Apparently, a few years back, he crossed paths with a disgraced banker named Charles Montgomery. The guy had lost his job and was desperate to make a quick buck. Eddie saw an opportunity and recruited him to help orchestrate elaborate Ponzi schemes."

As Nate absorbed the information, he couldn't help but marvel at Hewlett's cunning. The man was a chameleon, seamlessly adapting his tactics and exploiting every opportunity that presented itself.

"Charles gave Eddie access to a whole new world of victims," Amy continued. "Wealthy individuals who were willing to part with vast sums of money for a chance at even greater returns. That's how he ended up targeting Caterina and so many others like her."

Nate grimaced, thinking of the trusting, warm-hearted woman who had been victimized by someone she considered a friend. It wasn't just about the money; it was the betrayal of trust that stung the most.

"Damn," he muttered. "Eddie really is a piece of work."

"Unfortunately, Caterina's case is far from unique," Amy said, scrolling down the list of names they had uncovered. "We need to find a pattern, something that can help us predict Eddie's next move."

As the couple delved deeper into the web of deceit that Hewlett had spun, they couldn't help but feel a growing sense of urgency. They were up against a man who thrived on manipulation and possessed an insatiable desire for power and wealth. More than ever, they understood that stopping him was no longer just about helping Caterina – it was about preventing countless others from falling prey to his ruthless schemes.

"Everything we've learned about Eddie so far," Nate said, pausing to collect his thoughts, "just confirms how dangerous he is. How willing he is to do whatever it takes to get what he wants."

Amy nodded solemnly. "We need to be extra careful. He's not going to go down without a fight – and he'll take anyone he can with him."

They exchanged a determined glance, knowing that the road ahead would be filled with challenges and danger. But as they stared into each other's eyes, they found comfort and reassurance in their unshakeable bond.

Together, they would bring Edward Hewlett's reign of terror to an end. And justice would finally be served.

Chapter 13

Edward Hewlett sat in his lavish office, the dim glow from the multiple monitors casting eerie shadows on his finely chiseled features. His eyes darted between the screens, taking in the financial data displayed before him. He leaned forward in his leather chair, brow furrowed, fingers tapping impatiently on the mahogany desk as he studied the numbers of the High Yield Investment Program (HYIP). The more he analyzed the figures, the more a nagging suspicion gnawed at the back of his mind.

"Something isn't right here," he muttered under his breath, his usually smooth voice laced with irritation. He adjusted the cufflinks on his expensive suit, the frustration evident in the tightening of his jaw.

***

Several miles away, in their high-tech hideout, Nate and Amy Everhart observed Hewlett's activities through a live feed intercepted from his security cameras. Their covert base was an organized chaos of monitors, keyboards, and gadgets – a testament to their expertise and resourcefulness.

"Looks like Eddie's catching on," Amy said, her striking red hair framing her face as she cast a worried glance towards Nate.

Nate, tall and dark-haired, kept his gaze trained on the screen. He had seen this look on Hewlett's face before – the gears turning in that cunning mind, inching ever closer to the truth. "We need to stay ahead of him," Nate murmured, his military background showing in the tense set of his shoulders.

"Whatever he suspects, we can handle it," Amy reassured him, her journalistic instincts kicking in. She reached out and squeezed his hand, her confidence in their mission unshaken.

Nate met her gaze, a determined glint in his eyes. They had taken down the likes of Edward Hewlett before, and they would do it again. For justice, for Caterina, and for all those they sought to protect.

"Let's get to work," he said, and together they turned back to the screens, ready to outsmart the mastermind who threatened everything they held dear.

Edward Hewlett's fingers drummed impatiently on his mahogany desk as he dialed a number on his encrypted phone. "Vincent," he said, his voice cold and sharp, "I need you to look into this HYIP for me. The numbers... they're not adding up."

"Right away, Mr. Hewlett," Vincent replied, his tone a mix of respect and unease. Edward's instincts were rarely wrong, and the criminal underworld knew that all too well.

"Dig deep, Vincent. I want to know everything about their operations – their investors, their returns, any inconsistencies. And I want it done quickly." Edward's eyes narrowed as he spoke, his suspicions growing with each passing moment.

"Understood, sir. I'll get right on it." Vincent hung up, leaving Edward to contemplate the potential threat this investment posed to his empire.

***

Nate and Amy watched as Edward made his call, the audio feed crackling through their speakers. As they listened to their nemesis instruct Vincent to dissect the HYIP, Nate's mind began racing, calculating their next move. He turned to Amy, who was already anticipating his thoughts.

"We need to throw him off our scent," she said, her green eyes focused. "We could create a diversion – something unrelated but attention-grabbing."

"Or," Nate countered, his fingers tapping on the keyboard, "we could provide false evidence to support the HYIP's legitimacy. Make it look like his suspicions are unfounded."

Amy nodded, considering the options. "If we do it right, either plan could work. But we can't afford any mistakes. One slip-up and Eddie will have us cornered."

"Then let's make sure we don't give him that opportunity," Nate replied, his jaw clenched in determination. "Let's throw him off our trail and keep him invested long enough to bring him down."

Together, they set to work, their minds a flurry of strategizing and plotting as they attempted to outmaneuver the cunning Edward Hewlett. Little did they know that the greatest challenge of their lives was just beginning, and the game of cat and mouse had only just commenced.

Nate's fingers flew across the keyboard, the soft clicking of keys echoing in their dimly lit hideout. The glow from the monitors cast a blue hue on his face, highlighting the determination in his eyes. He was in the zone, expertly navigating through Hewlett's computer system, searching for the perfect place to plant false documents that would support the legitimacy of the HYIP.

"Got it," Nate muttered under his breath, his heart pounding with adrenaline. "Now for some creative forgery."

Amy, meanwhile, had her own mission. She sat at her desk, surrounded by stacks of financial reports and investment schemes. Her nimble fingers tapped away at her tablet, researching other successful ventures to provide Nate with additional material that would bolster the HYIP's credibility. Her eyes scanned the information, processing every detail, seeking patterns she could exploit.

"Did you find anything?" Nate asked, without taking his eyes off the screen.

"Several promising leads," Amy replied, her voice steady as she continued to sift through data. "I should have enough to make our little scheme look like a surefire winner."

"Perfect," Nate said, grinning with grim satisfaction. "Once I've planted these documents, they'll throw Eddie off our trail – at least for now."

As he spoke, Nate's fingers danced across the keyboard, adjusting dates, names, and figures within the fabricated documents. His past experience in ethical hacking had honed his skills to near perfection; he knew exactly how to cover his tracks, ensuring that the documents appeared authentic and untraceable.

"Almost done here," Nate announced, pausing to take a deep breath. His mind filled with thoughts of Caterina, the innocent girl caught up in this dangerous game. He couldn't afford any mistakes – her life, and countless others, depended on their success.

"Alright, I'm sending you the research now," Amy said, forwarding her findings to Nate's computer. "I've highlighted the most relevant points. Just make sure our scheme looks as good as these."

"Leave it to me," Nate replied, his voice full of confidence.

As he incorporated Amy's research into the forged documents, Nate couldn't help but feel a strange sense of exhilaration. They were playing a high-stakes game against a cunning opponent, and every move they made brought them closer to victory – or utter defeat.

"Done," Nate declared, hitting the enter key with finality. The false documents were now planted within Hewlett's system, waiting to be discovered. He glanced at Amy, who was watching him intently, her expression a mix of pride and anxiety.

"Let's hope this buys us some time," he said, allowing himself a brief moment of vulnerability. "We're going to need all the luck we can get."

"Or better yet," Amy added, her eyes gleaming with determination, "let's make our own luck."

Edward Hewlett reclined in his leather chair, one hand gripping the edge of his mahogany desk while the other held a tumbler of bourbon. His eyes scanned the documents displayed on his computer monitor – the ones Nate had so expertly planted within his system.

"Interesting," he murmured, taking a slow sip of his drink. The evidence seemed to support the legitimacy of the HYIP, yet something gnawed at him, a lingering sense of skepticism that refused to be silenced. He leaned forward, his brow furrowing as he examined the details more closely. "Yes, very interesting indeed."

***

Elsewhere in the city, Nate and Amy sat at a dimly lit booth in an upscale Italian restaurant, their fake investor friends gathered around them. Glasses clinked and laughter filled the air, but beneath the jovial surface, a serious conversation was unfolding.

"Alright, listen up," Nate began, his eyes flicking from one face to another. "Hewlett's suspicions are growing by the day. We need to maintain his investment without arousing further suspicion. Ideas?"

Amy chimed in, her voice low and steady. "We need to make sure our communication with him is consistent and convincing. No slip-ups, no signs of hesitation. He can't sense any weakness."

One of their fake investor friends, Marco, nodded in agreement. "I say we start talking about potential expansion plans for the HYIP. Get him excited about the future and the prospect of even bigger returns."

"Good point," Nate replied, tapping his finger on the table in thought. "But we also need to be careful not to overplay our hand. If we push too hard, he might become even more suspicious."

"True," Amy agreed, her eyes narrowing as she considered their next move. "But if we can strike the right balance, keep him engaged and invested...we might just be able to pull this off."

The others at the table exchanged nervous glances, aware of the immense stakes they were all facing. As their fake investor friends took turns pitching ideas and strategies, Nate's thoughts drifted back to Caterina. He knew that every decision they made – every move in this dangerous game – would ultimately determine her fate.

"Alright," Nate said finally, his voice firm and resolute. "Here's what we're going to do..."

As he outlined their plan, Amy watched him with a mixture of admiration and concern. She knew that beneath his confident exterior, Nate was grappling with the weight of their mission. But she also knew that together, they had faced seemingly insurmountable odds before – and emerged victorious.

"Let's do this," she said quietly, reaching across the table to squeeze Nate's hand. "For Caterina, and for all those who've suffered at Hewlett's hands."

"Agreed," Nate replied, his eyes meeting hers with steely determination. "We won't let them down."

And as their fake investor friends raised their glasses in a toast to their impending success, Nate and Amy knew that the real battle had only just begun.

Nate's fingers flew across his keyboard as he remotely accessed Hewlett's phone, intercepting and redirecting all incoming calls. As the final line of code fell into place, he glanced at Amy, who sat on the edge of her seat, her green eyes reflecting the glow of the computer monitors.

"Alright," Nate said, a determined glint in his eyes. "Phase one is complete. Let's keep Hewlett interested."

"Let's do it," Amy replied with a nod, her voice betraying equal parts excitement and anxiety.

Over the next few days, Nate and Amy orchestrated an intricate dance of deception. They monitored Hewlett's every move, adjusting their strategy to feed him just enough information about the HYIP's progress to keep him invested without raising suspicion. With each carefully crafted email, phone call, and meeting, they manipulated the situation, playing on Hewlett's greed and ambition like master puppeteers.

"Mr. Hewlett," Amy purred into the phone, her voice dripping with seductive charm. "We thought you'd like to know that our latest venture has yielded an impressive twenty percent return in just a week."

"Really?" Hewlett replied, his voice laced with intrigue. "That's quite impressive, I must say."

"Indeed," Nate chimed in, adopting his most convincing tone. "We're confident that this is just the beginning. The potential for profit here is virtually limitless."

"Interesting..." Hewlett mused, his skepticism momentarily assuaged but not completely eradicated.

However, Nate and Amy knew that even the most elaborate ruse couldn't withstand scrutiny forever. And as the days wore on, it became apparent that Hewlett was growing increasingly suspicious. He began to question the source of their information and demanded more concrete evidence to support their claims.

It was during one particularly tense video conference that the cracks in their façade began to show. Hewlett's hawk-like gaze bore into them through the screen, his voice cold and accusatory.

"Something doesn't add up," he said, leaning in closer to the camera. "I've noticed discrepancies between the documents you sent me and the public records I've been able to access independently."

Nate felt a bead of sweat trickle down the side of his face as his mind raced for a plausible explanation. Amy tensed beside him, her fingers gripping the edge of the table.

"Mr. Hewlett," Nate began, forcing himself to maintain eye contact with the criminal mastermind. "The reason for these discrepancies is that we have insider information on the companies involved. Our sources are privy to details that aren't yet available to the public."

"Really?" Hewlett challenged, his eyes narrowing. "And who exactly are these mysterious 'sources'?"

"Unfortunately, we can't reveal their identities," Amy interjected smoothly, her quick thinking kicking in. "But rest assured, they're highly reliable and well-placed within the companies in question."

"Besides," Nate added, "if our information were to become public knowledge, it would undermine our advantage and jeopardize the entire operation."

Hewlett studied them for a moment, his expression unreadable. Nate held his breath, praying that their shaky explanation would be enough to throw him off their trail.

"Fine," Hewlett finally said, his tone still laced with suspicion, but seemingly placated for now. "Just make sure your sources stay under wraps. I don't want any surprises."

"Understood," Nate replied, relief washing over him like a tidal wave.

As the call ended, Nate and Amy shared a look of quiet triumph. They had managed to deflect Hewlett's accusations, but they both knew that their victory was only temporary. The clock was ticking, and every second brought them one step closer to their ultimate confrontation with the cunning criminal mastermind.

Nate's fingers danced across the keyboard, his eyes flicking from screen to screen as he wove a web of urgency around the HYIP. Meanwhile, Amy sat hunched over her laptop, her red hair cascading down her back like a waterfall of fire, as she dug up impressive financial reports that showcased stellar returns on investment.

"Take a look at this," she said, spinning her laptop around for Nate to see. "A similar scheme that generated a 400% return in just three months."

"Perfect," Nate replied, a grin spreading across his face. "If we can convince Hewlett that these kinds of returns are possible, there's no way he'll back out now."

With their arsenal of information ready, Nate and Amy scheduled an urgent conference call with Edward Hewlett. The moment he answered, they launched into their carefully crafted pitch.

"Edward, I'm sure you've noticed the incredible returns our HYIP has been generating lately," Nate began, his voice steady and confident. "But what if I told you there's potential for even greater profits?"

"Go on," Hewlett said, his interest piqued.

"Based on our extensive research and insider knowledge, we believe that the next few weeks could see unprecedented growth in our investments," Amy chimed in. "We're talking returns in the triple digits, maybe even higher."

"Really?" Hewlett asked, skepticism creeping into his voice.

"Absolutely," Nate assured him. "We wouldn't bring this to your attention if we weren't certain about its potential. But in order to capitalize on this opportunity, we need to act fast."

"Fine," Hewlett agreed, albeit cautiously. "I'll allocate additional funds for the HYIP. Just make sure my investment pays off."

"Of course," Nate responded with a smile he knew Hewlett couldn't see. "You won't be disappointed."

As the call ended, Nate and Amy exchanged a look of relief. They had successfully stoked the flames of urgency, ensuring Hewlett's continued investment in their scheme.

But just as they began to celebrate their small victory, Hewlett's phone rang again. He picked it up, his expression shifting from annoyance to curiosity as the unknown caller divulged information that sent a chill down his spine.

"Are you certain about this?" he asked, his voice low and dangerous.

"Very well," he said after a pause. "Thank you for the information."

Hanging up, Hewlett stared at the phone in his hand, his eyes narrowing with suspicion. Someone had tipped him off about the true nature of the HYIP, and he now found himself questioning everything he thought he knew about Nate and Amy's operation.

As the pieces began to click into place, Edward Hewlett vowed to uncover the truth behind their lies – and make them pay for their deception.

The steady hum of their high-tech hideout provided a comforting backdrop as Nate and Amy sat huddled together in front of the monitors, watching the endless streams of data. Nate's fingers drummed anxiously on the table, his face a mask of deep concentration.

"Whatever that tip-off was," he muttered, "we need to stay one step ahead of Hewlett."

Amy nodded, her green eyes filled with concern. "We've come too far to let him bring us down now. We made a promise to Caterina, and we're going to keep it."

"Damn right," Nate agreed, clenching his fists. "He's not going to ruin anyone else's life like he did with Caterina. We'll make sure of that."

"Any ideas on how to handle this new development?" Amy asked, her voice tinged with worry.

Nate paused for a moment, his mind racing as he considered their options. "We'll have to be extra cautious. Monitor his every move, intercept any communications that might expose us. And if necessary, create more diversions to throw him off our trail."

"Sounds like a plan," Amy replied, determination etched across her face. "I'll start looking into other successful investment schemes we can use as inspiration. We need to make this HYIP even more convincing."

"Good," Nate said, a hint of a smile playing at the corners of his mouth. "And I'll work on improving our digital defenses, making sure Hewlett can't trace anything back to us."

As they set to work, Nate couldn't help but feel a renewed sense of purpose coursing through his veins. He knew that taking down a criminal mastermind like Edward Hewlett wouldn't be easy, but he also knew that with Amy by his side, they had a fighting chance.

"Hey," Amy said softly, placing a hand on Nate's arm. "We've faced tougher odds before, right?"

"Right," Nate agreed, giving her a reassuring smile. "We'll get through this, together."

With their resolve strengthened, Nate and Amy dove back into their mission, determined to bring Hewlett to justice and protect Caterina at all costs. But as they worked tirelessly to unravel the threads of deception they'd woven, they couldn't shake the nagging feeling that they were being watched – and that the stakes had never been higher.

"Let's do this," Nate whispered, his voice full of conviction. "For Caterina, for all the people he's hurt, let's bring him down."

"Agreed," Amy replied, her eyes blazing with determination. "No matter what it takes."

As they continued planning their next moves, Nate and Amy knew the road ahead wouldn't be easy. But they also knew that failure wasn't an option – not when the lives of those they cared about hung in the balance.

Chapter 14

The dimly lit room seemed to close in on Nate and Amy as they stood face to face with Eddie Hewlett, their eyes locked in a silent battle of wills. The tension between the trio was palpable, casting an ominous shadow over the otherwise unremarkable space.

Nate's fists clenched by his sides, his knuckles turning white from the effort it took to maintain control. Memories of his time in the military flooded his mind, reminding him that he had faced far worse situations than this. He took a deep breath, steadying himself for whatever might come next.

Amy's furrowed brow revealed her concern, but she refused to let any hint of fear show in her stormy grey eyes. Her past as an investigative journalist had trained her to remain composed, even under extreme pressure. She knew that revealing weakness now could cost them everything they had worked so hard to achieve.

Eddie, meanwhile, wore a smug smile that hinted at his growing suspicion. As a criminal mastermind, he had a knack for sensing when someone was trying to deceive him, and right now, his instincts were screaming that Nate and Amy were hiding something. His dark eyes bored into theirs, searching for any sign that would confirm his suspicions.

"Nice place you got here," Nate said, attempting to break the silence and diffuse some of the tension. "Very... intimate."

"Intimacy has its advantages," Eddie replied, his voice silky smooth, like oil sliding down a blade. "Especially when it comes to discussing delicate matters."

Amy nodded, swallowing hard, as she tried to read his true intentions. "Yes, we understand the need for discretion."

"Good," Eddie said, his gaze never wavering. "Now, I believe we have some business to discuss."

As Eddie continued to scrutinize them, Nate's mind raced, searching for the best way to steer the conversation away from their secret plan. He knew that if they were to succeed, they would need to keep Eddie off balance and maintain the illusion of trust, at least for a little while longer.

"Of course," Nate replied, his voice steady despite the pounding of his heart. "We're here to finalize the details of our... arrangement."

"Indeed," said Eddie, his smile widening ever so slightly. "And I'm looking forward to seeing just how well you can both deliver on your promises."

Eddie's eyes seemed to pierce through the dimness, a predator sizing up its prey. "You know, I've been in this business long enough to recognize when someone is playing me for a fool," he said, his voice dripping with venom.

Nate and Amy exchanged a quick glance, silently communicating their need to stay calm and composed. Nate clenched his fists, trying to channel the tension brewing within him, while Amy's furrowed brow betrayed her concern.

"Playing you for a fool?" Nate feigned surprise, raising an eyebrow. "Eddie, we're on the same side here."

"Are we?" Eddie asked, his tone accusatory. "Because I'm starting to think that this whole scheme of yours is just one big lie, designed to keep me off balance and distract me from what you're really up to."

Amy forced a laugh, trying to deflect the suspicion. "Eddie, we've spent months working on this plan together. Why would we deceive you now?"

"Maybe because you've got something even bigger going on behind my back," Eddie retorted, narrowing his eyes. "Something that could make you rich without having to share the profits with me."

"Come on, Eddie," Nate interjected, his voice steady but his heart pounding with anxiety. "We both know there's more than enough money to go around. We wouldn't risk everything we've built just to cut you out."

"Then explain this," Eddie demanded, tossing a piece of paper onto the table between them. "I found it in your office. It looks like a blueprint for some kind of hacking operation, complete with detailed instructions on how to bypass security systems and infiltrate financial accounts."

Nate picked up the paper, studying it carefully before responding. "This? This is just research, Eddie. You know, part of our due diligence to make sure we're prepared for any potential obstacles that might come our way."

"Really? And I'm supposed to believe that you just happened to leave it lying around where anyone could find it?" Eddie challenged, his voice growing colder with each word.

Amy stepped forward, her tone confident. "Eddie, you know how thorough we are. We wouldn't be in this position if we hadn't been meticulous in researching every aspect of our plan. This is just one of many documents we've used to prepare ourselves."

"Fine," Eddie said, his eyes still narrowed with suspicion. "But I'll be keeping a much closer eye on you both from now on. One more piece of evidence like this, and our partnership is over."

As the weight of Eddie's ultimatum hung heavy in the air, Nate and Amy knew they had to tread carefully, their every move being watched. Their quest for justice was far from over, and the stakes had never been higher.

Eddie's eyes burned into Nate and Amy, his gaze as sharp as a dagger. The dangerous glint in them sent chills down their spines, but they knew they couldn't let fear take hold. Nate clenched his jaw and focused on Eddie's love for power and influence, seeking the perfect deflection.

"Listen, Eddie," Nate began, his voice steady, "You know that our plan involves breaking into some high-level security systems. It's only natural we'd need to research everything possible to make sure we don't get caught. I mean, you wouldn't want any of us to end up behind bars, would you?"

Eddie's expression softened ever so slightly, his ego being stroked by Nate's words. "Of course not. But I still don't like it."

"Let's not forget, Eddie," Amy chimed in, "that with this operation, we'll be able to infiltrate some of the biggest corporations in the world. Think of the power and control we'll have once we pull this off."

Eddie's eyes lit up at the thought, momentarily distracted. Nate seized the opportunity, subtly steering the conversation towards another aspect of their scheme.

"Speaking of which," Nate said, nonchalantly adjusting his cufflinks, "we recently got our hands on a new piece of software that will help us bypass even the most advanced firewalls. It's going to be a game-changer for us."

"Really?" Eddie asked, curiosity piqued. "Tell me more about it."

"Top-secret stuff, Eddie," Amy replied with a slight grin, knowing full well how much he loved a good secret. "It's a one-of-a-kind program, custom-made just for us. And it's practically undetectable. Just imagine how unstoppable we'll be when we have that kind of access."

"Interesting," Eddie mused, his eyes narrowing again as he weighed their words, suspicion still lingering. The tension in the room was palpable, but Nate and Amy maintained their composure, determined to keep Eddie from discovering the truth.

"Look," Nate added, his tone reassuring, "we both know that trust is crucial for any partnership to succeed. We're all in this together, and we wouldn't be here without your expertise and connections. But in order for us to pull off something of this scale, we have to be one step ahead at all times."

For a moment, it seemed as though Eddie might relent, the temptation of power and influence tugging at his desires. But the shadows in his eyes betrayed his continued skepticism, and Nate knew they were far from safe. With each passing second, the noose around their necks tightened, threatening to strangle their mission for justice before it could fully take flight.

The room's air grew heavy, as if it were filled with the smoke of suspicion and treachery. Beads of sweat formed on Nate's forehead, and he clenched his fists to keep them from shaking. Eddie continued to scrutinize them, his gaze piercing through their defenses like a dagger.

"Undetectable, huh?" Eddie asked, his voice low and dangerous. "You two better not be playing me for a fool."

Nate held Eddie's stare, his heart pounding in his chest. 'Hold it together,' he thought, fighting the urge to look away. 'One slip, and everything we've worked for crumbles to dust.'

Amy, aware of the precariousness of their situation, studied the room with her peripheral vision. The dimly lit room offered little comfort, but she noted the placement of the windows and doors, mapping out potential escape routes. She could feel her pulse quickening, urging her to take action.

"Of course not, Eddie," she replied, injecting a hint of offense into her tone. "We're all in this together, remember? We wouldn't jeopardize our operation by double-crossing you."

"Prove it," Eddie demanded abruptly, leaning forward in his chair. The sound of his voice echoed off the barren walls, intensifying the atmosphere of uncertainty that had settled over the room.

"Fine." Nate forced himself to remain calm as he pulled out his laptop, opening up a series of files. He began to explain the intricacies of the program they had developed, using technical jargon to both impress and confuse Eddie.

Amy seized the opportunity to subtly glance at Nate, her eyes conveying silent reassurance. They had faced dangerous situations before, but the stakes seemed higher now. As they navigated the treacherous waters of their conversation, she felt an odd mixture of fear and exhilaration, knowing that every word spoken could either save them or seal their fate.

"Here," Nate said, gesturing to a line of code on the screen. "This part of the program ensures that we're completely invisible within the system. No alarms, no traces, nothing."

Eddie leaned in closer, his breath hot and foul as it mixed with the stifling air of the room. The three of them stood there, locked in a tense moment of scrutiny, each acutely aware of the unspoken threat that hung over them like a guillotine blade.

"Alright," Eddie conceded, sitting back in his chair. "But I'm warning you – if I find out that you've lied to me about any of this, there will be hell to pay."

Nate nodded, swallowing the lump in his throat. "Understood."

In that instant, they knew they had bought themselves some time, but the lingering doubt remained. As they continued to weave their web of deception, every word spoken and every gesture made carried the weight of their future – a life dedicated to justice, or an untimely end driven by revenge.

Eddie's fingers drummed on the table, a metronome ticking away the seconds of their rapidly thinning façade. Nate glanced at Amy, her eyes locked onto Eddie, and he knew they had to keep pushing forward. Their composure was now their only line of defense.

"Another crucial aspect," Nate began, his voice steady, "is the misdirection we've built into the scheme. By diverting attention elsewhere, it'll be nearly impossible for anyone to link us back to the operation."

"Interesting," Eddie said, his voice laced with skepticism. "And how exactly do you plan on achieving that?"

Amy chimed in, her tone confident. "We've set up a series of dummy accounts that appear legitimate but are ultimately disposable. If anyone does start digging, they'll find themselves chasing shadows."

"Shadows, huh?" Eddie leaned back in his chair, tapping his finger against his chin as he studied them. Nate could feel the weight of Eddie's stare, like a predator sizing up its prey.

"Exactly," Nate replied, forcing a smile. "It's an intricate web designed to keep our enemies confused and off-balance."

"Like I said, shadows," Amy reiterated, her voice unwavering.

For a moment, silence filled the room, punctuated only by the hum of the computer servers and the distant thrum of traffic outside. The tension was palpable, a live wire sparking between the three of them.

"Very well," Eddie finally said, his gaze piercing through Nate and Amy. It felt as if he were trying to peel back the layers of their deception, searching for any sign of weakness. They exchanged a brief glance, silently questioning if their plan was about to crumble before their eyes.

"Your plan seems... thorough," Eddie admitted, though the suspicion never left his eyes. "But remember, if you're playing me for a fool, the consequences will be dire."

Nate's heart raced, but his voice remained steady. "We understand, Eddie. We're not in the business of making enemies – especially not with you."

"Good," Eddie replied, his eyes narrowing further. "Because if I find out you've been lying to me..." He let the threat hang in the air, a dark cloud looming over them.

"Trust us, Eddie," Amy added softly, her gaze never leaving his. "We wouldn't dream of it."

As they continued to dance along the razor's edge, Nate couldn't help but feel a strange sense of exhilaration. They were walking a tightrope, and one misstep could send them plummeting into the abyss - but there was no turning back now. The pursuit of justice demanded their unwavering resolve, and they would see this through to the end, come what may.

Eddie's face loomed closer, the dim light casting sinister shadows across his features. Nate and Amy could feel the heat radiating from him as he leaned in, his voice dropping to a dangerous whisper that sent a shiver down their spines.

"Let me be perfectly clear," Eddie hissed, his breath warm and heavy on their faces. "I have eyes and ears everywhere. If you think for even a moment that I won't find out if you're lying to me..." He paused, letting the threat hang in the air like a noose.

Nate clenched his jaw, resisting the urge to take a step back. His heart thundered in his chest, a constant reminder of the high stakes they were playing with. Stay calm, he told himself. Don't give him any reason to doubt you.

"Like we said, Eddie," Nate replied, forcing a confident smile. "We're on the same side here."

"Are we?" Eddie countered, his eyes narrowing into slits. He looked back and forth between Nate and Amy, as though searching for any hint of deceit. "Because something doesn't quite add up."

Amy's mind raced, searching for the right words to deflect his suspicion. She knew Eddie was a master manipulator, constantly probing for weaknesses. It was crucial that they stay one step ahead of him, anticipating his every move. Her father's wrongful conviction had taught her the importance of being prepared for anything – and she couldn't let Nate down now.

"Look," she began, her voice steady despite the fear clawing at her insides. "We've done our research, Eddie. We know what you're after, and we know how to get it. Trust us – we wouldn't have come this far if we didn't think we could pull it off."

Eddie's gaze flickered between the two of them, his expression unreadable. For a moment, the room seemed to hold its breath, the stifling silence punctuated only by their pounding hearts.

"Alright," he finally said, his voice low and dangerous. "I'll give you this one chance. But if I find out you're double-crossing me..." He trailed off, a sly smile playing at the corners of his lips as he delivered a chilling ultimatum. "Well, let's just say the consequences won't be pleasant for either of you."

Nate and Amy exchanged a tense glance, the weight of Eddie's words settling over them like a suffocating fog. They had come too far to turn back now – but would they be able to maintain their delicate web of deception, or would it all come crashing down around them?

Only time would tell.

Chapter 15

The dimly lit living room flickered with the faint glow of a single candle, casting eerie shadows on the walls. Nate and Amy sat on their worn-out couch, the weight of their mission pressing heavily on their shoulders. The silence was palpable, punctuated only by the soft crackling of the candle's wick.

"Are we doing the right thing, Nate?" Amy's voice wavered as she looked at her husband, her green eyes filled with concern. "I mean, we knew this would be risky, but what if something happens to Caterina or any of our friends?"

Nate sighed, his dark eyes mirroring the worry in hers. He ran his fingers through his hair, trying to find the right words. "I know, Amy. But remember why we started all this – we've seen too many people like Caterina suffer because of men like Edward Hewlett. We can't just sit back and do nothing."

Amy stood up abruptly, her hands clasped tightly together as she paced back and forth across the small living room. Her red hair shimmered in the candlelight, her movements betraying her anxiety. Nate leaned forward, his brow furrowed in deep thought, considering the impact their actions might have on their loved ones and the potential backlash they could face.

"Of course I understand that, Nate. It's just..." She hesitated, swallowing hard before continuing. "What if our actions put them in harm's way? Are we truly ready to accept those consequences?"

Nate's gaze followed Amy as she continued pacing, her footsteps echoing in the silent room. He knew all too well the feeling of putting others in danger – it was something he had faced during his military days and still haunted him. He pressed his lips together, weighing the risks and benefits of their plan.

"Look, I won't lie to you. There's always a chance that things could go wrong," Nate admitted. "But if we don't fight for Caterina and everyone else who's been wronged, who will? We have the skills to make a difference, and I believe our mission is worth the risk."

Amy paused in her pacing, turning to face Nate with determination in her eyes. She nodded slowly, acknowledging the truth in his words. They both knew the stakes were high, but the potential reward of justice for Caterina and others like her outweighed the risks.

"Alright, Nate. Let's do this – together, like always," Amy said resolutely, her voice steady despite the thoughts racing through her mind. And with that, they shared a brief, knowing glance before standing up, ready to face the challenges ahead as a team.

The flickering glow of the fireplace cast eerie shadows on Nate's face, highlighting his furrowed brow and the dark circles under his eyes. He clenched his fists and took a deep breath, trying to steady his trembling voice. "Amy," he began, forcing himself to meet her gaze. "I can't shake the feeling that we might be putting Caterina and our friends in even more danger with this plan."

Amy's pacing slowed as she looked at Nate, her heart twisting at the raw vulnerability in his eyes. She knew that this mission was tearing him apart on the inside, and it pained her to see him so conflicted. "We've always tried to do what's right, Nate," she said, her own voice wavering. "But you're right, we have to consider the consequences of our actions too. What if something goes wrong? What if we only make things worse?"

A heavy silence settled between them, broken only by the crackling of the fire. The weight of their decision pressed down on them, suffocating and inescapable. Nate stared into the dancing flames, his thoughts racing as he grappled with the morality of their mission.

"Every time we act, there's a risk," Nate admitted, his voice barely audible above the fire's whispers. "But we can't let fear paralyze us. We owe it to Caterina and everyone else who's been hurt by Hewlett to fight back. If we don't, who will?"

Tears welled up in Amy's eyes as she considered the potential fallout from their actions – the legal battles that could ensue, the emotional toll it might take on their relationships with Caterina and their friends. She knew that they were walking a tightrope, one wrong move away from disaster. But the thought of standing by and doing nothing while others suffered was unbearable.

"Every time we act, there's a risk," Nate admitted, his voice barely audible above the fire's whispers. "But we can't let fear paralyze us. We owe it to Caterina and everyone else who's been hurt by Hewlett to fight back. If we don't, who will?"

Tears welled up in Amy's eyes as she considered the potential fallout from their actions – the legal battles that could ensue, the emotional toll it might take on their relationships with Caterina and their friends. She knew that they were walking a tightrope, one wrong move away from disaster. But the thought of standing by and doing nothing while others suffered was unbearable.

"Every time we act, there's a risk," Nate admitted, his voice barely audible above the fire's whispers. "But we can't let fear paralyze us. We owe it to Caterina and everyone else who's been hurt by Hewlett to fight back. If we don't, who will?"

"Is it worth it, Nate?" Amy whispered, her gaze locked on the floor. "Are we really doing the right thing here, or are we just playing God and putting our friends in danger because of our own crusade for justice?"

Nate sighed, running a hand through his dark hair. He wished he could give her a definitive answer, something that would put both their minds at ease. But he knew that life was never that simple.

"I don't know, Amy," he admitted, swallowing the lump in his throat. "All I know is that if we don't try to help, then Caterina and countless others like her will continue to suffer, and that's something I can't live with. We have the power to make a difference, and I believe it's our duty to use it."

Amy looked up at Nate, her eyes glistening with unshed tears. She understood his conviction, his unwavering belief in their mission. And as much as she feared the potential consequences of their actions, she knew deep down that he was right.

"Okay," she whispered, wiping away her tears with the back of her hand. "We'll see this through, for Caterina and everyone else who has been wronged by Hewlett. But we have to be careful, Nate. We can't let our own emotions cloud our judgment. We owe it to them to do this right."

Nate nodded, locking eyes with Amy. There was no turning back now. They would face whatever challenges lay ahead, united in their fight for justice.

The dim lighting in the living room cast deep shadows across Nate's face, accentuating his furrowed brow and the lines of worry etched into his features. His eyes flickered with the weight of their decision, the potential consequences threatening to consume them both.

"Listen, Amy," he said, reaching out to take her trembling hand. His fingers wrapped tightly around hers, offering a reassuring squeeze. Their eyes locked, sharing a moment of silent understanding: a mixture of determination and fear that bonded them together even as it threatened to tear them apart.

"Let's not forget who we are, what we've accomplished – the lives we've touched and the difference we've made," Nate murmured, his voice steadier than before. "We took down that human trafficking ring last year, remember? And what about the pharmaceutical company that was price gouging on life-saving medications?"

Amy nodded, her grip tightening on Nate's hand as she recalled their past victories. The memories washed over her like a wave, reminding her of the strength they had when they were united in purpose. "Of course I remember, Nate. Those people, they needed us. They didn't have anyone else to stand up for them. And now... Caterina needs us."

"Exactly." Nate's gaze held steady, never waning from the intensity of their shared resolve. "Caterina and our friends – they're counting on us. We can't let them down because of our own doubts and fears. We need to be smart, resourceful, and above all, cautious. But we can do this. We've done it before, and we'll do it again."

Amy blinked back fresh tears, her chest swelling with renewed determination. "You're right, Nate. We've faced worse adversaries, haven't we? We always find a way to make things right. As long as we stay true to ourselves – to our mission – we'll find a way to bring justice to Caterina."

"Damn right, we will." Nate's lips curved into a half-smile, his grip on Amy's hand unwavering. "Now let's get to work."

Together, they stood up from the couch, their movements fluid and purposeful as they prepared for the next phase of their plan. They exchanged a final glance, knowing that their decision to see the mission through would have far-reaching consequences. But for now, they focused on the task at hand: protecting those who had been wronged and bringing justice to Caterina.

Nate and Amy knew that the road ahead would be fraught with danger and uncertainty. The stakes were higher than ever, and the risks greater than any they had faced before. But driven by their shared sense of duty and the knowledge that they could make a difference, they pressed forward, undeterred by the obstacles that lay ahead. They would fight for justice, for revenge, and for the countless lives that depended on them – no matter what the cost.

The dimly lit living room flickered with the glow of a single candle, casting shadows on Nate's face as he took a deep breath. The tension in the air was palpable as the weight of their mission pressed down upon them.

"Listen, Amy," Nate said, his voice steady despite the uncertainty that lingered in the air. "We can't abandon Caterina and our friends now. We've come too far to turn back."

Amy wiped away her tears, her hand shaking slightly. Her resolve hardened, and her eyes met Nate's with renewed determination. "I know the risks, Nate," she replied. "But we have a chance to bring justice for Caterina. We can't let her down."

Nate leaned back in his chair, his fingers drumming against the armrest. His mind raced with memories of past missions and the lives they had changed for the better – all fueled by their relentless pursuit of justice. He knew that there was no turning back; they were in this fight together, and they would see it through to the end.

"Alright then," Nate said, nodding at his wife. "Let's get to work."

As they prepared to embark on the next phase of their plan, Nate's thoughts returned to Caterina. She was more than just a friend; she was a symbol of everything they fought for. Her warmth, generosity, and passion for life were a constant reminder of the good that remained in the world, even in the face of darkness.

It wasn't just about revenge or righting a wrong. It was about protecting the people they cared about and ensuring that those who sought to exploit others were held accountable for their actions. And as Nate considered the potential consequences of their mission, he couldn't help but feel a sense of responsibility – not just for Caterina, but for all of those whose lives had been touched by Edward Hewlett's greed.

"Hey," Amy called out, breaking Nate's reverie. "I found something interesting on Hewlett's financial records."

"Really?" Nate asked, his curiosity piqued as he moved closer to examine the documents she had pulled up. "What have you got?"

"Looks like some of the money Caterina invested was transferred to an offshore account," Amy explained, her tone serious but focused. "If we can trace it back, we might be able to find a way to recover some of her losses."

"Good work," Nate praised, a fire igniting in his eyes. "Let's dig deeper into this. It could be our key to taking Hewlett down."

With their resolve solidified and their determination unwavering, Nate and Amy delved into the intricate web of lies and deception that surrounded Edward Hewlett. They knew that the road ahead would be fraught with danger and uncertainty, but they also understood that the potential reward – justice for Caterina, and perhaps countless others – far outweighed the risks.

As their fingers flew across the keyboards, Nate and Amy exchanged glances that spoke volumes. They were in this together, bound by their shared mission and a fierce desire to protect those who had been wronged. And though the outcome remained uncertain, one thing was clear: they would stop at nothing to bring justice to Caterina and all who had suffered at the hands of Edward Hewlett.

The glow of the city lights filtered through the thin curtains, casting a soft, warm aura around the dimly lit living room. Nate and Amy exchanged a determined glance, their doubts momentarily pushed aside by a surge of resolve. They both knew what needed to be done.

"Alright," said Nate, his voice steady and focused. "Let's do this."

Amy nodded in agreement, her fiery red hair cascading over her shoulders as she stood up from the couch. "We've come this far. We can't back down now."

As they left the living room, Nate and Amy grabbed their laptops and gathered the necessary tools for the next phase of their plan. Their movements were purposeful and focused, their minds set on the task at hand. Amy's eyes darted to a small photograph on the mantle – a snapshot of them with Caterina and some of their closest friends. A pang of guilt tugged at her heart, but she quickly suppressed it. This was about more than just them; it was about justice.

"Remember when we first started all this?" Nate asked, his voice tinged with nostalgia as he slung a backpack over his shoulder.

Amy smiled faintly, recalling their earlier days of covert operations and cyber espionage. "Yeah, I never thought we'd end up here, working to save our friend from a ruthless manipulator like Hewlett."

"Me neither," Nate admitted, zipping up his bag. "But we've helped so many people along the way, and we can help Caterina too. We just need to stay focused and trust in our skills."

"Agreed," Amy replied, her resolve hardening once more. She glanced at the clock on the wall, its ticking a steady reminder of the time slipping away. "We don't have much time. Let's get to work."

Together, Nate and Amy moved through their apartment, gathering the essential items they would need for the next phase of their plan. The weight of their mission bore down on them, but they found strength in each other's determination.

"Hey," Nate said suddenly, pausing as he caught sight of Amy's worried expression. "We've faced tougher challenges before, and we've always come out on top. We can do this."

Amy inhaled deeply, her eyes locking with Nate's. In that moment, she knew he was right. They had faced seemingly insurmountable odds before, but their shared drive for justice and their unwavering belief in each other had always seen them through.

"You're right," she whispered, her voice barely audible above the din of the city outside. "Let's bring Hewlett down – for Caterina, for our friends, and for everyone else he's hurt."

With renewed purpose, Nate and Amy strode towards the door, ready to face whatever challenges lay ahead. As they stepped out into the night, they knew that their decision to see the mission through would have far-reaching consequences. But with each other by their side, they were prepared to fight for justice, no matter the cost.

Nate's fingers danced across the keyboard, the rhythmic tapping a staccato soundtrack to their pursuit of justice. The small room, bathed in the dim blue glow of multiple computer screens, hummed with energy as they dove headfirst into their mission. Amy sat beside him, her own hands a blur as she navigated complex data streams, her eyes unblinking and focused.

"Remember that time in Prague when we thought we'd reached a dead end?" Nate mused, his voice barely more than a whisper. "And then you found that backdoor into the system? That was brilliant."

Amy cracked a slight smile, her eyes never leaving the screen. "And what about you, using your military training to get us out of that warehouse in Mumbai? Talk about thinking on your feet."

The memories fueled their determination, each recollection a testament to their unique skills and unwavering commitment to their cause. In the low light of their makeshift office, Nate and Amy were a formidable team – two vigilantes driven by a shared desire to right wrongs and protect the vulnerable.

"Edward Hewlett won't know what hit him," Nate declared, his voice tinged with both confidence and a subtle hint of amusement. "We'll expose his schemes and bring justice to Caterina and everyone else he's crossed."

"Agreed," Amy responded, her tone firm and resolute. "He may be cunning, but he's underestimated us. We've taken down bigger fish than him before."

As they continued to work, Nate felt a familiar warmth wash over him. It wasn't just the knowledge that they were doing something important, or even the satisfaction of bringing people like Hewlett to account. No, it was the fact that they were doing it together – side by side, united by love and a passion for justice.

"Hey," Nate said, briefly pausing his rapid typing. "I just wanted to say... thank you. For always being there, for always having my back."

Amy turned her head, locking eyes with Nate for a moment. "Of course," she said softly, before breaking into a playful grin. "And thank you for never doubting my crazy plans. I know it's not easy."

"Your crazy plans are what make us great," Nate replied, his voice warm and affectionate. "Together, we're unstoppable."

With their resolve stronger than ever, Nate and Amy returned their focus to the task at hand. Hewlett wouldn't elude them for long – they were determined to bring justice to Caterina and everyone else he'd wronged. And as they sat side by side in that dimly lit room, fingers flying across keyboards and minds racing, there was no doubt in either of their minds that they would succeed.

"Ready?" Nate asked, sharing a final glance with Amy.

"Ready."

With a sudden, almost jarring silence, the clatter of typing ceased. Nate and Amy had been working feverishly for hours, chasing down leads, digging through data, and refining their strategy. Now, they found themselves at a crossroads – a critical point in their plan where they had to choose between multiple paths, each with its own set of risks and potential rewards.

"Okay," Nate said, breaking the silence. "We've got three possible ways to get to Hewlett. Each one has its pros and cons. We need to make a decision."

Amy leaned back in her chair, rubbing her temple as she mulled over the options. "What's your gut telling you?"

"Option one is the quickest, but it's also the most dangerous," Nate replied, his eyes scanning the screen before him. "Option two is safer, but it'll take longer. And option three... well, that's the wildcard. I can't guarantee it will work, but if it does, Hewlett won't know what hit him."

"Your gut has never failed us before," Amy said, her gaze meeting Nate's. "I trust you."

Nate gave a small, grateful smile and took a deep breath. He knew the weight of this decision; the consequences could ripple outwards, affecting not only Caterina but also countless others who had fallen victim to Hewlett's schemes. The instinct honed from years of military service and ethical hacking told him that one path stood out above the rest – he just needed the courage to act on it.

"Alright," he said, his voice steady and determined. "Option three it is. Let's do this."

Amy nodded, her fingers poised over the keyboard, ready to spring into action. But before they dove headlong into the next phase of their mission, they shared a brief moment of stillness, allowing the gravity of their decision to sink in.

"Remember," Nate said, his voice soft yet resolute. "No matter what happens, we're in this together."

"Always," Amy whispered, the words hanging in the air between them like a promise.

With that, they took a collective breath and plunged back into their work, each keystroke echoing through the makeshift office like a heartbeat. They knew the challenges that lay ahead would test their resolve to its breaking point, but they drew strength from their shared mission and the knowledge that, together, they could right wrongs and bring justice to those who needed it most.

As the night wore on and the hum of their high-tech equipment filled the room, Nate and Amy were keenly aware that their decision to see the mission through would have far-reaching consequences. But even with the unknown lurking just around the corner, they moved forward – fueled by love, determination, and an unshakable belief in the power of justice.

Chapter 16

The hypnotic ticking of the kitchen clock provided a metronome for Nate and Amy's thoughts as they sat, hunched over the polished oak table. The steaming cups of coffee before them had long gone cold, forgotten in the intensity of their conversation. Their furrowed brows and tense expressions were telltale signs of the weighty decisions that lay before them.

"Are we really going to do this?" Amy asked, her voice tinged with apprehension. "Keeping Hewlett invested in the HYIP is risky, and it could backfire on us."

Nate leaned back in his chair, rubbing his temples as he mulled over her words. His military background had taught him how to assess risks and strategies under pressure, but this situation was unlike anything he'd faced before. "I know, but what other choice do we have? Caterina deserves justice, and we can't let Hewlett walk away unscathed."

Amy sighed, her investigative instincts telling her that Nate was right. They needed to bring down Hewlett, but the stakes were high. She took a deep breath, steeling herself for the challenge ahead. "Alright, let's find the best way to keep Hewlett hooked, without putting ourselves or Caterina in further danger."

Just then, the sound of footsteps echoed through the hallway, and Caterina appeared in the doorway. Her dark hair framed her face, and her eyes shimmered with determination and gratitude. She glanced between Nate and Amy, sensing their hesitation.

"Please, my friends," she implored, her thick Sicilian accent filling the room. "I believe in you both more than anyone else. You have already done so much for me, and I know you can succeed in this mission too."

Nate exchanged a glance with Amy, who gave him a subtle nod. He turned his attention back to Caterina. "We're committed to helping you, Caterina. We just need to be careful and plan every step."

Caterina's face softened, her eyes welling up with tears as she stepped further into the room. "I understand your concerns, but I trust you both completely. If anyone can recover my lost investment and bring Hewlett to justice, it's you two." Her voice was unwavering, full of conviction.

Amy reached across the table, taking Caterina's hand in hers. "We won't let you down, Caterina. We'll find a way to make this right, no matter what it takes."

With their resolve strengthened by Caterina's faith in them, Nate and Amy turned their focus back to the task at hand. They knew that the road ahead would be fraught with challenges, but they were determined to see their mission through to the end. Justice for Caterina – and all those who had suffered at the hands of people like Hewlett – depended on it.

Nate drummed his fingers on the table, the rhythmic tapping echoing through the tense silence in the room. Amy's eyes flicked between him and Caterina, her brows furrowed in concentration as she considered their options. "Alright," Nate finally broke the silence, leaning back in his chair. "We need to maintain Hewlett's trust in the HYIP while keeping our own hands clean. Ideas?"

"Perhaps we could create a false narrative showcasing the program's success and reliability," Amy suggested, her emerald eyes meeting Nate's gaze. "We can invent fake investors who've supposedly reaped huge rewards from the program."

"Or," Nate mused, rubbing the stubble on his chin thoughtfully, "we can provide him with misleading information that supports the legitimacy of the scheme, drawing his attention away from any potential red flags."

Amy nodded slowly, considering both options. "What are the risks and benefits of each? We need to be absolutely certain we make the right choice here."

"Creating a false narrative gives us control over the situation," Nate replied, his military background showing through in his careful analysis. "If we play our cards right, it could lead Hewlett to believe that he's missing out on lucrative opportunities. The downside is that if he catches onto the deceit, we'll lose all credibility and our chance to recover Caterina's investment."

"Meanwhile, providing misleading information might not be as convincing, but it would be easier to pull off," Amy added. "The risk of exposure would still be there, but we'd have plausible deniability if things go south."

"Either way, we're playing with fire," Nate admitted, running a hand through his dark hair. "But we need to convince Hewlett that his suspicions were unfounded in order to keep him invested. And we need to do it without getting ourselves burned in the process."

"Agreed," Amy said with determination. "We have to be smart about this, Nate. We're walking a tightrope here, and the slightest misstep could send everything crashing down."

Nate locked eyes with Amy, a fire burning within him. "We'll make it work, Amy. For Caterina's sake, we have to."

"Si," Caterina whispered, her voice barely audible but full of gratitude. "Grazie mille, Nate e Amy. I know you will do what is best."

As Nate and Amy continued to weigh their options, they couldn't help but feel the weight of Caterina's trust on their shoulders. They were determined not to let her down, no matter the risks involved. And as the sun began to set outside, casting long shadows across the kitchen table, they knew that the battle for justice had only just begun.

Nate's fingers tapped rhythmically on the tabletop, mimicking the ticking clock that hung on the kitchen wall. The air was thick with tension and determination as he exchanged a glance with Amy. They knew what they had to do – it was time to put their plan into motion.

"Alright," Nate said, his voice steady and resolute. "We'll create a series of fabricated success stories from other investors, complete with fake testimonials and financial statements. That should be enough to alleviate Hewlett's doubts and reinforce his belief in the HYIP."

"Agreed," Amy replied, her eyes narrowing in concentration. "If we can convince him that others are profiting from this scheme, then he'll be more likely to stay invested himself."

"Exactly," Nate confirmed, his mind already racing ahead to the details of their plan. "We'll need to divide the tasks between us. I'll take charge of creating the false success stories, while you focus on designing convincing financial statements."

"Sounds good to me," Amy said, nodding decisively. "Let's make sure we work efficiently and utilize our respective skills to bring this plan to life." As she spoke, her journalistic instincts kicked in, and she began mentally organizing the structure of the financial statements.

"Si, si," Caterina chimed in, her eyes shining with gratitude and determination. "I know you two can do this. Just remember, for every lie we tell, we're getting closer to the truth."

Nate couldn't help but smile at Caterina's unwavering faith in them. Taking a deep breath, he opened his laptop and began typing away at a rapid pace. His fingers danced across the keyboard like a pianist playing a complicated concerto, each keystroke a carefully crafted note in the symphony of deception.

As Nate worked on the false success stories, he wove intricate tales of ordinary people achieving extraordinary wealth through the HYIP. He drew upon his experiences as an ethical hacker and used that knowledge to create believable narratives, right down to the specific details of each individual's investments.

"Hey, Amy," Nate called out, not taking his eyes off the screen. "How are the financial statements coming along?"

"Almost done," she replied, her focus equally unwavering. She had already created a series of convincing charts and graphs that painted a glowing picture of the HYIP's performance. Now she was working on the finishing touches – adding in just enough inconsistencies to make them appear authentic rather than perfectly engineered.

As they continued to work, the sun dipped lower in the sky, casting an orange hue across their workspace. The fading light seemed to symbolize the dwindling time they had left to convince Hewlett to stay invested.

"Alright, I've got the false success stories ready to go," Nate announced, triumphantly hitting the save button on his laptop. "How about you?"

"Done," Amy confirmed, closing her own laptop with a satisfying click. "These financial statements should be more than enough to keep Hewlett hooked."

"Perfect," Nate said, his lips curling into a satisfied grin. "Now let's put these fakes to use and get one step closer to justice for Caterina."

As they prepared to embark on the next phase of their plan, Nate and Amy shared a look of fierce determination. They knew the risks involved, but they also knew that sometimes, in order to expose the truth, you have to play by the rules of deception. And if there was one thing they were good at, it was bending the rules to their advantage.

The sun cast long shadows on the pavement as Nate and Amy walked briskly through the streets, their footsteps echoing in unison. With a satchel containing the fabricated success stories and financial statements slung over Nate's shoulder, they made their way to meet with the seed investors—friends who had been posing as current investors in the HYIP.

"Let's just hope they're all on board with this," Nate said, his brow furrowed in thought. "We need those testimonials to make this work."

Amy nodded, her eyes scanning their surroundings as they turned into a narrow alley that led to an inconspicuous side door. "I have faith in our friends, Nate. They've got our backs, just like we've got theirs."

As they entered the dimly lit room, they were greeted by the familiar faces of their trusted allies. The air buzzed with anticipation, and Nate could feel the collective energy and determination that always seemed to fill the space when they gathered together.

"Alright, everyone, listen up," Nate began, his voice carrying a sense of urgency. "We have a plan to convince Hewlett that the HYIP is legit, but we need your help. We need you to provide false testimonials to bolster the fake success stories we've created."

There was a moment of silence as the group took in Nate's words, before one of the seed investors—a man named Marco—spoke up. "Nate, Amy, you've helped us in more ways than you can imagine. We're in this together, and we'll do whatever it takes to bring Hewlett down."

"Thank you," Amy said, her voice filled with gratitude. "We wouldn't be able to pull this off without all of you."

Over the next hour, Nate and Amy discussed the specifics of their plan, providing each seed investor with a detailed backstory to accompany their false testimonial. The group worked diligently, honing their performances and ensuring that every last detail was perfect.

"Remember, the key is to be convincing but not too over-the-top," Nate advised as they wrapped up their preparations. "We want Hewlett to believe in the HYIP's success, but not become suspicious."

With the testimonials secured, Nate and Amy arranged a meeting with Hewlett. As they prepared for the confrontation, Nate couldn't help but feel a thrill of anticipation mixed with nerves. This was the moment they had been working towards, the culmination of their efforts to bring justice to Caterina and others like her.

As they sat in their car outside Hewlett's office building, Nate took a deep breath, centering himself before turning to Amy. "Are you ready for this?"

"Let's do it," she replied, determination written all over her face. "It's time to show Hewlett what we're capable of."

Nate nodded, his thoughts racing. They had one chance to convince Hewlett that his suspicions were unfounded, and they couldn't afford to fail. In that moment, he knew that they had to draw on every ounce of skill, cunning, and determination they possessed to see this through.

"Alright," Nate said, clapping his hands together. "Let's go make some history."

The city skyline glowed like a neon promise as Nate and Amy entered Hewlett's lavish office, high above the bustling streets below. The opulence of the space was matched only by the smug grin on Edward "Eddie" Hewlett's face, as he leaned back in his leather chair, fingers steepled beneath his chin.

"Ah, Nathaniel, Amelia," he drawled, eyes flicking between the two. "You've brought me something interesting, I hope?"

"Indeed we have," Nate replied smoothly, exchanging a look with Amy. They had rehearsed this moment countless times, and now it was time to put their plan into motion.

"Edward, may I present you with the latest batch of success stories from our HYIP?" Amy said, her voice steady and confident as she handed over a folder filled with fabricated tales of financial triumph. "These investors have seen impressive returns, far beyond their initial expectations."

"Is that so?" Hewlett mused, leafing through the documents with an air of calculated detachment. His eyes narrowed as he scanned the financial statements, searching for any hint of deception.

Nate watched him closely, every muscle in his body tensed, ready to react at a moment's notice. He knew that if they were to convince Hewlett of the HYIP's legitimacy, they needed to play on his greed and ambition. Now was the time to strike.

"Edward," Nate interjected, leaning forward and fixing Hewlett with a piercing gaze. "What if I told you that these returns are just the beginning? That there is potential for even greater profits, limited only by your own ambition and willingness to invest?"

Hewlett's eyes gleamed with interest, and Nate could see the gears turning in his mind. Carefully, he continued, "Our program has generated a buzz among investors, and more people are clamoring to get in. With the right moves, we can capitalize on this momentum and drive even greater success."

"Interesting," Hewlett replied, his voice dripping with intrigue as he considered Nate's words. "But what about my previous concerns? How can I be sure that this isn't just another scheme destined to collapse?"

Amy stepped in, her gaze unwavering. "These testimonials speak for themselves, Edward. They come from real people who have experienced real success. Our program is built on a solid foundation, and we are confident in its ability to weather any storm."

For a moment, silence hung heavy in the air as Hewlett weighed their words against his own suspicions. Then, slowly, a smile began to spread across his face.

"Very well," he said, setting aside the documents and extending a hand to Nate. "You've convinced me. Let's see just how far this HYIP can take us."

As they shook hands, Nate felt a surge of triumph course through him. Their plan had worked – for now. But he knew that the real challenge lay ahead, as they navigated the treacherous waters of Hewlett's greed and ambition, all in the name of justice and revenge.

Nate's keen eyes flicked between Hewlett and Amy, observing the subtle twitch at the corner of the criminal mastermind's mouth as he considered their words. Hewlett tapped his fingers on the table, a telltale sign of his growing interest in the HYIP. Nate knew they needed to strike while the iron was hot.

"Edward," Nate began, leaning slightly forward with an air of confidence, "We've recently expanded our portfolio, focusing on cutting-edge cybersecurity solutions. The demand for these products is skyrocketing, and early investors are already seeing huge returns."

Hewlett raised an eyebrow, clearly intrigued. "Cybersecurity, you say? It's true; I've heard that market is booming. How much have your investors made?"

Amy seized the opportunity, her mind racing to supply a convincing figure. "One investor saw a return of 85% in just six months. With the right investments and strategy, there's potential for even greater profits."

"85%, impressive," Hewlett mused, his fingers now drumming on the table, betraying his eagerness. "And how do you plan on maintaining this level of success?"

Nate sensed the need to provide reassurance and dove into the depths of his ethical hacking experience. "By continuously researching and analyzing market trends, we're able to stay ahead of the curve and identify promising investment opportunities. Our team's technical expertise ensures that we only back projects with the highest potential for success."

Hewlett leaned back in his chair, stroking his chin thoughtfully. Nate could see the wheels turning in his head, the allure of wealth slowly overtaking his initial skepticism. He exchanged a brief glance with Amy, both understanding the delicate balance they were trying to maintain.

"Alright," Hewlett finally said, nodding decisively. "I'll invest an additional $250,000 into this HYIP. But I expect regular updates on its progress and my returns. If what you say is true, then this could be a very profitable venture for all of us."

"Of course, Edward," Amy replied smoothly, her voice filled with gratitude. "We're committed to ensuring your success in this investment. You won't be disappointed."

As Hewlett stood to leave, Nate's mind churned with the weight of their precarious situation, knowing that they had managed to keep him invested for now. But the true test of their plan was still to come – weaving an intricate web of deception while staying one step ahead of the cunning criminal mastermind. All in the name of justice, revenge, and Caterina's lost investment. The game was on.

Nate watched as a bead of sweat rolled down Hewlett's temple, his decision hanging in the balance. Amy's hand found its way to Nate's under the table, gripping it firmly—a silent reminder that they were in this together. They held their breath, waiting for the final verdict.

"Alright," Hewlett said at last, his voice firm and resolute. "You've convinced me. I'll invest an additional $250,000 into this HYIP."

Nate and Amy exchanged a look, relief washing over them like a cool wave on a sweltering summer day. Their plan had worked—for now. They knew that the road ahead was riddled with uncertainty, but they also knew that Caterina's faith in them was not misplaced. They would see this through, together.

"Thank you, Edward," Nate said, his tone sincere as he maintained eye contact with Hewlett. "We appreciate your trust in us and the HYIP. We're confident that the returns will exceed your expectations."

"Absolutely," Amy chimed in, her smile warm and genuine. "And we'll make sure to keep you updated every step of the way. Your success is our priority."

Hewlett nodded, seemingly satisfied with their assurances. He rose from his seat, straightening the lapels of his expensive suit. "I expect nothing less," he said, flashing them a self-assured grin—the kind that sent a shiver down Nate's spine.

As Hewlett strode towards the door, Nate's thoughts raced. There was no room for error; they needed to stay one step ahead of him. He could feel a familiar fire ignite within him—the burning desire for justice that had fueled his military career and, later, his work as an ethical hacker.

"Edward," Nate called out just before Hewlett reached the door. The man paused, turning back to face them with raised eyebrows. "We just wanted to say...we're grateful for your continued support and investment. We know you won't be disappointed."

"Indeed," Hewlett replied, his eyes narrowing ever so slightly. "I certainly hope not." And with that, he exited the room, leaving Nate and Amy to their thoughts.

As the door clicked shut behind him, Nate turned to Amy, her green eyes reflecting the same determination that coursed through his own veins. They had taken a significant step towards recovering Caterina's lost investment, and each day brought them closer to bringing Hewlett to justice.

"Let's make sure we stay ahead of him," Amy whispered, her voice fierce and unyielding. Nate squeezed her hand in response, knowing that they were unstoppable as long as they stood side by side.

"Agreed," he said firmly, his mind already racing with strategies to outwit Hewlett at every turn. "We've got this."

The moment the door slammed shut behind Hewlett, Nate and Amy sprang into action. Their eyes locked onto each other's as they shared a nod of understanding, determination igniting within them like a spark turned to flame.

"Alright," Nate said, his voice low and steady. "We've got our foot in the door. Now it's time to bring him down."

Amy smirked, her green eyes gleaming with resolve. "Couldn't have said it better myself."

As they exited the building, the crisp evening air enveloped them, its cool embrace serving as a reminder that time was of the essence. The city lights around them flickered like stars against the dark canvas of night, casting long shadows on the pavement below.

"First things first," Nate began, his mind already racing ahead to their next move. "We'll need to keep a close eye on Hewlett. His greed will be our greatest advantage, but we can't underestimate him. He's cunning and knows how to cover his tracks."

"Agreed," Amy replied, her fingers drumming against her thigh as she considered their options. "I can start by digging deeper into his financials. There's bound to be something there we can use to trip him up."

"Perfect," Nate said, his gaze fixed on the horizon as they walked. "I'll focus on finding any loose threads in his operation – anything that might give us leverage."

"Let's not forget about Caterina," Amy interjected, concern furrowing her brow. "We need to make sure she's aware of the risks involved and that she's prepared for any potential fallout."

"Absolutely," Nate nodded, his thoughts drifting momentarily to the passionate Italian woman who had unwittingly found herself caught in the crossfire. "We owe her that much."

As they continued on their way, a shared sense of purpose drove them forward. Each step brought them closer to the justice they sought, not only for Caterina but for all those who had been wronged by Hewlett's schemes.

"Y'know," Amy mused, a playful glint in her eye as she glanced at Nate. "If we pull this off, we might just have a future in the vigilante business."

"Only if you promise to wear a cape," Nate quipped, his lips curling into a grin despite the gravity of their mission.

"Deal," Amy laughed, her hand slipping into Nate's as they strode side by side through the city streets, united in their quest for justice.

They knew the road ahead would be fraught with danger and uncertainty, but there was no turning back now. Together, they were a force to be reckoned with – and they wouldn't rest until Edward Hewlett paid for his crimes.

Chapter 17

The dimly lit room hummed with the whir of computer fans, casting eerie shadows over the stacks of neatly bundled cash piled high on the table. Nate and Amy stood side by side, emanating confidence like a force field, while Hewlett fidgeted uncomfortably in his expensive suit. Tension hung in the air, thick and suffocating, as the financial data on the screens danced to the silent music of deceit.

Nate took a step forward, his eyes locked onto Hewlett's as he spoke in a voice that was steady and commanding. "You see, Eddie, we knew exactly what you were up to. We created that fake HYIP just for you." He gestured towards the computer screens, their glow painting his face with a sinister hue. "We knew it would be irresistible bait for someone like you."

Hewlett's eyes darted between Nate and Amy, his agitation growing more visible with each passing moment. His lips curled into a snarl, but he remained silent, waiting for the damning revelations to continue.

"From the beginning, our plan was to lure you in and get back Caterina's lost funds. And you fell for it, hook, line, and sinker," Nate continued, his tone cold and unyielding. He couldn't help but recall Caterina's warm smile and generous nature, the way she had always made them feel welcome in her Sicilian cafe. Her dream of expanding the cafe had been crushed under the weight of Hewlett's greed, and now it was time for justice to be served.

"Of course, we needed someone like you – an expert in manipulation and deception – to make it believable," Nate added, his gaze never leaving Hewlett's face. He could see the gears turning in the criminal mastermind's brain, trying to find a way out of the trap they had set.

As Nate spoke, he couldn't help but think back to his military days, when he had uncovered similar schemes and brought those responsible to justice. Those experiences had taught him that sometimes, the only way to fight against evil was to understand it – to predict its moves and exploit its weaknesses. And now, standing in this room with Amy by his side, Nate knew that they were doing just that.

"Imagine our surprise when you took the bait," Nate said with a wry smile. "I must say, Eddie, you're not as smart as I thought."

Amy's fiery red hair seemed to glow in the dimly lit room as she stood by Nate's side, her green eyes resolute and unwavering. She was a force to be reckoned with, her background in investigative journalism making her a formidable ally for her husband.

"Allow me to elaborate on Nate's point, Eddie." Amy's voice was smooth like silk, but there was no mistaking the steel beneath it. "We spent months tracking down every last detail of your schemes – studying your patterns, your methods, even your preferred time zones for conducting your illicit business."

Hewlett's face contorted with anger and disbelief, his nostrils flaring as if he were some cornered animal. "You think you're so clever, don't you?" he hissed, trying to regain some semblance of control over the situation. "But you've got nothing on me. No evidence, no witnesses. You're bluffing."

Amy exchanged a knowing glance with Nate before reaching into her jacket pocket and producing a flash drive. She dangled it between her fingers, letting it swing back and forth like a hypnotist's pendulum.

"Bluffing? No, Eddie, we're not bluffing. This little device right here," Amy said, tapping the flash drive lightly with her other hand, "contains all the proof we need. Transactions, IP addresses, even encrypted messages between you and your accomplices. It's all here."

Nate couldn't help but feel a surge of pride at Amy's words, at the way she had managed to stay one step ahead of Hewlett throughout their entire operation. Even now, as she held the key to his undoing in her hand, she exuded an aura of confidence and determination that made him feel invincible.

"See, Eddie, we know how you operate," Amy continued, her voice steady and relentless. "We know how you prey on vulnerable people like Caterina, promising them the world and then leaving them with nothing. And we're not going to let you get away with it any longer."

Hewlett's face paled as he realized the extent of their knowledge, the enormity of his defeat sinking in. He looked from Nate to Amy, his eyes darting around the room as if searching for an escape route that didn't exist.

"Fine," he spat, his hands balling into fists at his sides. "You've got me. But don't think for a second that this is over. I'll find a way out of this, and when I do, you'll both pay."

Nate felt a shiver run down his spine, but he refused to be intimidated. He and Amy had fought too hard and come too far to back down now. They were on the side of justice, and they would see this through to the end – no matter what obstacles stood in their way.

Hewlett's face reddened, the veins in his temples pulsating with each furious beat of his heart. "You think you're so clever, don't you?" he snarled, eyes darting between Nate and Amy. "But you've got it all wrong. I didn't steal Caterina's money; she lost it through her own ignorance and greed."

Nate shook his head, unfazed by Hewlett's desperate attempt to deflect blame. "We have the records, Eddie," he said coolly, gesturing at the stacks of cash and computer screens filled with incriminating data. "Every transaction, every lie, every manipulation – it's all here. And it all points to you."

"Besides," Amy chimed in, her voice laced with contempt, "we've spent months studying your patterns, learning how you operate. We know you better than you know yourself. You can't wiggle your way out of this one."

Hewlett's frustration mounted as he realized that his usual tactics wouldn't work on these two adversaries who had anticipated his every move. His rage boiled over, and with a guttural roar, he lunged at Nate and Amy, fists clenched and ready to strike.

But Nate and Amy were prepared for his attack. As former military personnel, Nate had honed his reflexes to perfection, and Amy's background in investigative journalism meant she was no stranger to danger. They sidestepped Hewlett's wild swing with ease, their movements synchronized like dancers in an intricate waltz.

"Pathetic," Nate muttered under his breath, watching as Hewlett stumbled past them, his momentum carrying him off-balance. In his mind, Nate couldn't help but think of Caterina, whose warm smile and dream of expanding her cafe had touched him deeply. He knew he couldn't let this man continue to destroy lives unchecked.

"Is that all you've got, Eddie?" Amy taunted, her eyes gleaming with a mix of amusement and disdain. "No wonder you resort to scamming innocent people – you certainly don't have the skills to make it in any legitimate business."

Hewlett's face twisted into a snarl as he tried to recover his footing, but it was clear that he was trapped. Nate and Amy had outmaneuvered him at every turn, leaving him with nothing but the bitter taste of defeat.

"Alright," Hewlett growled, resignation creeping into his voice. "You win this round. But remember – I'm not the only one who plays this game. You may have taken me down, but there are others out there who won't be so easy to catch."

Nate exchanged a brief glance with Amy, acknowledging the truth in Hewlett's words. But they were undeterred. Together, they had faced adversity and emerged victorious. And as long as injustice continued to flourish, they would stand as a united front against it – driven by their shared desire for retribution, and fueled by the strength of their love and partnership.

The dimly lit room seemed to close in on Hewlett as he scrambled backward, his back hitting a stack of cash. Nate and Amy's eyes remained locked on him, their expressions unyielding. With every breath he took, they seemed to anticipate his next move, their knowledge of his schemes acting as a shield against any last-ditch efforts he might attempt.

"Face it, Eddie," Nate said coldly, his military training evident in the way he held himself. "We know all about your little operation here." He gestured to the computer screens displaying financial data. "You thought you could just keep scamming people without anyone catching on?"

"Your game is up," Amy added, her journalistic instincts lending an edge to her voice that made Hewlett flinch. "We've got enough evidence to bury you."

Hewlett's eyes darted between them, searching for even the slightest vulnerability to exploit. But there was none. In desperation, he tried to feign ignorance, but his voice trembled, betraying his fear. "I don't know what you're talking about. You've got nothing on me."

"Really?" Amy smirked, and with a flick of her wrist, she sent a series of incriminating documents flying into Hewlett's face. His eyes widened in panic as he realized the extent of the evidence against him.

"Like I said, Eddie," Nate continued, his voice dripping with disdain. "Game over."

In a final act of defiance, Hewlett shoved the papers off his chest and made a break for the door. But Nate and Amy had anticipated this. They moved in tandem, swiftly blocking his path like two predators cornering their prey. Hewlett skidded to a halt, his heart pounding in his chest.

"Give it up, Eddie," Amy advised, her tone sharp and unforgiving. "There's nowhere left for you to run."

Hewlett's eyes darted around the room, searching for any possible escape route. But he knew deep down that it was futile. He swallowed hard, his shoulders slumping in defeat as he turned to face Nate and Amy.

"Fine," he spat bitterly. "You've got me. But remember – there are more like me out there. You'll never stop them all."

Nate and Amy exchanged a glance, their resolve only strengthened by his words. They knew full well that their fight against injustice was far from over. But for now, they had won this battle.

"Maybe not," Nate conceded, stepping forward to grab Hewlett by the arm. "But we'll take them down one at a time, just like we did with you."

"Starting with you," Amy added, her voice filled with satisfaction.

As they led Hewlett away, his mind raced with thoughts of revenge, but it was drowned out by the certainty that he'd finally met his match in Nathaniel and Amelia Everhart.

Hewlett's face contorted with anguish as he realized there was no way out. Nate and Amy stared him down, their eyes filled with determination.

"Alright," Nate said, his voice steady but firm. "Time to make things right." He strode across the dimly lit room and located a hidden compartment just behind one of the computer screens displaying financial data. His fingers expertly worked at the lock, fueled by years of experience as an ethical hacker.

Amy glanced over at Caterina, who stood in the doorway, her expression a mix of hope and anxiety. The Italian woman clutched a worn apron in her hands, her knuckles white from the tension.

"Got it," Nate announced, extracting a thick stack of cash from the compartment. He turned to Caterina, his eyes softening as he held out the money. "This is yours, Caterina. Every last cent."

Caterina hesitated, her eyes filling with tears of relief and gratitude as she took the money from Nate. "Thank you," she whispered, her voice choked with emotion. "Thank you both so much."

"Hey, we couldn't let Eddie get away with what he did to you," Amy replied, placing a reassuring hand on Caterina's shoulder. "We're here to help those who can't fight back."

"You two are something else," Caterina said, shaking her head in disbelief. "How can I ever repay you?"

"Seeing you use this money wisely and fulfilling your dream of expanding your cafe is more than enough for us," Nate insisted, sharing a proud look with Amy. "Just promise us that you'll do that."

"Si, si!" Caterina exclaimed, clutching the money tightly to her chest. "I promise! My little cafe will become a franchise, and I'll make sure everyone knows how brave and resourceful you both are!"

Nate grinned, his mind racing with thoughts of future battles against injustice. There was satisfaction in knowing that they had made a difference in Caterina's life, but he was all too aware that there were still countless others who needed their help.

"Alright then," Nate said, clapping his hands together with newfound purpose. "Let's get started on the next chapter."

As they escorted Hewlett out of the room, Amy's eyes met Nate's, a silent understanding passing between them. They were partners in every sense of the word, and together, they would continue to fight for justice against criminals like Hewlett. And as long as they had each other, nothing could stand in their way.

The dimly lit room hummed with the quiet satisfaction of a job well done, as Nate and Amy exchanged a silent nod of mutual understanding. They could see the gratitude in Caterina's tear-filled eyes, the weight of worry lifting off her shoulders as she clutched the recovered funds to her chest. In that moment, they knew they had not only restored Caterina's faith in humanity but had also reaffirmed their own commitment to their mission.

"Hey, you two," Nate whispered to Amy with an amused smirk, his voice low enough for only her ears. "We make a pretty good team, huh?"

"Better than good," Amy replied, her green eyes sparkling with determination. "Unbeatable."

"Exactly," Nate said, his dark eyes meeting hers in a shared pledge to continue their fight for justice.

"Alright, lovebirds, break it up," Detective Tom Harding called out as he entered the room, his team of officers filing in behind him. He walked over to Hewlett, who was still cornered by Nate and Amy. "Edward Hewlett," he announced, his voice steady and authoritative, "you are under arrest for wire fraud, money laundering, and illegal operation of an unregistered investment scheme."

"Are you kidding me?" Hewlett spat, his frustration boiling over into fury. "This is all just a big misunderstanding!"

"Save it for the judge," Detective Harding said coldly, slapping handcuffs onto Hewlett's wrists with practiced ease. "You have the right to remain silent. Anything you say can and will be used against you in a court of law. You have the right to an attorney. If you cannot afford one, one will be appointed to you."

As Detective Harding continued reading Hewlett his rights, Nate couldn't help but feel a pang of sympathy for the criminal mastermind. Despite his reprehensible actions, there was something almost admirable about Hewlett's refusal to go quietly. But then Nate remembered the countless victims of Hewlett's schemes, people like Caterina who had suffered at his hands, and any sympathy he might have felt evaporated.

"Good riddance," Amy muttered under her breath as she watched the officers lead Hewlett away, her fiery red hair casting an ethereal glow in the dim light. She caught Nate's gaze, and they shared a knowing look – one that spoke volumes about their unspoken understanding, their partnership, and the battles yet to come.

"Another one bites the dust," Nate whispered back, his voice tinged with both humor and determination. He knew that there would always be more criminals like Hewlett out there, but as long he and Amy were together, they would never stop fighting for justice – one scam artist at a time.

The cacophony of sirens outside the building seemed to fade into the background as Nate handed Detective Harding a flash drive containing crucial evidence against Hewlett's schemes. "This should be enough to put him away for a long time, Tom," he said, his voice steady and confident.

"Thanks, Nate," Detective Harding replied, accepting the flash drive with a nod. "We'll make sure this gets to the right people. And I appreciate your offer to continue supporting the investigation. Your skills and commitment to justice are unmatched."

Amy chimed in, her voice assertive yet compassionate, "There are more victims out there, Tom. We won't rest until they all get the justice they deserve."

As the officers began clearing the room, Caterina clung to the briefcase that held her recovered funds, tears glistening in her eyes. She watched Hewlett being escorted to the waiting police car outside, a mixture of relief and disbelief visible on her face.

"Is it really over?" she asked hesitantly, seeking reassurance from Nate and Amy.

"Edward Hewlett is going away for a long time, Caterina," Nate confirmed, placing a gentle hand on her shoulder. "You don't need to worry about him anymore."

"Thank you," she whispered, her gratitude palpable. "I owe you both my life, my future."

"Hey, we're just doing what we believe is right," Amy responded, a faint smile gracing her lips. She glanced at Nate, who nodded in agreement, their bond unbreakable.

With the room now empty, save for the three of them, the weight of their victory settled upon their shoulders. An odd silence permeated the space, the gravity of the moment sinking in. Caterina's cafe had been saved, and countless others had been spared from becoming victims of Hewlett's schemes.

"Let's celebrate," Caterina suggested, her eyes sparkling with newfound hope. "I'll cook a feast for you at my cafe, the best Sicilian dishes you've ever tasted."

Nate's stomach growled in anticipation, betraying his excitement. He grinned sheepishly at Amy, who laughed softly. "I think that's a wonderful idea, Caterina," she agreed.

As they left the building, the dark sky seemed to lift and brighten, as if reflecting their triumph over Hewlett's darkness. Nate couldn't help but feel a renewed sense of purpose – there would always be more battles to fight, more wrongs to right. But with Amy by his side and allies like Detective Tom Harding, he knew that justice would prevail.

The dimly lit room, once filled with tension and danger, now held an air of camaraderie and unity. Nate, Amy, and Caterina stood amidst the stacks of cash, their eyes gleaming with determination as they faced the future.

"Alright," Nate began, his voice steady and commanding. "We've taken down Hewlett, but there's still a lot more work to be done. There are countless others out there, preying on innocent people like Caterina."

Amy nodded in agreement, her fiery red hair catching the faint glow of the computer screens that surrounded them. "I've been thinking about how we can expand our operations, Nate. We need to start tracking these criminals before they even have a chance to strike."

Caterina clasped her hands together, her dark eyes alight with passion. "Si, I want to help too. I may not know much about hacking or investigating, but I can provide support for your mission. My cafe can be a base, a safe haven for those you rescue."

Nate's eyes softened, warmed by Caterina's generosity. He knew she was sincere – her own experiences had made her fiercely protective of others. "That's a generous offer, Caterina. But we need to make sure you're safe first. We don't want to put you in danger again."

"Non preoccuparti, Nate," Caterina reassured him, waving her hand dismissively. "I can take care of myself. And besides, I have you two watching my back, no?"

Amy chuckled, her expression mirroring Nate's admiration for Caterina's indomitable spirit. "You certainly do, and we'll make sure nothing happens to you or your cafe."

As the trio discussed their plans, Nate found himself lost in thought, envisioning a world where justice reigned supreme through their combined efforts. It was ambitious, perhaps even unrealistic, but with Amy's keen investigative skills and Caterina's unwavering support, he knew they could make a difference.

"Okay," Nate said decisively, pulling himself from his reverie. "Let's start by compiling a list of potential targets. We'll monitor their online activities and gather intel on their operations."

"Sounds like a plan," Amy agreed, already mentally cataloguing the countless leads they had encountered during their time tracking Hewlett. "I'll use my journalistic connections to help us stay ahead of the curve."

Caterina beamed at her newfound allies, her determination only growing stronger in the face of adversity. "And I will make sure you both are well-fed and rested while you fight for justice."

The room may have been dimly lit, but the spark that ignited within them shone brightly, casting away any lingering shadows. With Nate's strategic mind, Amy's adaptability, and Caterina's unwavering support, they were ready to embark on their mission – united in the pursuit of justice and driven by an insatiable desire to protect those who had been wronged.

Chapter 18

Nate stared at the wall of evidence that he, Amy, and Detective Tom Harding had painstakingly assembled. The dimly lit room seemed to crackle with electricity as photographs of Hewlett and his associates were pinned alongside detailed financial records, communication logs, and witness testimonies. Nate's eyes flicked from face to face, each one a piece in the intricate web of deception and crime that Edward "Eddie" Hewlett had woven.

"Looks like we've got him this time," said Detective Harding, breaking the silence with his rough voice. He rubbed his graying temples, looking tired but determined. "You two did an amazing job gathering all this."

"Couldn't have done it without your help, Tom," replied Nate, his dark eyes glinting with satisfaction. Amy, her red hair gleaming like a beacon of hope, nodded in agreement.

"Alright, let's strategize our next move," Tom said, clapping his hands together and pulling up a map of the city. "We need to catch them off guard."

Nate leaned in, studying the map thoughtfully, while Amy stood by his side, her hand instinctively reaching for his. Their shared passion for justice had brought them together, and now they were about to take down one of the most notorious criminal masterminds of their time.

"Here's what I'm thinking," Nate began, tracing a finger along the streets on the map. "We know Hewlett has a penchant for luxury, so we can assume he'll be holed up somewhere upscale. We also know he's paranoid, which means he'll have multiple escape routes planned."

Amy's mind raced, calculating possible scenarios and outcomes. "What if we use that paranoia against him? Make him think we're closing in from multiple directions, force him into a trap?"

"Brilliant," Tom agreed, a smile spreading across his weary face. "We can coordinate with the police, get units in position around his suspected hideouts, and give him no choice but to run right into our waiting arms."

"Exactly," Nate said, his eyes filled with determination. "And we'll be there to make sure he doesn't slip through our fingers."

The three of them shared a look of grim resolve, knowing that bringing down Hewlett and his associates would not be an easy task. They were about to go head-to-head with a criminal empire that had managed to stay one step ahead of the law for so long. But they also knew that their unique skillsets, combined with their unwavering dedication to justice, gave them a fighting chance.

"Let's do this," Amy whispered, her green eyes shining with conviction as she squeezed Nate's hand. Together, they began to plan the operation that would finally bring Edward Hewlett and his network of criminals to their knees.

The steady hum of Nate and Amy's computers filled their dimly lit makeshift office as they sat side by side, eyes glued to their screens. The tension in the room was palpable, with only the occasional click of a mouse or tap of a keyboard breaking the silence.

"Got it," Nate whispered, leaning back to stretch the stiffness out of his neck. "I've managed to hack into Hewlett's security system. I can monitor all of his cameras and alarms from here."

"Great job, babe," Amy replied, her fingers flying over her own keyboard as she cross-referenced data. "I'm tracking the movements of his associates. One is heading for a meeting with an unknown contact near Piazza Navona. Another seems to be setting up a new account at the bank in Via del Corso."

"Keep me posted on their activities," Nate said, his mind racing with strategies and possibilities. A slow grin spread across his face as he realized that, for the first time in ages, he was genuinely enjoying the thrill of the chase. His military background had taught him the value of being one step ahead, and he knew that with each piece of information they gathered, Hewlett's world was slowly crumbling around him.

Meanwhile, Detective Tom Harding stood in front of a group of skilled officers, his voice clear and authoritative as he briefed them on the operation. "Ladies and gentlemen, we are dealing with a highly intelligent and dangerous criminal network led by Edward Hewlett. It is crucial that we apprehend him and his associates without any complications. Your cooperation and professionalism will be key to ensuring the success of this operation."

"Sir, what do we know about Hewlett's organization?" a young officer asked, her pen poised above her notepad.

"His operation spans across multiple industries, from cyber security to investment schemes," Tom explained. "We have reason to believe he's been involved in numerous illegal activities, and that's why we're working closely with Nate and Amy Everhart. They've been instrumental in gathering evidence against Hewlett and his associates."

"Are they reliable, sir?" another officer questioned, a hint of skepticism in his voice.

"Absolutely," Tom replied without hesitation. "I've known them for years and trust them completely. Their skills are invaluable to this case, and you'll be expected to coordinate with them throughout the operation."

Back at their computers, Nate and Amy continued to monitor the movements of Hewlett and his associates. As they shared updates on their findings, they could feel the pieces of the puzzle falling into place. With each new piece of information, their confidence grew, knowing that the net was tightening around Hewlett's criminal empire.

"Tom," Nate said into his headset, his voice steady and calm. "We have eyes on Hewlett and his crew. We'll provide real-time updates as the situation unfolds."

"Copy that, Nate," Tom replied, his own determination mirrored in Nate's words. "We'll be ready to move when the time comes."

As Nate and Amy watched the movements of their targets from behind the safety of their computer screens, they couldn't help but feel a sense of satisfaction at the progress they had made. Their unique skillsets, combined with their shared passion for justice, had brought them to this moment – the moment when Edward Hewlett and his associates would finally face the consequences of their actions.

A torrent of rain lashed against the window, the sound providing a fitting backdrop to the tense atmosphere in the room. Nate leaned back in his chair, fingers drumming an impatient rhythm on the table as he watched Detective Tom Harding and his team scrutinize the evidence they had painstakingly collected.

"Here," Amy said, handing over a stack of financial records with an air of triumph. "These show the illegal transactions Hewlett's been making. Laundering money through shell companies, investing in criminal enterprises – it's all here."

Harding sifted through the documents with a steady hand, absorbing each detail with the precision of a seasoned detective. As he reached for the communication logs, Nate could see the satisfaction in his eyes, the knowledge that their case was tightening like a noose around Hewlett's neck.

"Good work," Harding finally said, nodding in approval. "This will be invaluable in bringing him down."

"Let's not forget the witness testimonies," Amy added, sliding a carefully organized binder toward the detective. "They confirm Hewlett's connections to various criminal schemes and implicate his associates as well."

"Excellent. With this evidence, we'll have them cornered in no time." Harding looked at Nate, his eyes filled with determination. "We've set up surveillance on Hewlett's known locations. We just need to wait for the right moment to strike."

Nate understood the importance of patience, but the weight of anticipation settled heavy on his chest. *We're so close,* he thought, his mind racing through each step of the operation. *The day of reckoning is almost here.*

"Keep us updated on any new information you uncover," Tom instructed. "Your hacking skills have proved invaluable in tracking their movements and activities."

"Of course," Nate replied, his voice firm. "We won't let Hewlett slip through our fingers."

"Remember, we're all in this together," Harding said, glancing between Nate and Amy. "Our goal is to bring Hewlett and his associates down, once and for all."

As the planning continued, Nate couldn't help but reflect on how far they had come. Their pursuit of justice had led them to this very moment; a moment brimming with potential, where every piece of evidence, every witness testimony, and every surveillance operation would converge into one decisive action.

"Stay sharp," Tom warned, as he prepared to leave the room. "We'll need to act quickly and decisively when the time comes."

"Understood," Nate and Amy said in unison, their voices resolute.

As the door clicked shut behind Detective Harding, Nate allowed himself a small grin. The anticipation crackled in the air like electricity, each heartbeat drawing them closer to the endgame.

Edward Hewlett, he thought, clenching his fists with determined resolve. *Your time is running out.*

The glow of the laptop illuminated Nate's face as he leaned in, fingers flying across the keyboard. Beside him, Amy listened intently to the chatter of the police radio, her eyes flicking between the screen and the scene unfolding below them. They were perched atop a building overlooking the warehouse district, a bird's-eye view of the police operation. The air was thick with tension, but it was also tinged with excitement; justice was within reach, and they could almost taste it.

"Anything new?" Nate asked, his voice barely audible over the hum of the city.

"Nothing yet," Amy replied, adjusting the radio's frequency. "But they're closing in on Hewlett."

Nate gave a small nod, his thoughts racing. *We've come this far, we cannot let our guard down now.*

"Keep an eye out for any unexpected moves," he said, his eyes never leaving the screen. "Hewlett is cunning, and we can't underestimate him."

"Understood," Amy acknowledged, her gaze fixated on the officers below. She knew just how important it was to stay vigilant, especially with someone like Hewlett involved. The reddish hue from the setting sun cast an eerie glow on the scene, amplifying the urgency of their mission.

The crackle of the police radio interrupted the silence. "We've got a tip," an officer announced. "Hewlett's been spotted inside one of these warehouses."

"Copy that," Tom Harding's voice responded. "Surround the area and move in cautiously."

"Finally," Nate muttered under his breath, heart pounding in his chest. He shifted his focus back to the laptop, ready to offer any support necessary.

"Remember, we're here to help," Amy reminded him, gripping his hand tightly. "We've got their backs."

"Right," he agreed, squeezing her hand in return. His fingers returned to the keyboard, expertly navigating through various security systems and feeds.

"Team One, move in," Harding's voice crackled over the radio. "Take no chances."

As they watched the police operation unfold, Nate couldn't help but think about all that had led them to this point. The countless hours spent gathering evidence, the sleepless nights, and the danger they'd faced – it was all for this moment. It was for justice, not just for them, but for every victim of Hewlett's twisted schemes.

"Stay sharp," Amy whispered, her eyes never leaving the scene below. "This is it."

Nate nodded, his fingers poised above the keyboard. *We've got you now, Hewlett.*

The world seemed to hold its breath as the police moved into position around the warehouse. There would be no escape for Edward Hewlett and his associates this time.

"Let's bring them down," Nate murmured, feeling a surge of adrenaline. His fingers danced across the keys, ready to strike at any moment.

"Agreed," Amy said, her voice filled with fierce determination. "Justice will be served."

The warehouse door exploded open, sending splinters of wood flying through the air. Armed officers swarmed in with military precision, their weapons drawn and ready. Nate and Amy watched intently from a distance as the scene unfolded before them.

"Police! Don't move!" Detective Tom Harding bellowed, his voice echoing throughout the cavernous space.

Edward Hewlett stood at the center of the chaos, a wicked grin plastered on his face. His associates scrambled around him, panic rising like a thick fog.

"Did you really think it would be this easy?" Hewlett taunted Harding, his voice dripping with condescension.

Nate's fingers flew across the keyboard, hacking into the warehouse's security system. He could feel the tension mounting as the standoff continued. *Come on, come on,* he thought, *give me an opening.*

"Drop your weapons!" Harding ordered, his voice firm and unwavering. "You're all under arrest!"

"Detective, I believe you have sorely underestimated my resourcefulness," Hewlett sneered. As if on cue, a series of steel shutters began to descend over the windows, plunging the warehouse into darkness. The sound of machinery whirred to life, signaling the activation of some unseen escape plan.

"Dammit!" Amy cursed under her breath. "Nate, can you do anything?"

"Working on it," Nate replied tersely, his fingers moving even faster now. He bypassed firewalls and encryption, seeking out the control system that governed the warehouse's defenses. *There!* With a triumphant grin, Nate tapped one final key, and the shutters abruptly halted in their descent, leaving the room bathed in an eerie half-light.

"Nice work," Amy whispered, relief evident in her voice.

"Thanks," Nate replied, though his attention remained focused on the situation unfolding below. He knew they couldn't let their guard down just yet; Hewlett was a master of deception and manipulation.

"Harding, it seems you've brought some friends. How delightful!" Hewlett mocked, his voice dripping with sarcasm. "But I'm afraid you won't be taking me today."

Amy's eyes narrowed. "He's stalling. He must have another escape route."

"Got it," Nate responded, already hacking into the warehouse's architectural schematics. He scanned the blueprints, searching for any hidden exits or passageways. *There! A tunnel leading to the sewer system.* He quickly disabled the access panel, sealing off Hewlett's last chance at slipping through their fingers.

"Your move, Eddie," Amy murmured, her voice cold and hard as steel.

Hewlett's eyes darted around the room, his confidence faltering as he realized the extent of their control over the situation. The air crackled with tension as the two sides faced off, neither willing to back down.

"Checkmate, Mr. Hewlett," Detective Harding declared with steely determination. "You're not getting away this time."

Nate and Amy exchanged a solemn glance, knowing they had done everything in their power to bring this dangerous criminal to justice. As the police closed in on Hewlett and his associates, they knew their pursuit for justice was far from over – but this was one significant victory.

"Good job, partner," Nate said softly, a sense of pride swelling within him.

"Couldn't have done it without you," Amy replied, giving his hand a reassuring squeeze as they watched the criminals being apprehended.

With a heavy bead of sweat trickling down his temple, Detective Tom Harding surveyed the scene before him: Hewlett and his associates, cornered and desperate, like caged animals. The air was thick with tension, and one wrong move could send everything spiraling into chaos.

"Listen up," he barked into his earpiece, addressing his team. "I want you to take them down slowly and methodically. No heroics. We don't need any casualties." His voice was steady, but his heart raced with anticipation.

"Roger that, Detective," came the response, as officers took their positions around the warehouse, guns drawn and ready to apprehend the criminals.

"Knock it off, Eddie," Tom called out to the criminal mastermind, who was still trying to regain control of the situation. "You're only making things worse for yourself."

"Detective Harding, always the optimist," Hewlett sneered, his eyes darting around in search of an escape. "You might have me cornered, but I'm not going down without a fight."

"Suit yourself," Tom replied coolly. "Just remember, we've got the place surrounded, and Nate and Amy have disabled every possible exit."

Hewlett's face darkened at the mention of the two hackers, but he said nothing. Instead, he glanced over at his associates, who were growing increasingly restless. They knew the game was up.

"Alright, men," Tom instructed his team. "Move in. Remember, slow and steady."

As the officers advanced, Tom's mind raced with thoughts of justice, revenge, and the countless lives ruined by Hewlett's schemes. *This is it,* he thought. *We're finally bringing this monster down.*

"Hey, Detective," Hewlett called out suddenly. "What do you call a fake noodle?"

Tom frowned, irritated by the interruption. "A what?"

"An impasta!" Hewlett burst out laughing, his associates joining in, their laughter strained and unnatural.

"Very funny," Tom muttered, rolling his eyes. But he couldn't help but crack a small smile, despite himself. *Even in the face of defeat, this guy's got a sense of humor.*

"Enough!" Tom bellowed, his humor evaporating as quickly as it had come. "Hands on your heads, all of you!"

Hewlett and his associates reluctantly complied, and one by one, the officers moved in, securing them in handcuffs and reading them their rights.

"Edward Hewlett, you have the right to remain silent. Anything you say can and will be used against you in a court of law..."

As the familiar words echoed through the warehouse, Tom allowed himself a moment of satisfaction. It wasn't often that he could savor such a clear-cut victory – and never before with so much at stake. He glanced over at Nate and Amy, who were watching from a safe distance, their expressions mirroring his own relief and pride.

"Good job, everyone," he whispered into his earpiece, knowing that this was only the beginning of the battle against cybercrime and investment schemes. But for now, justice had been served – and that was enough.

The warehouse air hung heavy with the acrid scent of fear and defeat as Hewlett and his associates were led away, their polished shoes scuffing against the concrete floor. Detective Tom Harding stood tall amidst the chaos, his gray eyes scanning the scene, ensuring that everything was under control.

"Alright, people, let's wrap this up," he called out to his team, his voice a steady anchor in the storm of activity. He caught Nate and Amy's gaze from across the room. "Nate, Amy, over here."

The duo approached, their expressions a mix of relief and determination. Nate held a laptop tightly under one arm, while Amy clutched a folder filled with documents, her red hair like a beacon in the dim light.

"Detective Harding," Nate began, his voice tinged with exhaustion but firm. "We've got more evidence for you. It'll make sure Hewlett and his crew won't see the light of day for a long, long time."

Tom raised an eyebrow, impressed despite himself. "Let's see it, then."

Amy handed over the folder, which contained financial records, communication logs, and further witness testimonies. "This should tie up any loose ends and make it clear that Hewlett was the mastermind behind the whole operation."

Tom flipped through the pages, his eyes widening as the weight of the evidence became apparent. "This is... incredible work, you two. I don't know how you managed to find all this, but it's going to make our case bulletproof."

"Long nights and a lot of espresso," Nate quipped, offering a wry smile. His dark eyes twinkled with a hint of mischief as he glanced at Amy. "Plus, we make a pretty good team."

"More than just 'pretty good,'" Tom interjected, his gratitude evident in every word. "You two have been invaluable in bringing down Hewlett and his criminal operation. I can't thank you enough."

"Seeing them cuffed and off the streets is thanks enough, Tom," Amy replied, her voice firm yet gentle. She knew all too well the cost of unchecked crime and injustice. "Besides, we couldn't have done it without your help and that of your team."

"Right," Nate chimed in, nodding his agreement as he tapped a few keys on his laptop, sending the last of their digital evidence to Tom's inbox. "We're just glad we could play our part in making sure Hewlett and his associates face the consequences of their actions."

Tom studied their faces for a moment, struck by the resolve and dedication that shone through their exhaustion. He was lucky to call them friends and allies – a fact he didn't take lightly.

"Still," he said, clasping a hand on each of their shoulders, a rare display of affection from the typically stoic detective. "I want you both to know how much I appreciate you. Your skills, your commitment... it's made all the difference."

"Thank you, Tom," Nate replied, his voice thick with emotion. "That means more than you know."

"Indeed," Amy agreed, meeting Tom's gaze with fierce sincerity. "But remember, this isn't just about us. It's about justice and protecting the innocent. And together, we'll keep fighting the good fight."

As they stood amid the remnants of their hard-won victory, the unspoken bond between them stronger than ever, they knew that nothing could stand in their way. They were a force to be reckoned with – and the world would be a better place for it.

Hewlett's cold eyes stared back at Nate through the one-way mirror, his once confident demeanor now replaced with a barely concealed fear. The criminal mastermind was finally cornered, and he knew it. Nate couldn't help but feel a twisted sense of satisfaction as he watched Hewlett squirm under the weight of the evidence against him.

"Can't say I'll miss that smug look on his face," Amy remarked, her arms crossed as she stood next to Nate, both of them observing the interrogation room. Detective Tom Harding entered the room, a stern expression etched onto his features.

"Let's see how he likes the taste of justice," Nate whispered under his breath, his fingers tapping rhythmically on the glass.

"Remember, this is only the beginning," Amy reminded him, her voice soft but determined. "There's still a long road ahead for us."

"Indeed," Nate agreed, his mind already racing with thoughts of the trials and investigations yet to come.

In the interrogation room, Tom fixed Hewlett with an unwavering stare. "Edward Hewlett, you are under arrest for multiple charges, including fraud, money laundering, and conspiracy to commit murder," he announced, his tone leaving no room for doubt.

"Your little empire has crumbled, Eddie," Tom continued, relishing the opportunity to see the man who had eluded justice for so long finally pay for his crimes. "And you have Nathaniel Everhart and Amelia Everhart to thank for that."

Nate felt a surge of pride at Tom's words, knowing that all their hard work and sacrifice had led to this moment.

"Damn right," Amy murmured, a fierce smile tugging at her lips. "No one messes with our city and gets away with it."

As they listened to Tom read out the list of charges, Nate and Amy exchanged a knowing glance, their connection stronger than ever. They had faced countless challenges and overcome insurmountable odds, but together, they had triumphed.

"Can't wait to see what's next for us," Nate said quietly, his eyes never leaving Hewlett's defeated form.

"Whatever it is, we'll face it head on," Amy replied, her hand finding Nate's and giving it a reassuring squeeze. "As long as we're together, there's nothing we can't handle."

Tom looked up from the table, catching their reflection in the mirror. He nodded in agreement, knowing that with Nate and Amy by his side, they would continue to bring down the criminals who threatened their city.

"Here's to justice," Tom whispered, his voice carrying just enough for Nate and Amy to hear.

"Salute," Nate and Amy murmured back, their eyes filled with determination and hope for the future.

As the chapter closed on Hewlett and his associates, a new one began for Nate, Amy, and Tom – one where they would continue to fight for justice and protect the innocent, no matter the cost. And as they stared into the darkness beyond the mirror, they knew that together, they were unstoppable.

Chapter 19

The clink of espresso cups and low chatter filled the cozy Sicilian café as Caterina Bianchi approached Nate and Amy's table, her dark eyes shimmering with gratitude. She clutched a small tray bearing three steaming cups of coffee, the rich aroma wafting through the air.

"Signor Nate, Signora Amy, please," she began, her voice thick with emotion, "I cannot thank you enough for everything you have done for me. Recovering my lost investment has truly changed my life." She placed the coffees on the table, her hands trembling slightly.

Nate took a sip of the rich, velvety espresso, his military-trained senses absorbing every detail of the café – the scent of freshly baked cannoli, the soft melody of Italian music playing in the background, and the warmth of the people around him. He looked up at Caterina, his deep-set blue eyes filled with empathy.

"Believe me, Caterina, it was our pleasure to help you. No one should have to go through what you did. I'm just glad we could bring justice to your situation," he said, the corners of his mouth turning up in a reassuring smile.

Amy nodded in agreement, her red hair glinting in the afternoon sunlight that streamed through the café windows. Her investigative journalist's mind raced with thoughts of how far Caterina had come since they first met her, from a vulnerable and trusting woman to someone who had learned to navigate the treacherous waters of investment schemes.

"Your success is our success, Caterina," she chimed in, her green eyes reflecting the same empathy as her husband's. "You've worked so hard to make this café what it is today, and we're honored to have played a part in that."

Caterina's eyes welled up with tears as she gazed at the couple seated before her. The weight of her gratitude seemed to fill the small café, enveloping them like a warm embrace. She dabbed at her eyes with the corner of her apron, then straightened up, determined not to let her emotions get the better of her.

"Thank you, my friends," she whispered, clenching her fists in a gesture of resolve. "I will never forget what you have done for me."

As Nate and Amy exchanged appreciative glances, they knew that their mission for justice had been accomplished – at least for now. And as they sipped their coffee and listened to Caterina's laughter ring through the café, they couldn't help but feel a deep sense of satisfaction in knowing that they had made a real difference in someone's life.

Caterina's eyes sparkled like the Mediterranean Sea as she leaned in closer to Nate and Amy, excitedly sharing her vision for the future. "I have been thinking about this for quite some time, my friends," she began, her voice filled with passion. "This café has always been a dream of mine, but I want to take it further. I want to bring the taste of Sicily to more people – not just here, but everywhere!"

Nate exchanged a look with Amy, both intrigued by Caterina's enthusiasm. He took a sip from his espresso, feeling the rich flavor dance on his tongue, while Amy nodded encouragingly. "That sounds like a fantastic idea, Caterina. And given how incredible your food is, I'm sure it'll be a huge success."

"Si, si!" Caterina beamed, her hands gesticulating wildly as she spoke. "The world needs more of our beautiful culture and cuisine. With your help, I know I can make this dream come true."

Amy put a hand on Caterina's arm, her eyes filled with sincerity. "We believe in you, Caterina. You've already built something wonderful here, and we're confident that you can do the same on a larger scale."

"Absolutely," Nate chimed in, his military background kicking in as he assessed the situation. "Expanding a business is certainly a challenge, but it's nothing compared to what you've already accomplished. We'll be here to support you every step of the way."

"Thank you –" Caterina paused, searching for the right words and then continued, her voice wavering slightly, "– You both have shown me that there are still good people in this world, willing to fight for justice. You've helped me regain my faith in humanity."

As Nate and Amy listened to Caterina's heartfelt words, they couldn't help but feel a renewed sense of purpose. They had dedicated their lives to helping others, and in Caterina's eyes, they could see the fruits of their labor.

"Your success is our success," Nate assured her, his dark eyes reflecting the determination that had driven them both for so long. "We'll be here for you, Caterina. Whenever you need us."

"Si, si!" Caterina repeated, her voice thick with emotion. "Grazie mille, my friends. Together, we will create something truly special – and bring the heart of Sicily to the world!"

With that, the trio raised their cups of espresso, toasting to the bright future ahead. As the warmth of the coffee filled their bodies, they couldn't help but feel that same warmth radiating from the friendship they had forged – a connection built on trust, hope, and a shared love of Italian culture.

The golden afternoon sun streamed through the cafe's window, casting a warm glow over the bustling room. The clatter of dishes and the hum of conversation blended with the unmistakable sound of laughter, creating an atmosphere that felt like home. Nate watched as a mother at a nearby table wiped tomato sauce off her young son's cheek while he giggled in delight. He couldn't help but smile at the scene, knowing that this was more than just a cafe – it was a sanctuary for people seeking solace in the comforting embrace of Sicilian culture.

"Amici," Caterina began, addressing Nate and Amy with a warmth that seemed to radiate from her very soul, "I cannot express my gratitude enough. You both have done so much for me already, but I must insist on doing something for you."

"Really, Caterina, there's no need," Nate said, his voice carrying a hint of humility. Amy nodded in agreement, her red hair catching the light as she did so.

"Please," Caterina insisted, her dark eyes shimmering with sincerity, "allow me to show my appreciation by treating you to the delicious dishes we serve here at the cafe. Unlimited free visits, whenever you like!"

Nate and Amy exchanged glances, momentarily speechless. It wasn't every day that someone offered them such a generous token of gratitude. But they knew Caterina well enough to understand that refusing her offer would be akin to denying her the chance to give back.

"Alright," Nate conceded, meeting Caterina's gaze with a genuine smile. "We'd be honored to accept your generous gift."

"Thank you, Caterina," Amy added, her eyes softening with emotion. "Your cooking is truly exceptional, and we'll definitely take you up on your offer."

"Buono!" Caterina exclaimed, her face lighting up with joy. "You are always welcome here, my friends. My cafe is your cafe."

As Nate and Amy basked in the warmth of Caterina's gratitude, they couldn't help but feel a deep sense of satisfaction. They had used their unique skills to right a wrong, restore justice, and bring joy back into the life of someone who truly deserved it. And in return, they had gained something priceless – the knowledge that they had made a real difference in someone's life and the promise of many more delicious Sicilian meals to come.

"Here's to the future," Nate declared, raising his glass in a toast. "To new friends, amazing food, and dreams coming true."

"Salute!" Caterina beamed, clinking her glass against theirs as they celebrated the path that had led them all to this very moment.

And somewhere in the background, amid the laughter and the chatter, the sound of a traditional Sicilian song began to play, its melody weaving through the air like a gentle reminder that even in the darkest of times, there was always hope, love, and good food to be found.

The sun dipped low in the sky, casting a warm golden glow over Caterina's cafe. The aroma of fresh espresso mingled with the scent of the sea breeze, evoking an idyllic Sicilian afternoon. Nate took a sip from his cup and turned to Caterina.

"Let's talk about your plans for expansion," he said, setting down his cup. "I think we can help you turn this dream into reality."

"Ah, grazie mille," Caterina replied, her eyes shining with determination. "I want to bring authentic Sicilian cuisine to more people, let them experience the flavors of my homeland."

"Location is key," Nate began, tapping a finger on the table thoughtfully. "You'll want to target areas with high foot traffic, but also consider the demographics. Places where people appreciate good food and have some disposable income."

"Si, I agree," Caterina said, nodding enthusiastically. "I was thinking of starting with one or two locations, see how they do, and then expand further."

"Smart move," Nate encouraged. He couldn't help but feel invested in Caterina's success, her passion contagious. "Now, marketing will be crucial. We'll need to create a strong brand identity and get the word out there." He paused, considering his next words carefully. "I can offer my expertise in cybersecurity to ensure the safety of your business. Protecting customer data and financial transactions is vital in today's world."

"Thank you, Nate," Caterina said gratefully. "I know so little about this, so your help means a lot."

Amy, who had been listening intently, chimed in. "With my background in investigative journalism, I've learned a thing or two about creating buzz. To attract potential investors, we can craft a compelling story around your journey and your dedication to authentic Sicilian cuisine."

"Stories like that can go a long way," Nate agreed, impressed with Amy's insight. "Especially if we highlight how you bounced back from the investment loss and turned adversity into opportunity."

"Si!" Caterina exclaimed, her excitement growing. "I love that idea!"

"Additionally," Amy continued, "we should emphasize the importance of building a strong reputation. The quality of your food and service will speak for themselves, but we'll also need to engage with customers, both online and offline."

"Social media is an excellent place to start," Nate added. "We can create profiles for your franchise, showcasing mouthwatering photos of your dishes and sharing glowing testimonials from satisfied customers."

"Brilliant!" Caterina clapped her hands together, her face aglow with enthusiasm. "I can see it now – my little cafe becoming a beloved destination for Sicilian food lovers everywhere!"

"Believe in your vision, Caterina," Amy said warmly. "With determination, hard work, and a bit of luck, anything is possible."

"Thank you both, truly," Caterina said, her eyes glistening with unshed tears. "Your support means the world to me."

As they continued brainstorming ideas for Caterina's future empire, Nate couldn't shake the thought that this was more than just a business venture. It was a testament to the power of resilience, hope, and friendship – a reminder that even in the darkest moments, there was always a chance to rise above and emerge stronger than ever before.

Caterina's eyes shone with determination as she surveyed the blueprint of her dream cafe, laid out on a table before her. She could almost taste the mouthwatering arancini and hear the cheerful chatter of satisfied customers in the air. Her fingers traced the outline of a potential new location, her mind racing with possibilities.

"Thank you both for your guidance and expertise," Caterina said, her voice laced with genuine gratitude. "I couldn't do this without you."

"Hey, it's our pleasure," Nate replied, giving her an encouraging smile. "You've got something special here, Caterina. We're just glad we can be a part of it."

"Your success is important to us," Amy added, placing a reassuring hand on Caterina's shoulder. "We'll be there for you whenever you need us. Just say the word."

Caterina nodded, drawing strength from their unwavering support. She knew that with Nate and Amy by her side, nothing could stand in her way. The thought filled her with a newfound confidence, prompting her to square her shoulders and fix her gaze on the horizon.

"Alright," she declared, a fiery resolve sparking within her. "Let's make this happen."

"Before we move forward, let's ensure that we have all the necessary precautions in place," Nate cautioned, his military background surfacing. "It's essential to keep your intellectual property and customer information secure. I'll help you set up robust cybersecurity measures to protect your business from any potential threats."

"Great thinking, Nate," Amy agreed, nodding approvingly. "And remember, Caterina, building a strong brand takes time and effort, but it's crucial in today's world. We'll work together to create a marketing strategy that highlights the unique qualities of your franchise while attracting the right investors."

"Si, si," Caterina breathed, her heart swelling with gratitude. "I am so fortunate to have you both on my team. I feel as if I can conquer the world."

"Let's start by conquering the food industry," Nate quipped, a playful glint in his eyes.

As they continued discussing strategies and plans for Caterina's franchise, her unwavering faith in her vision was bolstered by the presence of her newfound allies. Nate and Amy's support had given her the courage to chase her dreams, even when the odds seemed insurmountable. Together, they would build something extraordinary

– an empire that would stand as proof of the resilience of the human spirit, and the power of friendship to triumph over adversity.

As the sun began to set outside, casting warm hues of orange and pink across the cafe, Caterina uncorked a bottle of prosecco and poured it into three glasses. The effervescent bubbles danced in the liquid like tiny fireworks, symbolizing the newfound hope she felt. Nate and Amy watched her with tender smiles on their faces, their eyes reflecting the same warmth that filled the room.

"Come," Caterina said, handing Nate and Amy their glasses. "Let's toast to our partnership, and the bright future that awaits us."

Nate raised his glass, his dark eyes sparkling with anticipation. "To Caterina's Cafe – may it become a beacon of Sicilian culture around the world."

Amy chimed in, her red hair glowing like embers in the dying sunlight. "And to justice, for without it, we would never have found each other."

"Salute!" Caterina exclaimed, as they clinked their glasses together and took a sip of the crisp, refreshing prosecco. The joyous occasion was punctuated by laughter and chatter from the cafe customers, who were enjoying the culinary delights of Caterina's homeland.

In that moment, Caterina knew she had found more than just allies in Nate and Amy; she had found true friends. She turned to them, her eyes brimming with tears of gratitude. "I cannot thank you enough for everything you've done for me," she said, her voice trembling with emotion. "You not only recovered my lost investment but helped me find the strength to pursue my dreams. You two will always have a special place in my heart – and in my cafe."

Touched by her words, Nate placed a comforting hand on Caterina's shoulder. "We're honored to be a part of your journey, Caterina," he said earnestly. "And we'll continue to support you and your vision every step of the way."

"Absolutely," Amy agreed, her eyes shining with pride. "We believe in you and what you're creating. And we can't wait to see where this adventure takes us all."

As the evening wore on, the trio continued to discuss the intricacies of Caterina's plans, their camaraderie a testament to the power of human connection. With Nate's cybersecurity expertise and Amy's investigative journalism background, they formed an unstoppable force that would guide Caterina through the challenges ahead. And despite the uncertainty that lay before them, one thing was clear: they were united in their quest for justice, and together, they would change the world, one Sicilian dish at a time.

The sun dipped below the horizon, casting an otherworldly glow over the bustling Sicilian cafe. Nate and Amy exchanged a knowing glance, their shared sense of fulfillment palpable in the dimly lit room.

"Time flies when you're changing lives," Nate mused as he finished his espresso, savoring the last sip of the bitter brew.

"Or when you're enjoying the best cannoli in town," Amy replied with a grin, wiping away a stray crumb from the corner of her mouth. "Caterina has really outdone herself."

Caterina approached them, her eyes sparkling with gratitude. "It's getting late, my friends. I know you must be tired after helping me so much today. But remember, my door is always open to you."

"Thank you, Caterina," Amy said warmly. "We'll definitely take you up on that offer. And we promise to check in on your progress, too."

"Si, grazie mille," Nate added, his Italian accent surprisingly convincing. "We'll stay in touch, and if you ever need anything – anything at all – don't hesitate to reach out."

"Of course," Caterina assured them, her voice filled with emotion. "I couldn't have come this far without you two. Your support means the world to me."

As they stood to leave, Caterina enveloped each of them in a heartfelt embrace, leaving no doubt about the depth of her appreciation. Nate and Amy returned the gesture, the bond between them stronger than ever.

Stepping out into the cool night air, they paused for a moment, taking in the sights and sounds of the vibrant city. The distant chatter of cafe customers mingled with the rhythmic hum of passing cars, creating a symphony of life that echoed through the narrow streets.

"Feels good, doesn't it?" Nate asked, breaking the silence. "Knowing that we made a real difference in Caterina's life."

"More than good," Amy agreed, her eyes reflecting the joy in her heart. "It feels like we're finally using our skills for something truly meaningful."

Nate nodded, his thoughts swirling with memories of past adventures and the promise of future triumphs. Together, they had faced seemingly insurmountable odds and emerged victorious – all in the name of justice.

"Here's to many more successes," he said, offering his arm to Amy as they began their journey home. "And to the people whose lives we'll change along the way."

"Cheers to that," Amy replied, linking her arm in his. As they walked through the cobblestone streets, a renewed sense of purpose carried them forward, igniting a fire within that would continue to burn long after the sun had set on this unforgettable day.

Chapter 20

Nate leaned back in his leather armchair, swirling a glass of bourbon as the dim glow of the fireplace reflected in his eyes. Amy sat on the plush sofa opposite him, her red hair cascading over her shoulders, as she absentmindedly flipped through a magazine. Their living room, filled with the warm scent of burning wood, seemed to embrace them like a cocoon, shielding them from the chaotic world outside.

"Can you believe it?" Nate said, breaking the comfortable silence. "We actually managed to recover Caterina's investment and take down Hewlett."

Amy looked up from her magazine and smiled. "I knew we could do it. We just needed the right strategy and a bit of good old-fashioned teamwork."

"Teamwork, indeed," Nate agreed, raising his glass in a toast. "To us, and to justice."

"Cheers," Amy replied, clinking her own glass of wine against his. As they drank, Nate couldn't help but feel a deep sense of satisfaction wash over him.

"Y'know, I can't help but think about how many lives we've changed for the better," he mused. "Caterina can finally breathe easy knowing that her cafe is secure and that she has a chance at making her dream come true. And we've put a stop to Hewlett's schemes, preventing countless other people from falling victim to his manipulations."

Amy nodded thoughtfully. "It's a good feeling, isn't it? Knowing that we're making a difference in the world."

"Absolutely," Nate affirmed, taking another sip of his bourbon. "And we did it using my hacking skills for something positive, instead of just causing chaos for the sake of it. It's amazing what we can accomplish together when we put our minds to it."

"Speaking of which," Amy interjected, setting her magazine aside. "What do you think our next move should be? There's no shortage of injustice in the world, and I'm eager to see what kind of impact we can make on other lives."

"Whatever it is," Nate replied, setting his glass down on the coffee table, "I know that together, we'll continue to fight for those who need us most. We've proven time and time again that we're a force to be reckoned with, and I don't intend to stop now."

As they sat there in the glow of the fire, Nate and Amy knew that they had only just scratched the surface of their potential to bring about change. With each new challenge, they would grow stronger, more determined, and more united in their shared mission to right wrongs and help those in need.

Amy leaned forward in her seat, her green eyes reflecting the flickering flames of the fireplace. "You know, Nate," she began, her voice soft and contemplative, "I think what we're doing here is really important. I mean, our work not only helps people like Caterina get their lives back on track, but it's also about fighting for justice."

"Definitely," Nate agreed, his gaze meeting hers. "There's something incredibly fulfilling in standing up for those who have been wronged, especially when it feels like the world is against them."

As Amy listened to the crackling fire, memories of her father's unjust conviction swirled through her mind. She thought of the countless hours she spent poring over evidence, trying to find a way to set him free. That experience had ignited a fire within her – a relentless determination to fight injustice wherever she encountered it.

"Growing up, I always wanted to make a difference," she confessed, tucking a strand of red hair behind her ear. "Being an investigative journalist gave me that opportunity, but working with you, Nate... it's taken that passion to a whole new level."

Nate reached out and took her hand, gently squeezing it. "I feel the same way, Amy. My time in the military and my hacking skills taught me how to navigate the darker side of humanity. But this mission – our mission – has given me a renewed purpose. We're fighting for something bigger than ourselves."

"Exactly." Amy nodded, her expression resolute. "And together, we'll continue to help those who need us most, no matter what challenges we face along the way."

"Agreed," Nate said, his tone equally determined. "We're a team, and there's nothing that can stop us from bringing perpetrators of injustice to their knees."

Their eyes met, two kindred spirits bound by a shared commitment to righting wrongs and protecting the innocent. They knew that their journey was only just beginning, but together they would face whatever challenges lay ahead – united in their fight for justice.

"Here's to our next adventure," Amy said, raising her glass in a toast.

"May we continue to make a difference," Nate replied, clinking his glass against hers before they both took a sip, sealing their vow. And with that, they embraced the unknown future, eager to see where their mission for justice would take them next.

The sun dipped below the horizon, casting a warm glow over the living room as Nate and Amy lounged on the couch, their fingers intertwined. The flickering screen of the television cast a pale light on their faces, but neither seemed particularly interested in what was playing. Instead, their thoughts were already on the next mission.

"Any ideas on what our next case should be?" Amy asked, breaking the silence. Her green eyes sparkled with excitement at the prospect of their next adventure.

Nate leaned back, his dark hair brushing against the soft fabric of the couch. "I've been doing some research," he began, scrolling through his tablet. "There's a small town up north where people have been mysteriously disappearing." His voice took on a grave tone, underscoring the seriousness of the situation.

"Sounds like something we should look into," Amy agreed, her investigative journalist instincts kicking in. "But are we prepared for the challenges that come with investigating a missing persons case?"

"Nothing we can't handle together," Nate reassured her, squeezing her hand. "We've faced danger before, and we'll face it again. But we can't let fear hold us back from helping those who need us."

Amy smiled, appreciating his unwavering determination. "You're right. We have a duty to use our skills and resources to fight injustice, no matter how risky it might be."

"Besides," Nate added with a grin, "we've got an ace up our sleeve – your knack for uncovering hidden truths and my hacking abilities give us an edge most investigators don't have."

"True," Amy conceded, her lips curving upwards. "So, what's the plan? Do we go undercover as tourists or perhaps locals?"

"Let's start by getting a feel for the town and its people," Nate suggested, pulling up an aerial view of the area on his tablet. "We can use our cover as a couple looking to move there, maybe even buy a house. It'll give us an excuse to talk to the locals and ask questions without raising suspicion."

"Sounds like a solid plan," Amy said, leaning in to examine the map on Nate's tablet. Her red hair fell over her shoulder in a cascade of fiery curls, and she absentmindedly tucked a strand behind her ear.

"Let's just hope we don't have to deal with local law enforcement getting in our way," Nate mused, his brow furrowed in thought. "We'll have to be careful not to step on any toes while we're investigating."

"Agreed," Amy replied, her expression serious. "But if it comes down to it, we'll do what we have to in order to protect the innocent and bring those responsible to justice."

Nate nodded, knowing full well that their commitment to their mission would sometimes require them to walk a fine line between right and wrong. But as long as they had each other's backs, he was confident they could face whatever challenges lay ahead – together.

"Alright then," he said, closing his tablet and setting it aside. "Tomorrow, we start our next adventure. Are you ready?"

"Absolutely," Amy responded, her eyes shining with determination. "There's nothing I'd rather do than fight for justice by your side."

The sun cast a warm, golden glow on the cobblestone streets as Nate and Amy strolled through the bustling Italian town. Around them, locals chatted animatedly, the scent of fresh-baked bread and brewing espresso wafting through the air. The lively atmosphere seemed to hum with the promise of new beginnings – fitting, considering the recent events in Caterina's life.

"Seems like everything is back on track for her," Nate observed quietly, his eyes scanning the array of vibrant storefronts that lined the street. "I'm glad we could help make that happen."

"Me too," Amy agreed, her emerald green eyes sparkling with satisfaction. "It's not often we get to see the direct impact of our work like this."

As they approached Caterina's cafe, they couldn't help but notice the subtle changes that had taken place since they'd last been there. A newly painted sign swung gently above the entrance, proudly displaying the cafe's name in elegant script. Beneath it, tables draped in red and white checkered cloth spilled out onto the sidewalk, surrounded by cheerful patrons sipping espresso and savoring their Sicilian pastries.

Stepping inside, Nate couldn't help but feel a swell of pride at the sight of Caterina standing behind the counter, her dark hair pulled back into a neat bun. She looked every bit the confident business owner she was meant to be – thanks, in part, to their efforts.

"Buongiorno, Caterina!" he called out, offering her a friendly wave as they made their way over to the counter.

"Ah, Nate, Amy! Come stai?" Caterina greeted them warmly, her face lighting up with genuine happiness at the sight of her two saviors. "Please, sit, sit! I will bring you something special!"

"Actually, Caterina," Amy interjected, holding up a hand to halt her eager host. "We wanted to thank you for trusting us with your case and giving us the chance to make a difference in your life."

Caterina's eyes welled up with tears as she reached across the counter to grasp both of their hands tightly. "No, I should be thanking you," she insisted, her voice thick with emotion. "You saved my dream, and for that, I am eternally grateful. Please, let me repay you – unlimited free visits to my cafe! It is the least I can do for the two of you."

Nate squeezed her hand gently, his dark eyes filled with warmth as he met her gaze. "Caterina, your trust in us was a gift in itself. Just knowing that we've made a positive impact in your life is more than enough repayment for us."

"Exactly," Amy chimed in, her own eyes shining with unshed tears. "Helping people like you is the reason we do what we do."

"Then at least promise me you'll come back to visit," Caterina implored, dabbing at her eyes with the corner of her apron. "I want to hear all about your future adventures and the lives you continue to touch."

"Of course," Nate assured her, exchanging a knowing glance with Amy. "We wouldn't dream of staying away."

As they left the cafe, Nate couldn't help but ponder the powerful bond they'd forged with Caterina and the countless others like her whose lives they'd been fortunate enough to touch. While the path they'd chosen was fraught with risks and challenges, there was no denying the profound sense of fulfillment it brought them – and together, there was nothing they couldn't overcome.

As Nate and Amy walked side by side down the bustling street, they couldn't help but feel the weight of their most recent mission still lingering in the air. The cityscape seemed to hum with a newfound energy, a testament to the lives they had touched and the justice they had helped bring about.

"Sometimes I wonder if we're making a difference, you know?" Nate mused, his gaze locked on a family passing by – a father hoisting his daughter onto his shoulders, her laughter ringing out like music. "With all the risks we take, the sleepless nights, the constant fear of being caught... is it worth it?"

Amy glanced at him, her stunning red hair catching the sunlight just so, and she smiled. "You know it's worth it, Nate. Just look at Caterina, and all the others we've helped. We've made a tangible impact on their lives. That's something not many people can say."

"True," he admitted, his fingers brushing against hers as they walked. "But sometimes I worry that the price we pay is too high. What if one day, we can't protect ourselves or the people we love?"

"Then we'll face that challenge when it comes," she replied with a quiet determination, her grip on his hand tightening ever so slightly. "Together, like always. Besides, the work we do is important. You know that better than anyone – your background in ethical hacking, your time in the military... all of that has led you here, to this moment. Our purpose is clear, Nate. We have a unique set of skills, and instead of using them for personal gain, we're fighting for justice."

Nate sighed, knowing deep down that she was right. "I suppose you're right, Amy. It's just... sometimes the weight of it all can feel overwhelming."

They continued on in silence for a few moments, the city pulsing around them like a living, breathing entity. Eventually, they reached their modest home, tucked away on a quiet side street that seemed to exist in a world all its own.

As they stepped inside, Nate couldn't help but feel a sense of peace wash over him – this was their sanctuary after all, a place where they could leave the chaos of their missions behind and focus on the lives they had rebuilt together.

"Look at us," Amy murmured as she closed the door behind them, her eyes scanning the familiar surroundings with a hint of nostalgia.

"Who would've thought that a former ethical hacker and an investigative journalist would end up here, fighting for justice in our own unique way?"

"Life is full of surprises," he agreed, wrapping his arm around her waist and drawing her close. "But I wouldn't trade what we have for anything in the world."

"Neither would I," she whispered, resting her head against his chest.

Together, they stood there in the warmth of their home, reflecting on the progress they had made and the countless lives they had touched through their mission. And as they looked toward the future, they knew one thing for certain: they were ready to face whatever challenges lay ahead, united in their fight for justice and driven by the powerful bond they shared.

The warm glow of the setting sun bathed their living room in a golden hue, casting elongated shadows across the floor. Nate leaned against the windowsill, his eyes focused on the horizon as he took in the last remnants of daylight. Amy sat on the couch, her legs tucked under her, gently cradling a steaming cup of coffee in her hands.

"Remember that time in Rome?" Nate began, his voice low and pensive. "When we first realized what we wanted to do with our lives?"

Amy glanced up at him, her green eyes reflecting the sunlight. "Of course. That was the turning point for us, wasn't it?"

Nate nodded, lost in thought. "It's amazing how far we've come since then. And yet, every mission still feels like the first."

"Because it's personal," Amy added, taking a sip of her coffee. "We're not just going after criminals, we're fighting for people like Caterina – for justice."

"Exactly." Nate turned to face her, his gaze intense. "We can't bring back what they've lost, but we can make sure no one else suffers the same fate."

"Every life we touch, every wrong we right..." Amy trailed off, her eyes welling up with unshed tears. "It's worth all the risks we take."

"Speaking of risks..." Nate's lips curled into a wry smile as he walked over to their desk, tapping away at the computer keyboard. "I've been doing some research on our next potential case."

"Already?" Amy raised an eyebrow, amused by her husband's enthusiasm. "What have you found?"

"Let's just say it involves a pharmaceutical company, high-stakes investment fraud, and a family torn apart by greed." Nate's fingers flew across the keys, pulling up a cluster of documents and news articles on the screen. "It's right up our alley."

Amy set her coffee down and joined him at the desk, her curiosity piqued. As she skimmed through the information, her expression shifted from intrigue to determination.

"Looks like we have our work cut out for us," she mused, glancing over at Nate. "But together, we can make a difference."

"Always." Nate reached for her hand, giving it a reassuring squeeze. In that moment, their shared purpose seemed to resonate between them, an unbreakable bond forged by their commitment to justice.

The sun dipped below the horizon, shrouding the room in darkness. But as Nate and Amy delved into the details of their next mission, they felt a renewed sense of excitement and anticipation – for they knew that each adventure brought with it the chance to change lives and bring light to even the darkest corners of the world.

More?

If this book has captured your imagination and left you yearning for more, I am thrilled to share that it is part of a larger series. Each book delves into the lives of the characters and the plotlines that unfold.

To continue the journey, you can find the other books in the series available for download at http://idsfa.co.uk/where you'll find links to all major online publishers

***

CheckMate

https://books2read.com/b/bwQLj9[1]

In the heart of the city, a vulnerable soul is exploited by a powerful tycoon. But when a husband and wife team takes up the fight for justice, they embark on an elaborate and risky mission to extract money from the tycoon and right the wrongs committed.

With their impeccable reputation as high-profile consultants, they cunningly position themselves as experts in the tycoon's interests and values. Orchestrating a meeting that captivates his attention, they unveil an irresistible offer that seems to align perfectly with his ambitions. As the stakes rise, they skillfully tap into his fear of missing out and desire for greatness, gradually escalating the investment with promises of astronomical returns and exclusive perks.

But this elaborate con isn't just about money. The husband and wife team's ultimate goal is to expose the tycoon's exploitation and demand restitution for the victim. With undeniable evidence in their hands, they confront the tycoon, threatening to expose him publicly and unleash legal and reputational consequences.

---

1. https://books2read.com/b/bwQLj9

As the tycoon faces the potential ruin of his empire and confronts his own moral compass, he undergoes a transformation. But can the husband and wife team trust him to fulfill his promises? With every twist and turn, they must stay one step ahead of the tycoon and navigate a treacherous path to justice.

Will the husband and wife team succeed in their mission and bring justice to the victim? Or will their plan crumble, leaving them with regrets and the tycoon unscathed? Discover the truth in this gripping tale of revenge, redemption, and the pursuit of justice.

***

The Great Escape

https://books2read.com/u/bPzqXx[2]

In a world where justice is elusive, Nate and Amy emerge as an unstoppable force against the dark forces of human trafficking. Nate, an ex-military white-hat hacker, and Amy, a fearless investigative journalist, join forces to form a modern-day A-Team.

Their latest mission takes them deep into the heart of a religious commune, where young girls are held captive under the guise of spirituality. With the cult leader using twisted interpretations of the Bible to justify his heinous acts, Nate and Amy must infiltrate the operation and expose the truth.

They gain the trust of the cult leader and unravel the intricate web of his trafficking ring. But as they dig deeper, they discover that this is just the tip of the iceberg, with a larger operation lurking in the shadows.

Armed with intelligence and cunning, Nate and Amy race against time to dismantle the operation and save as many lives as possible. There are no guns in this battle, only the power of their minds and unwavering determination.

---

2. https://books2read.com/u/bPzqXx

This action-packed thriller takes readers on a heart-stopping journey through the depths of human trafficking. With every page, they witness the atrocities and feel the adrenaline-fueled pursuit of justice.

With a gripping climax that will leave readers breathless, this novel is a testament to the resilience of the human spirit and the unwavering fight against injustice. A must-read for those seeking a thrilling and morally charged adventure.

Acknowledgements

You.

First and foremost, I would like to express my heartfelt gratitude for choosing to embark on this journey with me. Your decision to purchase this book means the world to me, and I am truly honored to have you as a reader.

Writing this book has been an incredible labor of love, filled with numerous late nights, countless cups of coffee, and unyielding determination. However, it is your presence here that gives my words purpose and breathes life into the pages.

I humbly ask for a moment of your time to share your thoughts and experiences with this book. If you found solace within its pages, if it made you smile, laugh, or shed a tear, please consider leaving a review. Your feedback is invaluable, not only to me but also to other potential readers who may be searching for their next read.

Your review, whether it be a few heartfelt words or a detailed analysis, has the power to influence others and guide them towards this world I have created. By sharing your thoughts, you are not only supporting my work but also helping to create a community of readers who can connect and engage with one another.

I understand that time is precious, and writing a review may seem like a small task in the grand scheme of things. However, I assure you that your words have the ability to make a significant impact, allowing this book to reach even greater heights and touch the lives of more readers.

Once again, thank you for your trust and for joining me on this adventure. Your support means everything to me, and I am forever grateful.

With deepest appreciation,

- Shane

Andy

I've known Andy for more than a decade. We used to work together and he lives a short walk away from me, which is handy for dog walks. Andy is inscrutably honest and a great person to brainstorm plot ideas with. Andy helped with the plot for this book, both introducing questions and answering them. Without him, this book wouldn't exist.

Alison

Alison is one of the coolest people I know. She is humble and plays bass guitar, apparently thinking that's normal and not realising how cool it is. Alison told me that having a book published is a major achievement, somehow not knowing how agog I am when I hear her play.

Don't miss out!

Visit the website below and you can sign up to receive emails whenever Shane Reed publishes a new book. There's no charge and no obligation.

https://books2read.com/r/B-A-LSDAB-CFMYC

BOOKS 2 READ

Connecting independent readers to independent writers.

Did you love *The Sicilian Defense*? Then you should read *The Queen's Gambit*[1] by Shane Reed!

[2]

In a world where justice hangs in the balance, Nate and Amy, a formidable couple armed with unique skills, embark on a mission to right the wrongs of their community. As an ex-military hacker and investigative journalist, they become an unstoppable force, seeking retribution for the victims of injustice.

Their latest assignment takes them undercover into a seemingly harmless community theater group. Little do they know, a sinister plot is unfolding behind the scenes. Sapphire, one of the drag queens, is using their theatrical talents for nefarious purposes, stealing identities and unleashing chaos upon the unsuspecting members.

---

1. https://books2read.com/u/49aaZw

2. https://books2read.com/u/49aaZw

As Nate and Amy dive deeper into the secrets of the theater group, they uncover a web of deceit, betrayal, and hidden agendas. With each revelation, the stakes grow higher, and the danger becomes a palpable presence. But Nate's keen eye catches a crucial detail—an opportunity to expose Sapphire's true identity.

With the power in their hands, Nate and Amy walk a tightrope, balancing their personal lives and their mission. They must confront their own vulnerabilities and make sacrifices for the greater good. In a game of cat and mouse, they chase justice while their adversaries fight to maintain control.

In this heart-pounding thriller, Nate and Amy's relentless pursuit of retribution will keep readers on the edge of their seats. With unexpected twists and turns, they race against time, determined to protect the innocent and expose the truth. In the end, their dedication to justice will prevail, but not without facing the ultimate test of their strength and resolve.

Also by Shane Reed

A Conning Couple Novel
Checkmate
The Great Escape
The Queen's Gambit
The Sicilian Defense